THE COMPLETE BOOK OF

Bible Trivia CROSSWORDS

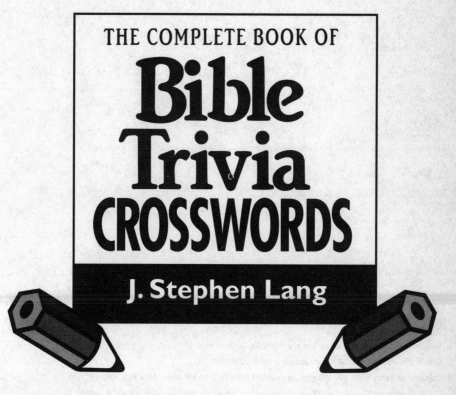

THE COMPLETE BOOK OF Bible Trivia CROSSWORDS

J. Stephen Lang

Tyndale House Publishers, Inc.
WHEATON, ILLINOIS

Visit Tyndale's exciting Web site at www.tyndale.com

Puzzles created by Terry Hall, Media Ministries, 516 E. Wakeman Ave., Wheaton, Illinois 60187.

Designed by Brian Eterno.

ISBN 0-8423-0324-3

Printed in the United States of America

04 03 02 01 00
9 8 7 6 5 4 3 2

The Naked Truth

ACROSS

1 Psalm ending
6 Small marine animal
10 What father lay naked and intoxicated in his tent, which so disturbed his sons that they came and covered him?
14 Refiner
15 Overly precious, to a Briton
16 Hole punchers
17 Where did a follower of Jesus escape an angry mob by running away naked?
19 "___ Dinah" (Avalon hit)
20 Regard
21 ___ vis (one in a million)
23 Low-grade wool
25 Waning
29 Make the grade
33 Straightened bed covers again
36 Ancient city of Edom
37 Island off Alaska
38 Not *nah*, but
39 Attention-getters
41 Who went naked as a way of wailing over the fate of Jerusalem?
44 One of Job's "comforters"
45 ___-Oberstein (German town)
46 Sock necessity
47 One of the Bobbsey twins
48 A Gandhi
50 *New York Times* reviver Adolph
51 Decoction of herbs
53 Twitch
55 Quarterback Brett
58 Burr and Hank
63 What king of Israel, struck with the power to prophesy, stripped off his clothes and lay naked for a whole day and night?
66 What disciple, busy at his daily work, was caught naked by Jesus?
68 Wild cat
69 Strongest part of castle
70 Mongolian range
71 British manorial court
72 Short example?
73 Abnormal sacs

DOWN

1 Cooking herb
2 Dutch uncles
3 Dole's Senate successor
4 After stomach or tooth
5 What prophet threatened to take away the flax that covered his wife's nakedness?
6 Seminary deg.
7 ___ of words
8 Capp's hyena
9 Looked
10 Aaron's priestly son
11 See red?
12 Local pol.
13 Health, Safety, and Envir. Mgt. Council
18 Life, in the early days
22 At right angles
24 Called pager
26 Poison remedy
27 Broadway Joe of the Jets
28 Flows freely
29 Inventor's quest
30 Bebai's son
31 Yarn packages
32 Philistine giant

34 Moslem messiah
35 "Have ___!" (be sympathetic)
40 Kumi ___ braiding
42 One run will ___ stocking
43 Roman emperor
49 Russian Alexander
52 Musical key
54 Early Inca leader
56 Cambodian money
57 Rhea's cousin
59 Depend on
60 Baseball Mel's family
61 Spiffy
62 Calcutta misters
63 Maxim's seasoning
64 "___, matey"
65 *Sons and Lovers* actress May
67 Photo ___ (camera sessions)

Laughers and Dancers

ACROSS

1 Pugilist's weapon
5 Play-___
8 Von ___
13 "___ boy! Way to go!"
14 Hawaiian victorfish
15 Cavalry swords
16 Hebrew tribe
18 New Orleans cuisine
19 Champagne name
20 Hardly any
21 Van ___ of theater and film
25 What prophetess led the women of Israel in a victory dance?
28 Julia, on *Seinfeld*
29 Salinger dedicatee
31 Major mail ctr.
32 Reviewed by Nielsen
33 What epistle tells Christians to turn their laughter to mourning?
34 *The Simpsons* storekeeper
35 Biblical suffixes
36 Star-to-be
37 Tenor John
38 Prussian pronoun
39 Cast
40 Jewish month
41 *High* ___ (Anderson play)
42 Light beams
43 Bristly
44 Words before "toes" or "best behavior"
46 Disney head
47 Typestyle
48 First model, for short
50 Ostrich or kiwi
52 Who had his decree for a Passover celebration laughed at by the men of Israel?
57 *Sleepless in Seattle* writer-director
58 Crater Lake st.
59 ". . . one ___ two!" (Welk intro)
60 Envy color
61 Concealed
62 Rooney of *60 Minutes*

DOWN

1 Terrif!
2 Native suffix
3 B&O stop
4 ___ Mahal
5 Entertainer Vic
6 '30s migrant worker
7 Peck's partner
8 Wingdings perhaps
9 "Cross as ___"
10 Continued from 23-Down
11 Lamprey, for one
12 Trio of wind dirs.
15 Con artist
17 "I have half ___ to . . ."
21 Start of a toast
22 Jubilance
23 Who held a feast with dancing when his son returned? (answer continued in 10-Down)
24 Fishy tales?
26 Conciliate
27 Lamenter
29 Kind of chair
30 Saw-billed duck
33 Old-time film actor Victor
36 Reprimand
37 British isles
39 New Jersey's capital

40 Mont Blanc covering
43 Confiscated
45 Bete's *couleur*
48 "Whoops!"
49 Grist for the operatic mill?
50 Norm.

51 Loan computation meth.
53 *Jungle Book* hisser
54 A keeper may keep it
55 Put two and two together
56 Horse food

1
2
3
4
5
6
7
8
9
10
11
12
13
14
15
16
17
18
19
20
21
22
23
24
25
26
27
28
29
30
31
32
33
34
35
36
37
38
39
40
41
42
43
44
45
46
47
48
49
50
51
52
53
54
55
56
57
58
59
60
61
62

They Did It First

ACROSS

1 What was the first city called?
6 Wife of King Ahaz
9 ___ Valley, California
13 Maui neighbor
14 Travel account
15 Rim that holds a gem
16 Who used the first pseudonym? (answer continued in 54-Across)
19 Lead actor in *Thief*
20 Galley slave's tool
21 *Mr. Holland's Opus* actor Glenne
22 Recipe meas.
23 "Am ___ brother's keeper?"
24 Auto racer Teo
25 Connection between bump and log
26 Sort of show
27 Christian singer Price
30 Who were the first exiles?
34 Macaws
35 Who was the first apostle to be martyred?
36 Female sandpiper
37 River of Syria
38 Khan and others
39 Who was the first disciple chosen by Jesus?
41 Illiterates' signatures
42 WWI German admiral
43 Oil, in Hamburg
44 Prot. denomination
45 Spell
46 Popular test on *ER*
49 ___ *of No Importance* (Wilde play)
52 Short or long weight
53 Waterway of Espana
54 16-Across, continued
57 What is the first color mentioned in the Bible?
58 Sale item marking: Abbr.
59 ___ *Down Staircase*
60 Turkish official
61 Who planted the first garden?
62 What was the first animal out of Noah's ark?

DOWN

1 Choose by ballot
2 Belongs to USA space cmd.
3 Waiting in the wings
4 "All the Way" lyricist Sammy
5 "Get a move on!"
6 Forever in old times
7 Nobel-winning physicist Niels
8 "Here ___ Again": 1964 song
9 Caravansary
10 Author and atom enders
11 Lunch or brunch
12 Badly
15 Pioneer bathyspherist
17 Caesar's empire
18 Tint
23 Claire and Balin
24 ___clock shadow
25 Of masses
26 The Beatles' "You Won't ___"
27 College gp.
28 Lover's or Lois
29 Glacial ridges
30 Comet competitor
31 ___ Evans Rogers
32 Grant and Carter
33 Helps with the dishes
34 First homicide victim
37 Summit

39 Caesar's backbone
40 Limitlessly
42 Hatch
44 Arab chieftain
45 Stockpile
46 *Promised Land* venue
47 Astronomer Tycho
48 Secretary of Defense William ___
49 Soissons seraph
50 Sincere
51 Buddhist sacred mountain
52 "Comin' ___ the Rye": Burns song
53 Casual shoe
55 Actor Ruman of *Ninotchka*
56 Gold: Prefix

Kings, Pharaohs, and Other Rulers

ACROSS
1 Favor one foot
5 Spa: Abbr.
9 Luia lead-in
13 Austr. Boating Ind. Assoc.
14 Ken of *thirtysomething*
15 ____bronn, Ger.
16 Who refused to let the Israelites pass through his country on their way to Canaan?
19 Granada greeting
20 Bond
21 What Philistine king did David seek refuge with when he fled from Saul?
23 What evil king of Judah was humbled and repentant after being taken to Babylon in chains?
25 Guam is one
29 High peak
30 A.M. TV offering
33 Something to take out
34 What man, one of Solomon's officials, had his reign over Israel foretold by the prophet Ahijah?
36 ____ *mieux* (so much: Fr.)
37 Currency in Iceland
39 River in Spain
40 Who was the last king of Judah?
42 What king of Hazor organized an alliance against Joshua?
43 Prefix with meter
44 Med. deg.
45 Idaho recreation area
47 Fistfuls
49 ___re (joint holding)
52 Obligated
57 Latin love
58 Who attacked the Israelites on their way into Canaan, only to be completely destroyed later?
60 Drug shipment, maybe
61 Lion of Hollywood
62 Spy ____ Hari
63 ____e (musical exercise)
64 Opening
65 "An apple ____ . . ."

DOWN
1 Mighty ____ Rose
2 As before, in footnotes
3 Ho Chi of Vietnam
4 Call a beeper
5 Bulgaria's capital: adj.
6 Bulgarian city
7 ____ *Wild Pony*
8 ____-Cat
9 Super-satisfied sound
10 Start of a string of 13 popes
11 Diamond and Abner
12 What king of Israel was murdered while he was drunk?
17 Ottoman dynasty founder
18 Jewish Old Testament commentary
22 King mackerel
24 *Nana* star Anna
25 Passover food
26 In the style of actor Asner
27 Sonata section
28 "I can't believe ____ the whole thing!"
30 Opera baritone Tito
31 Golden Gate's headlands
32 Surrounded by
34 Fourth Gospel
35 Abacus unit
37 Nome neighbor

38 McNally's partner
41 Hooded hoodlums
42 Composer Franz ____ Haydn
45 Very enthusiastic
46 Moldy morsel?
47 What king wanted to see miracles when the arrested Jesus was sent to him?
48 Certain
49 Dessert
50 Fail to mention
51 Balsamic solvent: Abbr.
53 Where Bear Bryant's boys played
54 Jazz, revived by the Brits
55 "Do I dare to ____ peach?": T.S. Eliot
56 WWII turning point
59 Aeron. low visibility aid

So Many Dreamers

ACROSS

1 Mennonite
6 Ski lifts, sometimes
11 Air rifle ammo
14 Death-related
15 Mir's path
16 Need a doctor's care
17 Daniel had a dream of four beasts rising out of the sea. What did they look like? (answer continued in 59-Across, 24-Down, 28-Across, and 43-Across)
19 Initials on a food label
20 Paul Revere was one
21 Beruit's country: Abbr.
22 Severe shortages
26 Poet Fardd et al.
28 24-Down, continued
29 Triffling
32 TV's warrior princess
33 Ground pine
35 Advice dispenser
38 ___ and outs
39 Apple remains
40 Actor Stephen ___
41 Delicate handmade laces
43 28-Across, continued
44 Social-page word (pl.)
45 French star
47 Auto racer Teo
48 Biblical wilderness
50 Burn without a flame
53 *Charlotte's Web* initials
54 Follows skeet or straight
58 French pronoun
59 17-Across continued
64 Piglet
65 "Lead, follow, ___ out of the way!"
66 Bottled water brand
67 Follows no for direction
68 Whip marks
69 Jewish scholar

DOWN

1 ___pest meter
2 Director Brooks
3 French place
4 Packed house letters
5 Province of China
6 Future things
7 Fox or Rabbit
8 "Blind as ___"
9 To laugh, in Lyons
10 Looked impolitely
11 A Midianite soldier dreamed of his tent being overturned by an unlikely object. What was it?
12 Senator Al
13 Thick slices
18 Ginger is one
22 Repair
23 Sports center
24 59-Across continued
25 "Once ___ blue moon"
27 Col. deg.
29 Blender setting
30 "___ a Kick Out of You"
31 Morse *T*
33 Play start
34 What Old Testament prophet said there will come a day when young men will see visions and old men will dream dreams?
36 Pioneer bathyspherist
37 Mr. Arafat
42 D.C.'s Union ___

44 Sports org.
46 Ship's speed
48 Who repeats the words of 34-Down in an early Christian sermon?
49 Like ___ from the blue
50 Photocopies
51 Debussy's "La ___"
52 Instruct the waiter
55 Roll-call response
56 Certain horn
57 Auto import from Europe
60 Actress Gardner
61 Writing tip
62 Tiny amount
63 A Vanna turnover

1
2
3
4
5
6
7
8
9
10
11
12
13
14
15
16
17
18
19
20
21
22
23
24
25
26
27
28
29
30
31
32
33
34
35
36
37
38
39
40
41
42
43
44
45
46
47
48
49
50
51
52
53
54
55
56
57
58
59
60
61
62
63
64
65
66
67
68
69

What's in a Name?

ACROSS

1 What Bible character's name means "praise of the Lord"?
5 Black follower
10 Restaurant chain's letters
14 Queen of Eng.
15 Start of the "Sailor's Song"
16 Ingrid's *Casablanca* role
17 Winglike parts
18 Of the moon
19 Tax-free bond, briefly
20 China cotton
22 What Bible character's name means "peace"?
24 P___ (aviator)
25 Make a change for the verse?
26 TV's Soupy
29 *2001* computer
31 Onetime *60 Minutes* journalist Alexander
35 What Bible character's name means "affectionate"?
37 Earlier form of a word
38 Space-age approval
39 Tread heavily
41 Food antioxidant init.
42 Harry S.
45 What Bible character's name means "the Lord has consoled"?
48 Assassinated Egyptian president
49 Greek archit. style
50 Dillon and Groening
51 Behind schedule
53 Army rank: Abbr.
55 What Bible character's name means "God has helped"?
58 Playpen toys
62 Sir Guinness
63 Send elsewhere
65 Actor Lukas of *Witness*
66 What Bible character's name means "something worth seeing"?
67 Tolkien character
68 What Bible character's name means "help"?
69 Japanese winter sports center
70 Mug, in Munich
71 Bridge position

DOWN

1 Sturdy twilled fabric
2 *Smiles of a Summer Night* star ___ Jacobsen
3 Primatologist Fossey
4 What Bible character's name means "God is strong"?
5 His feast day is April 11
6 Biblical elevation
7 Intl. Stds. No.
8 Herb
9 Gideon's campsite
10 What Bible character's name means "honored of God"?
11 Down at the mouth
12 "Money ___ object!"
13 Gladly, to Shakespeare
21 "What ___ is new?"
23 Santa checks it twice
26 Petty quarrels
27 Now, in Nogales
28 Israeli political party
30 "That's ___!"
32 Circumference
33 Bareheaded
34 Belonging to hot springs discoverer

36 Quite a hgt.
37 New Testament bk.
40 Wednesday, in Paris
43 What Bible character's name means "messenger"?
44 Sweet smeller: Var.
46 Follows pre to displace
47 What Bible character's name means "gift of the Lord"?
49 Sahara is one
52 Gang territories
54 What Bible character's name means "enlightened"?
55 Actress ___ Flynn Boyle
56 Cattle-breeding African people
57 Greek letter
59 Take it easy
60 Prominent rabbit features
61 H.S. exam
64 Giant, to Jack

1 2 3 4 5 6 7 8 9 10 11 12 13
14 15 16
17 18 19
20 21 22 23
24 25
26 27 28 29 30 31 32 33 34
35 36 37
38 39 40 41
42 43 44 45 46 47
48 49 50
51 52 53 54
55 56 57 58 59 60 61
62 63 64 65
66 67 68
69 70 71

The Runners

ACROSS
1 Macho party
5 What prophet ran after another prophet to accept the appointment as his successor?
11 Private eye
14 Hawaiian coffee
15 Became insipid
16 Id starter, for sharp
17 Conclusion of 23-Across
19 Former Stooge
20 Take care of
21 Dough dispenser
22 Opposite of sings.
23 According to Isaiah, what sort of people can run and not be weary?
28 Diary
31 Eskimo knife
32 Whale intro
33 Israeli port
35 Past hist.
38 Necklace units
42 "___ like sheep have gone astray" (Isa. 53:6)
44 Neath's opposite
45 What man ran to meet Abraham's servant at the well?
46 What boy ran into the Philistine camp to confront their best warrior?
47 Spiffy
49 New Zealander
50 Grammy category
52 Navigation hazard
54 Total U.S. output
55 When the man of Benjamin saw the ark of the covenant captured by the Philistines, what Israelite did he run to tell?
61 Initials of a U.S. poet
62 Pathet ___ (Asian party)
63 Light metal maker
67 D. L. Moody's school
68 What two women ran from Jesus' empty tomb to tell the disciples what had happened?
71 Movie, for short
72 "Relax!"
73 Famous Robert
74 School for Lts.
75 Sign of good weather tomorrow
76 The Cornhusker st.

DOWN
1 Inventory tag codes
2 Frequent bars
3 Starts sis, a mind state
4 Common corporate chart
5 N.T. bk.
6 New Guinea port
7 ___ ease (nervous)
8 Laziness
9 Bandleader Woody
10 Put two and two together
11 Buccaneer's base
12 Dangerous bacteria
13 Colgate rival
18 ___bohu: chaos
24 Add ow and push aside
25 Territory bordering Alaska
26 Shelved, with ed
27 Vent with frenzy
28 X-ray stopper
29 Pueblo pot
30 Zincked, as steel: Abbr.
34 Cheep
36 First letter in Creator's name

37 Air current
39 "Speak softly and carry ___ stick": Teddy Roosevelt
40 It breaks every day
41 Cut a little
43 ___-Oberstein (German town)
48 Part of Italy
51 What aviator is mentioned in the Bible?
53 Tickled pink
55 Musical speed
56 Sister's clothes
57 Cast-of-thousands films
58 Equipped for sound
59 Nutritious beans
60 Southern Ural Mountains range
64 Singer J. J.
65 Midianite general
66 Advertiser Francis Wayland ___
68 Just scratch the surface
69 Date with "out"
70 Marshal at Waterloo

Names Made in Heaven

ACROSS

1 Pugilist's weapons
6 Motor oil grading code
9 South American Indians
14 Hebrew military general
15 *The ___ Couple*
16 Mercury model
17 What was Hosea told to name his daughter?
19 "Li'l ___"
20 Possessive Latin pronoun
21 Highland headwear
22 "___ for apple"
23 Father of Queen Jezebel
26 Col. deg.
27 *The Simpsons* storekeeper
30 Lord High Treas.
31 Team cheer
32 Put on
33 ". . . as lovely as ___": Kilmer
36 Coffee or vanilla
38 Starts on for fast flyers
39 Who told Mary that her son was to be named Jesus?
42 Small dam
43 Actors Alejandro and Fernando
44 Peter of *Casablanca*
45 Prince Valiant's son
46 Suffix with cash
47 Throw or Oriental
48 Apt. divisions
49 Part of CBS
50 Church cry room
54 Pepper and others
55 Orchestra's location
56 Payment abbreviation
57 What prophet was told by God to name his son Lo-ammi?
60 Who was told by an angel that his son was to be named John?
63 Proximate
64 DIN's counterpart
65 Tehran resident
66 Honey badger
67 Son of Jacob
68 Seven-time Emmy winner

DOWN

1 Imitation
2 "That's it for me," in cards
3 What was Sarai's name changed to?
4 Current starter
5 Measure
6 Corporeal
7 What did God call his human creation?
8 Old English crossed *d*
9 Who was told by God to name his son Maher-shalal-hash-baz?
10 Arrests
11 Cable network
12 Guinness specialty
13 Church talk, for short
18 Rat-___
22 River of Syria
24 Obscure to view
25 "Like ___ on a hot griddle"
26 Crows
27 Firefighter Red
28 Raft helmsman
29 ___ Sam
33 Fighting
34 Heat combiner
35 Equestrian's controls
36 Miller and Becks
37 English cathedral city

38 Water lily pad riders
40 Middle tones
41 Become indistinct
46 What did God change Jacob's name to?
47 Legendary Yankee
50 Rechargeable battery
51 NA geologic epoch
52 Tennessee county and college
53 PLO leader
54 "___ Bones Gwine ter Rise Again" (old song)
55 "Que ___?" ("What's going on?")
57 Postal code
58 Commercial suffix with Motor
59 Drunkard
60 Zig's companion
61 Athletes in Action (Christian gr.)
62 Monopoly props.

Notable Women, and Some Less Notable (Part 1)

ACROSS

1 Dieter's concern
5 For what Old Testament prophet did Gomer bear Lo-ruhamah, Lo-ammi, and Jezreel?
10 What widowed prophetess was 84 years old when she saw the young Jesus in the temple?
14 They follow so
15 ___ *for Adano* (movie)
16 Superman's sweetie
17 Pitcher ___ Hershiser
18 Illinois town
19 Seaweed
20 What two women refused to commit infanticide in Moses' time?
23 Pertaining to ecological stages
24 Top-of-the-line
25 Repeated letters in German poet's first and last name
28 What woman of Corinth had a household that Paul described as being full of strife among Christian leaders?
33 Pt. of old Russia
36 Kind of house
40 Average grades
41 What congregation was Julia part of?
44 Performing without ___ (taking risks)
45 Who is the first daughter mentioned by name in the Bible?
46 Bible eds.
47 What daughter of Saul was promised as a wife to David for slaying Goliath?
49 Professor 'iggins, to Eliza
51 After Eve, who is the first woman mentioned in the Bible?
55 Type of orange
59 Role of 20-Across
64 What Israelite woman aided her people by murdering the Canaanite general Sisera in her tent?
65 Lizard
66 "___ Where My Money Goes" (early 1900s song)
67 ___-Seltzer
68 "Walk Away ___": 1966 hit song
69 A covering of hoarfrost
70 Daring deed
71 ___ Rice Burroughs
72 Author Robert ___ Butler

DOWN

1 Duds
2 Lash of old westerns
3 On ___ (overindulging)
4 What handmaid of Rachel bore Jacob sons Dan and Naphtali?
5 Actress Goldie
6 Shortest Old Testament bk.
7 Hurry, to Shakespeare
8 ___ Island, Australia
9 Medicinal plant extract
10 Controversial orchard spray
11 Vincent Lopez theme song
12 Almost
13 What king of Judah was the husband of Azubah?
21 First Hebrew letter
22 Chest muscle
26 "___ a tight ship"
27 Tiber feeder
29 Postal code

30 Emperor called "The Armenian"
31 Computer system vendors
32 Suffixes relating to nationality
33 Before ford in Connecticutt
34 Without, in Worms
35 Change course
37 Fellowship of Christian Athletes: Abbr.
38 Cry of woe
39 *Back to* ___ (Wayne film)
42 Windy City's pub. transportation
43 Kind of pillow
48 Candy follower
50 San ___, California
52 *The Wreck of the Mary* ___
53 Bearded, like some grasses
54 Some Vietnamese
56 Benefit
57 "___ to the Church on Time"
58 City on the Ruhr
59 Nathan, American revolutionary
60 Cries in the comics
61 Sound from the meadow
62 Intestinal parts
63 Bambi, for one
64 Popular sports car, informally

More Kings, Pharaohs, and Other Rulers

ACROSS
1 Oil money?
6 Showy rugs
10 What king of Israel experienced a long famine and drought during his reign?
14 "___ in peace"
15 ___ *Peach* (Allman Brothers album)
16 Hot-dog holder
17 Who was reigning in Judah when the Babylonians besieged Jerusalem and exiled the nobles?
19 1201, to Livy
20 ___ even keel
21 Vietnamese coin
22 Keyboard phone
24 ___pick
25 Actress Maryam
26 ___ *Fables*
30 This is one, in brief
31 Fall behind
32 Notice of intent: Abbr.
33 Actress Maureen
36 Beginning of a virus?
38 Hawaiian seaport
39 What Babylonian king's ambassadors were shown all of Hezekiah's treasures?
42 Limp as ___
43 What Egyptian king fought against Judah and killed King Josiah?
44 Peter and Paul, but not Mary
45 Coal porter
46 Masses, in brief
47 Garlic, in the Southwest
48 Renee, of old movies
50 Trade language, for short?
52 Kegler's org.
55 O.T. book
56 Duty cmdr.
57 L-o-n-g time
58 Airhead
61 What king of Assyria sent foreigners to settle in Israel after the Israelites had been taken away?
64 What king of Israel built the city of Samaria and made it his capital?
65 Italian actress Eleonora
66 Of course, Caesar
67 Hammer head
68 Anglo-Saxon letters
69 Pen name

DOWN
1 Mustard style
2 Early Britons
3 Bareheaded
4 Egyptian god of the gods
5 Defendants at law
6 Ish-bosheth's assassin
7 Internet search engine
8 When some lunch hours start
9 California city
10 Not Navy's
11 Ad ___ committee
12 Distillery prod.
13 Bible Lit. Int.
18 What evil king of Judah sacrificed his son as a burnt offering and built a Syrian-style altar in Jerusalem?
23 Young sheep
25 Couple
27 South Dakota city
28 Regions reached by Peary
29 Ten or pen followers
30 Short improvement?
31 ___-Hamath, Israel

33 City near Boys Town
34 What king lied to the magi about his desire to worship Jesus?
35 Pyrenees plough
36 King toppers
37 Pos. of 13-Down
38 Son of Milcah and Nahor
40 Predate
41 Naval off.
46 Green univ. dept.?
47 St. Louis landmark
49 What king of Syria joined the king of Israel in attacking Judah?
50 What king of Judah was hidden as a boy to protect him from wicked Queen Athaliah?
51 Buenos ___s
52 Spanish playwright Calderon
53 Rain gear
54 Two wives of King Henry VIII
57 Son of Beriah
58 Lapidary tool
59 "___ Mine" (Beatles song)
60 Lockheed ___-Star
62 South, in Seville
63 Bookkeeper, for short

Most Mentioned Men

ACROSS

1 What king has one less reference than the answer to 28-Down and ranks fifth?
5 What man would, if his famous nickname were considered in all contexts, outrank all the others in this list?
10 Place ___ in the paper
14 Elbe feeder
15 Debate
16 Scent sensor
17 Region in Ethiopia
18 Hairdo
19 Was certain
20 Insect nests
22 What military man ranks eleventh with 197 references?
24 Uneasy
27 1040 line
28 What patriarch, with 306 mentions, ranks seventh?
31 What king, mentioned 1,118 times in the Bible, is the second-most-mentioned man?
36 Computer-aided instr.
37 Composer ___ Stravinsky
39 A clean ___
40 Provo neighbor
42 What man, as if you don't know, is the most mentioned man in the Bible?
44 Pressure measurements, for short
45 Not at all, vernacularly
47 *General Hospital* regular Sofer
48 Motel extra
49 Chou of China
50 Who is eighth with his 295 mentions?
53 Bible chap. divs.
56 Egyptian pharaoh
57 What government leader in a foreign land ranks tenth with 208 references?
60 Signal Corps VIPs
63 Enameled metal
64 Prep school alternative in France
68 Stumble
70 Part of spy org.
71 Fable writer
72 *The Windsor Beauties* painter
73 Immigration's
74 *The Sound of Music* family
75 Jedi teacher

DOWN

1 Titanic message
2 "Like ___ on a hot griddle"
3 To the city, in old Italy
4 Beginning of a tape
5 Pointed criticism
6 Opposite of dep.
7 Computer display type
8 ___ board
9 Hound
10 Symbol of life in Cairo
11 Unfit for highborn Brits
12 Drifting
13 Drops on the lawn
21 Crete's highest mount
23 Baby danger, in brief
25 G-string?
26 European hunter
28 What priest ranks fourth with a total of 339 references?

29 Chile Ambassador John
30 What leader, with 740 mentions, ranks third?
32 Matterhorn is one
33 ___ Nunez de Balboa
34 Suffix with add or part
35 ORD or LAX, e.g.
36 Baskin-Robbins purchase
38 Kind of sentence
41 Memo of agr.
43 Red-tag event
46 Marry
51 Already taken: Abbr.
52 By and large
54 Rotten-tomato sound
55 More timid or bashful
57 Enroll in
58 Palm leaves used for writing
59 Meeting
61 Creme cookie
62 Small herring
63 Cable TV giant
65 Lee side?
66 End of paragraph marker
67 Bible teacher Theodore ___
69 Burmese currency

Most Mentioned Women

ACROSS

1 Sloppily
8 Jason of film
15 Shipwreck remains
16 What wife of both Nabal and David ranks seventh with 15 mentions?
17 What mother of twins ranks fourth with 31 mentions?
18 Bullfight
19 Tiber feeder
20 Elevs.
21 Courtier of King Josiah
24 A foot wide?
25 Health center
28 Old Glory, for one
29 Arlene and Roald
32 What relative of number 2 (8-Down) ranks third with 34 mentions?
33 Good angel in Frank Peretti's books
34 Safety agcy.
35 Packers' Keith
36 What follower of Jesus is mentioned 14 times?
40 Factotum
41 ___ part (play on stage)
42 Turner's channel
44 Derelicts
45 What Old Testament woman bore a child at age 90 and is the most mentioned woman in the Bible (56 mentions)?
47 Columbian river
48 This year's grads
49 *Beverly Hillbillies* character
50 Young lady's property
51 Caleb's oldest son
52 Helicopter inventor Sikorsky
54 What evil woman ranks fifth with 23 mentions?
58 Most like Felix Unger
62 Attire
63 Mrs. Roosevelt
64 Surgeon's stitches
65 Milk gland

DOWN

1 Mass maker, for short?
2 Engineer's course, in brief
3 Whimper
4 Short shorthand?
5 Siberian city
6 Dutch artist of Hals's time
7 Men's org.
8 What wife of a patriarch ranks second with 47 mentions?
9 Ugandan president's possession
10 Short hair, to Burns
11 Cabinet dept.
12 BBC's Italian counterpart
13 Past do?
14 Hearst's abductors: Abbr.
21 Ship's stern
22 Persistent outcry, in England
23 Prophet ___ donkey
25 Psychic sessions
26 Folks
27 Satisfied sounds
29 District sales mgr.
30 Eureka!
31 What servant woman is mentioned 14 limes?
32 Heavy-duty cleanser
34 Popeye's Olive
35 Col. deg.
37 *Treasure Island* initials

38 Bing Crosby's record label
39 Olympian, for short
40 Home signal sender
43 TV's *Emerald Point* ___
45 Tranquil
46 Grown-ups
47 What sister of a famous leader ties with number 7 (16-Across)?
49 Windsurfer's action
50 Computer-phone link
52 Menu entry
53 ___ monster
54 Petite sizes, for short
55 ___ Claire, Wisconsin
56 Face problem?
57 Grounded bird
59 Former queen of Spain
60 Starts dessert bet
61 Take a stab at

Still More Kings, Pharaohs, and Other Rulers

ACROSS
1 Parsley pieces
7 Coxcomb
10 Alts.
14 Continental breakfast?
15 What saintly king of Judah was crippled with a foot disease in his old age?
16 Great Lake
17 What son of Saul was made king over Israel by army commander Ahab?
19 Traveled by donkey
20 "Easier said ___ done!"
21 Common Market cont.
22 Blood letters
24 Same, for short
25 Parts of airplane seats
27 Effigies
31 Mauna ___
32 E.T.'s transport
34 Indo-European root run
35 Persian Gulf sheikdom
38 Architect Saarinen
40 Chinese politico Li
41 What king sent his son to David with expensive presents that David decided to use in worship?
44 Yarn
45 Leprechauns: Var.
46 Reminder lists
47 Icel., for one
48 It's after pi
49 Early PCs
50 Rebuke
52 Scruffs
55 Vietnamese New Year
58 Yes votes
60 Cent or capita leader
61 Walt Kelly's creation
62 Ex-host Griffin
65 Who reigned in Persia when Nehemiah heard the sad news about the walls of Jerusalem?
68 Fire prefix
69 Persian Gulf gp.
70 1955 children's heroine
71 Connecticut Senator
72 Head man: Abbr.
73 Sweet spice

DOWN
1 *NYPD Blue* actor Jimmy
2 Aggressive
3 Actress Ada
4 Book code
5 ___-Coat (wax)
6 Canaanite captain
7 ". . . ___ lands forlorn": Keats
8 German compass point
9 Glacial hill
10 What king had the apostle James executed with a sword and had Peter arrested?
11 Doz. doz.
12 Prescription abbr.
13 Bishop's territory
18 ___ Hin (Thai resort)
23 Pers. summary
25 Permanent brand
26 Roams, as the Internet
28 Daphne or Echo
29 Slowly, in music
30 Sad sounds
31 Superior, for one
33 "Fie, ___, and fum"
35 Upper story
36 What king of Judah became king

at age seven and was aided in his reign by the saintly priest Jehoiada?
37 Rock's ___ Vanilli
38 What fat king of Moab was murdered by the judge Ehud?
39 End of file marker
40 Chief mil. doctors
42 O.T. wall bldr.
43 Lawmen: Abbr.
48 Wilder's *Bridge of San Luis* ___
49 What Persian king was embarrassed by his disobedient wife?
51 Who was the first Hebrew king to reign from Jerusalem?
53 More fitting
54 Black-eyed or sweet
55 EPA word
56 Cast out
57 "We're off ___ the Wizard . . ."
59 What king broke his own law when he called on a spiritualist to bring up the ghost of Samuel?
61 Malay outrigger
62 ___term exam
63 Part of the psyche
64 Three min., in boxing
66 X-ray unit
67 Young sow

A Herd of Prophets

ACROSS

1 What prophet predicted that Jeroboam would be king over ten tribes of Israel?
7 Seize
10 Weakens
14 Latin Bible translator
15 Dots per in.
16 "___ a Song Go . . ."
17 Under legal age
18 City area, in brief
19 Crazy
20 UPS competitor
21 Some women's const. desire
23 What Old Testament patriarch was revealed as a prophet to King Abimelech?
25 Mama grizzly is one
28 Yoga position
29 What false prophet wore a yoke, which Jeremiah broke?
32 German lady
35 Actress Merrill
36 Contraction
39 Ushers
43 What prophet spoke of the need to purify temple worship after the return from exile in Babylon?
45 Madelaine Albright was one: Abbr.
46 Viet ___
48 This king of Israel was, early in his career, associated with a group of prophets?
49 Record or measure
53 King of Kings
57 The only female judge of Israel, this woman was considered a prophetess
60 What prophet wrote a brief book against Edom?
63 Tayback of *Alice*
64 Prune
66 North, to Pierre
67 Which was to be done: Lat. abbr.
69 Playful manner
71 Aweather's opposite
72 Ulan-___: Russian city
73 In a row: Var.
74 Pierre's yesterday
75 Preacher William Ward
76 What prophet, associated with Zechariah, was active at the time of the rebuilding of the temple in Jerusalem?

DOWN

1 Open a crack
2 Cordage plants
3 Type of linen
4 Provost of TV's *Lassie*
5 Protozoan
6 Sirs: Ger.
7 So. Bend campus
8 Guam's capital
9 Lettuce type
10 What traveling companion of Paul's was considered a prophet?
11 Wailuku welcome
12 Nut type
13 Plant pore
22 Auto club letters
24 1986 Indy winner Bobby
26 Hebrew who brought King Eglon "a message from God"
27 Circ.
30 998 in Rome
31 Santa ___ (Pacific wind)

32 Miami's st.
33 Sleep-study wd.
34 Army air base: Abbr.
36 Peruvian city
37 Day of the wk.
38 Weaken: Abbr.
40 "Pardon me, Marcello"
41 Greek island
42 Pilot's heading, in brief
44 Hebrew tribe: Var.
47 What prophet took David to task for numbering the people of Israel?
50 Today's English Version letters
51 King Rehoboam's son/successor
52 Oklahoma town
53 What reluctant prophet was thrown overboard in a storm?
54 Levi's *Christ Stopped at* ___
55 Bengali wrap
56 Milk source
58 "___ came a spider . . ."
59 What prophet was famous for his marriage to a prostitute?
61 Sea shade
62 Lamarr, of Hollywood
65 Foot prefix
68 Suffix that bears
70 Smoke stick, for short

Notable Women, and Some Less Notable (Part 2)

ACROSS

1 Who came to Jesus at the wedding of Cana and said, "They have no wine"?
5 "Nor iron bars ___": Milton
10 McDonald's founder Ray ___
14 Oxfordshire, for short
15 Philanthropic one
16 Mineral vein
17 What woman saved her city by negotiating peacefully with Joab?
20 Code-breaking org.
21 Ground-floor apartment
22 Up, to Ty Cobb
23 Make a day ___
24 Parisian oasis
26 What little girl was referred to as "Talitha" by Jesus?
33 Synthetic fiber
34 "Money ___ object!"
35 *Norma* ___ (Sally Field movie)
36 Cameroon volcanic lake
37 Charge
39 ___ D. (Doctor of Letters)
40 Velvet finish
41 Tortilla flour
42 Lariat
43 What unnamed woman broke the king's law by order of the king himself?
47 "Shake ___!"
48 Grandmother, affectionately
49 Bolivian popular capital
52 Follows am or Point-au-
53 Ecol. watchdog
56 Who helped David by hiding two of his messengers in her cistern?
60 Bk. data
61 Hebrew letter
62 Birds up from Down Under
63 Andrew of *Melrose Place*
64 Island next to Leyte
65 Over hill and ___

DOWN

1 Cut down
2 Central pivot
3 Parks who wouldn't take discrimination sitting down
4 Chem. ending
5 Aphrodite's love
6 Bill Haley's backup
7 Canaanite city of giants
8 Poly follower
9 Ranch follower
10 Coffee ___ (gathering)
11 Virginia Senator
12 Greek concert sites
13 Stonehenge builder
18 Unhappy
19 Moorehead's mate
23 Mining metals
24 "Que ___?" ("What's going on?")
25 Jemima, for one
26 Jamie Lee's mom
27 Rebel against King Pekah of Israel
28 Hole ___ (ace)
29 What daughter of Jacob caused major problems by venturing into strange territory?
30 Any Tom, Dick, and Harry
31 "One should ___ live not . . .": Molière
32 Do some roadwork
37 Taxi door info
38 Rescuers on the briny: Abbr.

39 Actresses Horne or Olin
41 A ___ minute
42 Get new lease
44 Canary's song
45 City in central New York
46 Outstanding in his field?
49 Motor oil additives
50 "Forget it!"
51 Philippine island or its seaport
52 Baby carriage, in England
53 Jane Austen novel
54 What apostle had a sister whose son informed soldiers of a murderous plot?
55 Handle, in Paris
57 Elevated place, for short
58 Nafta signatory
59 Largest lexicon, in brief

1
2
3
4
5
6
7
8
9
10
11
12
13
14
15
16
17
18
19
20
21
22
23
24
25
26
27
28
29
30
31
32
33
34
35
36
37
38
39
40
41
42
43
44
45
46
47
48
49
50
51
52
53
54
55
56
57
58
59
60
61
62
63
64
65

They Heard Voices

ACROSS

1 What blind father recognized Jacob's voice but was deceived by his covered hands?
6 Missing GI
10 Remove from a ms.
14 ___ Antoinette
15 Egoist's refrain
16 "What ___!" ("Groovy")
17 According to Isaiah, what noble person will not lift up his voice in the streets?
20 Female fowls
21 Nuclear watchdog's letters
22 Swines' sounds
23 Backwards brew?
24 Internet info. server
25 Tear apart
27 It turns out Its.
28 Actress Stapleton
29 *Atlas Shrugged* author Rand
32 According to Psalm 19, what has a voice that goes out to all the world?
36 "Like a bolt out of the ___"
37 Infloresence
38 O.T. maj. prophet
39 Coal carriers
40 Hockey score
41 Where did God speak to Moses in a voice like thunder?
43 Common ID
44 *I Spy* costar
45 Starts cough or cup
46 Whale groups
47 Inlet
48 Person with a beat?
51 Mongolian monks
54 Big name in guerrilla warfare
55 Muslim's House of God
56 Who cried out at the top of her voice when she saw Samuel raised from the dead?
60 Great dog?
61 Aussie tennis great
62 What bird did John hear crying in a loud voice, "Woe, woe to the inhabiters of the earth"?
63 Framing timber
64 *The Empire Strikes Back* mystic
65 Dime store founder Samuel

DOWN

1 "Oh, ___ kind of guy . . ."
2 South Sahara area
3 Omni or Forum
4 Feels sick
5 Company head
6 Staff members
7 Children's IQ test
8 Bus. course
9 Stretch the truth
10 What king heard the voice of God in the temple—although there was no temple at the time?
11 Richard of *A Summer Place*
12 Like young Abe Lincoln
13 Superlative endings
18 Mikhail's mate
19 Speckled horse color
24 Reykjavik is its cap.
25 French theologian Ernest
26 Eastern Airlines Syst.
27 Child of Zerubbabel
28 YMCA founder
29 Cranston or Greenspan
30 Arizona city
31 '40s theater director James

32 Boats
33 Med. care providers
34 Abba of Israel
35 Seventeenth cent. stringed instruments
36 ___-a-brac
39 Chinese tea
41 Indian tree
42 Larcenist
44 Mozart's "___ fan tutte"
46 Caressed clumsily
47 Who recognized Peter's voice after he was miraculously delivered from prison?
48 Sponge
49 Ancient Greek coins
50 Cuts down
51 Former Fords
52 At the drop of ___
53 Bill of fare
54 Large African lake
55 Tree burl
57 "Lord's Prayer" pronoun
58 Talk amorously
59 Cousin of "Yikes!"

1
2
3
4
5
6
7
8
9
10
11
12
13
14
15
16
17
18
19
20
21
22
23
24
25
26
27
28
29
30
31
32
33
34
35
36
37
38
39
40
41
42
43
44
45
46
47
48
49
50
51
52
53
54
55
56
57
58
59
60
61
62
63
64
65

Sleepers and Nonsleepers

ACROSS

1 Calculating snake?
6 Pentecostal denom.
9 To be, to Brutus
13 Mohandas Gandhi's religion
14 Rapper Dr. ___
15 Classic cars
16 Which epistle urges believers to be alert, not asleep?
19 Caesar's garb
20 Worked for
22 Mispelling like this
26 Cygnus's brightest star
28 Last Supper pl.
29 According to Jesus, what person was not dead, but only sleeping?
32 Dominick's Food Stores, e.g.
33 Capital of Norway
34 FICA funds mgr.
35 USA lexicon
38 Tyson tidbit?
39 Cockney residence
42 Add table to make flammable
44 S.S. Kresge, today
49 Who sneaked into Saul's camp while he was asleep?
53 Tennis score
54 River by the Louvre
55 Wildebeests
56 France's War of the Three ___
58 Spaniard's other
60 Which epistle chapter uses sleep as a metaphor for physical death?
66 Do-___ (scale tones)
67 French corp.
68 What MP seeks
69 Enzymes
70 Step after scanning txt.
71 ___ lazuli

DOWN

1 One casual greeting
2 Dah's counterpart
3 Letters after Gov. Jeanne Shaheen's name
4 Netherlands city
5 Metal attacker
6 Proverbs
7 Disney World gateway city
8 Small Chevrolet
9 Silkworm
10 Use AltaVista, e.g.
11 14-liners
12 Dead Sea Scrolls monastics
17 Lays down a lawn
18 Spiral ___
21 British liner sunk in Persian Gulf
22 Assoc. deg. site (with the)
23 Shout of derision
24 Daughter of Ingrid
25 "___ will throw thee from my care . . .": Shakespeare
27 Life of Riley
30 Dealt a severe blow
31 Russian author Maxim
36 Tennis champ Andre
37 Feminine suffix
39 Turkish chamber
40 Amber dessert wine
41 Displays clearly
43 Asinine
45 Chinese food additive
46 Army health nurse: Abbr.
47 Writer Santha Rama ___
48 Third word of "America"
50 Where to do as others do

51 Pollen bearer
52 Half a rice diet disease
57 Eye shutter
59 Amer. Acad. of Arts and Letters
61 Drafted officer
62 Minneapolis-based airline's initials
63 Dinner dipper
64 Last year of Caligula's reign
65 Eds.

1 2 3 4 5 6 7 8 9 10 11 12
13 14 15
16 17 18
19 20 21
22 23 24 25 26 27 28
29 30 31
32 33 34
35 36 37 38
39 40 41 42 43 44 45 46 47 48
49 50 51 52
53 54 55
56 57 58 59
60 61 62 63 64 65
66 67 68
69 70 71

People in Exile

ACROSS

1 Who was exiled to the land of Nod?
5 Shaving aid
9 Lolled
14 Amer. Radiological Nurses Assoc.
15 ___*hling*: David Bowie album
16 Bless, old-style
17 Who stayed in Egypt until Herod died? (answer continued in 62-Across)
19 What some fences are
20 Short friar?
21 Ottoman symbol
22 Kitchen attachment
23 Who sent Moses to Pharaoh?
24 Cert. of Adv. Studies
25 Gov't. annual stat
26 Kara ___ (Turkmenistan desert)
29 Colorado county
31 Creeping crusher
32 Artist's paints
33 Who was in exile three years after killing his brother Amnon?
36 Tyndale House author J. Stephen ___
37 Best Picture of 1958
40 "It takes a ___ livin' to make a house a home": Edgar Guest
41 Apothecary's pl.
42 Passed with flying colors
43 What nation carried Israel into exile?
45 ___ Bridge, St. Louis
46 Cot or cow follower
47 ". . . ___ body cry?": Burns
51 ___ carte menu
52 Where to hear *All Things Considered*
53 B-ball score
55 Org. for Nasser
56 Creator of Lorelei Lee
58 Puccini's ___ *Angelica*
59 He yielded to GRF
60 Wire cutter is one
62 17-Across, continued
64 Former Gold Coast
65 Precedes phone or polis
66 Tropical tree of the soapberry family
67 Hurt
68 Eccentric person: Slang
69 Third highest USN rank

DOWN

1 Currency exchange
2 Where Noah dropped anchor
3 "When ___, do as the . . ."
4 Denial
5 "I ___ Song Comin' On"
6 Rest stops
7 Calla lily family
8 Rocky and Alps, for short
9 Christine, of *Chicago Hope*
10 Work without ___ (take risks)
11 Who was king when Jerusalem fell to the Babylonians?
12 '50s musical star Taina ___
13 Hamlin's *L.A. Law* costar
18 Ebenezer's partner
22 Charm
25 Mawkishly sentimental
27 Wrist-elbow tie
28 RCC prelate
30 Fridge forays
31 Indifferent
32 Greek flasks

34 Needles, e.g.
35 Norse gods
37 Greek earth goddess
38 Med or rad add-on
39 Who was appointed governor of Judah after the people went into exile?
44 Short preface?
48 Finder's cry
49 Retarded, as an action
50 Dutch city on the Rhine
52 "War Games" org.
53 Stir
54 Lollipop cop
57 Prefix for wine
58 Snick's partner
60 Golf org.
61 Loc. of 1-A and 1-D
62 Allied Mil. Govt.
63 Patriotic org.

Violent People and Things

ACROSS

1 What evil king of Judah was killed by his servants?
5 Forcible impact
9 Hungarian river and city
14 Actor Wilder
15 Hoboes hit it
16 Big name in drugs
17 Coll. of writings
18 Airline from Lod airport
19 Minute stinging organ
20 Who killed Hamor and Shechem because of their sister Dinah?
23 Col. deg.
24 Biblical affirmative
25 Passover fare
29 Hooks
31 Sweet potato
34 Pewter, in Paris
35 Wine: Prefix
36 Study, with over
37 What did Ehud use to kill fat King Eglon of Moab?
40 State where M. L. King was killed
41 Noted *Harper's Bazaar* illustrator
42 Like *USA Today*
43 Curve in ship's timber
44 Open delight
45 Archeologist's find
46 Wild river of Borneo
47 Common DC license letters
48 Where did Cain kill Abel?
55 Circular
57 Islands off New Guinea
58 To him, to Babette
59 Commit arson
60 Crossword publisher
61 Hollywood's Ryan O'___
62 Japan's third-largest city
63 Caps Lock neighbor, on a computer
64 Who threw a javelin at David?

DOWN

1 "I've Got ___ in Kalamazoo"
2 Handwriting on the wall
3 Airing
4 Royal Crown Cola brand
5 Murder weapon in Clue
6 Detains, as for questioning
7 Amer. Assoc. for the Adv. of Science
8 Year in Ivan the Terrible's reign
9 Program hosts
10 Birthplace of Columbus
11 Thomas Moore's country
12 Accepted, in brief
13 Jamaican pop music
21 ". . . to get her poor dog ___"
22 Jesus' cry from the cross
25 Butcher's offerings
26 Time for coffee break, often
27 Lion-colored
28 Jerusalem's temple hill
29 Golfer Calvin
30 Cologne conclusion
31 Hindu mystics
32 Son of Gad
33 Streep of the screen
35 Mean person
36 Belongs to golfers' org.
38 New ___, India
39 Mr. Hitler
44 Nabber's cry
45 In an unconstrained manner
46 General Motors product
47 Wild Asian dog
48 Work, in Madrid

49 Zippo
50 Long journey
51 Actors McKellen and Holm
52 Zeno's home town
53 Hawaiian banquet
54 Seasoning herb
55 Sioux Indian
56 *L.A. Law* villainess

Taxes, Extortion, and Bribes

ACROSS

1 What empire's taxation led to Jesus being born in Bethlehem?
5 Zuider ___
8 Syrian plain
12 Chicago paper, familiarly
13 Product ID
14 "Take ___ your leader"
15 What did hungry Esau give up to Jacob in exchange for food?
18 Star Wars, initially
19 Pleading
21 Superhighways: Abbr.
25 Behave like a brat
28 Intl. Conf. for Itinerant Evangelists
29 According to the Law, how much tax did adult Israelites have to pay when the census was taken?
32 Number in NASA-speak
33 Shoe width
34 Allow
35 Computer display type: Abbr.
38 Mil. goods functionary
39 Denver's time zone: Abbr.
42 Ride the waves
44 "I have ___": Essays of Elia
49 Who bribed the guards at Jesus' tomb to say that the disciples had stolen the body?
53 Actress with a *Tootsie* role
54 Heavenly phenomena
55 Amino acid
56 Minor accident result
58 Usual, in brief
60 Who laid a tax on the whole Persian Empire?
66 *Star Wars* princess
67 Honshu city
68 Who held a feast for Jesus that was attended by many tax collectors?
69 Time-line divisions
70 Map lines, for short
71 Pre-college exam: Abbr.

DOWN

1 Follows no for direction
2 "___ will throw thee from my care . . .": Shakespeare
3 Wrong prefix?
4 Wanes
5 Swiss banking center
6 Clumsy "in" follower?
7 Level of hierarchy: Abbr.
8 Old song "Abdul Abulbul ___"
9 Celery or carrots
10 Morally right
11 On the nasty side
16 McKinley and Lupino
17 Indian money
20 Goes, in Germany
21 Beige
22 ___ Beta Kappa
23 Topeka's st.
24 Lupus letters
26 Casual shirt
27 Guitar player
30 Just-baked
31 Italian sculptor, 1509–90
36 21 shillings, to Brits
37 Mars: Prefix
39 Short sessions?
40 Ball and chain is one
41 Boston and Manchester are two
43 First Families of Virg.
45 British ref. book set

46 Pueblo pronoun
47 Pete Sampras's org.
48 Cape Town's land: Abbr.
50 Skulls
51 Admission permits
52 Four before vee
57 Belongs to Wood's org.
59 Singers Shannon and Reeves
61 Heston role
62 Near: Abbr.
63 Abbr. next to a telephone number
64 Dutch col.
65 Command to Rex

1
2
3
4
5
6
7
8
9
10
11
12
13
14
15
16
17
18
19
20
21
22
23
24
25
26
27
28
29
30
31
32
33
34
35
36
37
38
39
40
41
42
43
44
45
46
47
48
49
50
51
52
53
54
55
56
57
58
59
60
61
62
63
64
65
66
67
68
69
70
71

Military Men

ACROSS

1 Courtyard
6 Police radio msg.
9 El ____, California
14 Revise a text
15 Schoolboy
16 "You ____ Beautiful"
17 What Roman soldier was led to Christ by Peter?
19 Tear to shreds
20 Plop or plunk starter
21 Tablecloth label letters
22 Sound at the circus
23 What brother of Joab was famous for having killed 300 enemy soldiers in battle?
26 Outstanding athlete
30 Minos's man of brass
31 Doctors' gp.
32 Without, in Wittenberg
33 What soldier was in charge of David's bodyguard?
36 Dog's papers
37 American stamp maker
40 "It's ____ Unusual Day"
41 Migrating fish
42 Confucian path
43 Lethargic feeling
45 "Is it" Latin?
47 Buz clan leader
48 Morals standards
52 Who was the commander of Abimelech's army?
54 What Philistine soldier was slain by a boy carrying a bag of stones?
56 Presbyterian Church in Amer.
57 Newsman Armstrong
58 11 seceders, for short
59 Wedding attendant
61 What Assyrian field commander tried to intimidate King Hezekiah by speaking propaganda to the people of Jerusalem?
64 Oak offering
65 Hawaiian instr.
66 Popular watch brand
67 Used a paddle
68 Styling stuff
69 Trial's partner

DOWN

1 Eat like a bird
2 Unicellular creature
3 Sharon Green's fantasy leader
4 Hilton is one
5 Praise poem
6 Suspect's need
7 Who had a nephew that informed the Roman soldiers of a plot to kill a prisoner?
8 Governing gps.
9 Seasonal song
10 Musical passage
11 What judge from Gilead was called to be a commander against the Ammonites?
12 Buckeyes' sch.
13 Alphabet sequence
18 Length over all: Abbr.
24 Convulsive cries
25 Health, Safety and Envir. Mgt. Council
26 What foreign king had Nebuzaradan as commander of his troops?
27 TV actress Christine
28 "Lonely Boy" singer
29 Shipping dept. stamp

31 Garlicky mayonnaise
34 Sturgeon River, to native Edmontonites
35 Hero of the first opera written for TV
37 BYU gridiron foe
38 Waist product
39 What captain of the palace guard did Joseph serve under?
41 What commander led a successful revolt against the ill-fated King Zimri?
44 Choice gp.
46 Give consent
49 Computer enthusiast
50 Susquehanna's source
51 Mountain town of Reuben, Zereth-____
53 Went swiftly
54 Lonesome George of early TV
55 Antiquated, in brief
57 Clear leaves
59 GI's R & R spot
60 TV's ____ Na Na
61 Carpet
62 Weeding tool
63 American Airlines's parent co.

The Anointed Ones

ACROSS

1 What apostle told the early Christians that all believers were anointed by the Holy Spirit?
5 Causes of some scratches
10 Tabula ___ (blank slate)
14 A phobia lead-in
15 Wash cycle
16 French summers
17 Who, according to James, should anoint the sick believer with oil?
20 Neptune's realm
21 See eye to eye
22 Ancient land on the Aegean
23 Anti-narcotics grp.
24 Perfumed
26 Supernatural marvels
31 *Wheel of Fortune* request
32 Unnamed ones
33 *Fly Away Home* flock
35 Denial expression
38 Persian king Cyrus was considered to be ___
42 Baden Baden, e.g.
43 Party game
44 "The ___ lama, he's a priest": Nash
45 Once owned
46 What substance was usually used for anointing in Israel?
49 Deciphers
53 Add ame for a famous Street
54 Ex-Mrs. Trump
55 Words on a diner ad
58 Blind charity initials
61 Who did Moses anoint with the blood of a ram?
64 Snarl
65 *Gandhi* setting
66 Hebrew month
67 JFK sights
68 Bog
69 "If I ___ you . . ."

DOWN

1 Sajak and Summerall
2 Tooth trouble
3 Fertilizer compound
4 Whereabouts, for short
5 The TV Gourmet
6 NYC commuter line
7 Suffix with exist
8 What scattered from Jeroboam's altar when he ordered his men to seize a prophet in front of it?
9 Envision
10 Newly decorated
11 Pitch ___
12 Fin de ___ (remainder): Fr.
13 Syrian president
18 Hic ___ hoc . . .
19 One with a mortgage
23 From nine to five, in the classifieds
25 Bone holder
26 Short sessions?
27 Popular food chain, informally
28 The scarlet letter
29 Last East German Communist party leader Krenz
30 Watchmaker
34 Carbon compound
35 Taboo
36 "Dedicated to the ___ love"
37 Archer William
39 Island and city at head of Persian Gulf
40 Skin-colored
41 Accomplishes

45 Advanced classes
47 Old Testament major prophet
48 Dog docs
49 Analyses, in brief
50 Swimming gold medalist Janet
51 Gold weight
52 Medicinal plant
56 Dest.
57 ___ *Old House*
58 In one—good; in roof—bad
59 Tree protuberance
60 Capri, for one
62 Ambition
63 Put in stitches

Houses of Worship

ACROSS

1 God and the ___ are the temple in the New Jerusalem
5 Sicily's volcano
9 What king tricked the followers of Baal by gathering them in Baal's temple and then slaughtering them?
13 Wings, to Pindar
14 Which goddess had a notorious temple at Ephesus?
16 Commotions
17 Mozart's "___ Pastore"
18 Looks happy
19 Mane setting
20 What famed religious structure was at Ephesus?
23 Agreements
24 Keep a date
25 Prophet Samuel's hometown
29 What king issued an order allowing the Jews to rebuild the temple in Jerusalem?
34 "So that's it!"
37 Scrabble pieces
39 "___ a man who wasn't there"
40 What did Ezekiel receive a vision of while he was in exile in Babylon?
44 Who had an Assyrian-style altar made for the Hebrews' worship center?
45 Mumblings
46 Tennis match unit
47 Baal-___ (Philistine god)
50 Former East German secret police
52 Spar
54 "___ if I care!"
58 Who asked Elisha's forgiveness for worshipping in the temple of the god Rimmon?
65 "___ each life . . ."
66 Tot
67 The "A" in A.D.
68 *Gone With the Wind* setting
69 Apply sequins to
70 "___weiss": *Sound of Music*
71 Who built a temple for Baal in Samaria?
72 Academic periods, in brief
73 Amphibious vehicles, for short

DOWN

1 Nonclergy
2 Formal avenue
3 Schoolteachers of old
4 Pager
5 Sharp side
6 Novice
7 Unaffected
8 Karenina and Pavlova
9 A Fonda
10 What's wrapped up in the whole ball of wax?
11 Arizona native
12 Functions
15 ___ as a beet
21 Attorney-to-be's exams, in brief
22 Boston party
26 Ms. Farrow (Allen's ex)
27 "___ Well That Ends Well"
28 Shoe parts
30 Basket boundary
31 Rascals
32 African river
33 Let it stand
34 Take ___ at (criticize)

35 Foolish giggle
36 Sandarac tree
38 Plant fungus
41 Automatic weapon
42 Sing-a-long syllable
43 Theme paper
48 As yet undisclosed info.
49 Trumpets, in traffic
51 Country where 9-Across was king
53 Support timbers
55 Varieties
56 French impressionist
57 Chemical compounds
58 Silent actress Naldi
59 Esau's in-law
60 Gillette product
61 Land of ancient Jordan
62 Ho. repair store
63 Ancient Dead Sea region
64 They say the same things, in brief

1
2
3
4
5
6
7
8
9
10
11
12
13
14
15
16
17
18
19
20
21
22
23
24
25
26
27
28
29
30
31
32
33
34
35
36
37
38
39
40
41
42
43
44
45
46
47
48
49
50
51
52
53
54
55
56
57
58
59
60
61
62
63
64
65
66
67
68
69
70
71
72
73

Horns of the Altar (Part 1)

ACROSS

1 Phys. or Psych.
5 Cry of delight
10 Hankering
14 Celebes ox
15 ___ Doone (cookie brand)
16 British liner sunk in Persian Gulf (1962)
17 What was the altar in the tabernacle made of?
19 Lincoln, and the like
20 Ulan ___, Mongolia
21 *Knots Landing* actress Park Lincoln
22 Animal often sacrificed on an altar
23 *Homo erectus,* for one
25 *Ripley's Believe ___ Not!*
26 Current starter
29 Suffix with drunk or tank
30 TV adjunct
31 TV's *Emerald Point* ___
34 Bearer of bad tidings to Nehemiah
36 What priest of Judah placed a money box near the temple's altar?
38 Ms. Sommer of *The Oscar*
39 ___ *Gay* (famed warplane)
41 Cupcake topper
42 What wicked Hebrew king built altars for the worship of Baal and the stars?
44 Cooked in hot water
46 Old Tokyo
47 Six-time home run champ
48 PC mem.
49 Capitol-___ (music company)
50 Compass pts.
52 In what country did evil King Ahaz build an altar modeled on the altars of Syria?
54 What did King Josiah take out of tombs and burn on an altar to defile it?
56 Encyc. component
57 Falters
61 Future fowl?
62 What book of the Bible mentions a talking altar?
64 Ever so much
65 Nintendo's precursor
66 What Bible book records Joshua rebuilding the Jerusalem altar when the exiles returned to Israel?
67 Sneaker brand
68 Building bus.
69 Caroled

DOWN

1 Aircraft and auto maker
2 Mid-Atlantic or midwestern sch.
3 Gravy holder
4 Who built an altar and named it for El, the God of Israel?
5 Ending for pay or Cray
6 Bayed
7 Penpoint style
8 ___ off (switch choice)
9 ___ Vashem (Jerusalem museum)
10 Boise's state
11 Where was the Hebrews' altar of incense first located?
12 American Indian
13 Door fastener
18 West New Guinea
22 Add be for photo light
24 Who offered sacrifices on the brazen altar?

25 "The glory has departed" (Hebrew name)
26 This puzzle has one
27 Waldorf, for one
28 In Athens Paul saw an altar inscribed "To an ___"
30 Calfskin ms.
32 Revoke, at the bar
33 Famed New York restaurateur
35 Actors' assn.
36 Fourth Gospel, in brief
37 The third
40 Take home
43 Plants seeds
45 Nebraska city
48 Kings, e.g.
51 Birds build them
52 Men's fragrance brand
53 Detests
54 Bird feature
55 Leer
56 Controversial line item
58 Gershwin tune
59 Undecided
60 Unexpected obstacle
62 British motorists' org.
63 Ignited, as a bottle rocket

A Bevy of Priests (Part 1)

ACROSS

1 What the high priest ordered his men to give Paul
6 What priest Zacharias was made because he did not believe an angel's prophecy
10 Twosomes, for short
13 Unverified news
14 Don Juan's mother
15 Actor Stephen, of *The Crying Game*
16 Royal title of 52-Across
19 Rev. Paisley
20 Carrots' companions
21 Took a humbling position
23 What priest was told by Jeremiah that he would be taken to Babylon as a prisoner?
27 Cross-shaped figure
29 Detach
30 Caiaphas's occupation
31 Priest Jehoiada made the ___ piggy bank
32 What priest of Midian taught Moses how to administer justice among the Hebrews?
33 Conway, Ark. sch.
36 Musical symbol
37 Having handles
38 Bobby, of hockey, and namesakes
39 Capitol Hill VIP
40 Argumentative words
41 Walt Disney's middle name
42 Arrives, as a bus or train
44 Tarzan's transport
45 First Christian martyr
47 A chief city of Samaria
49 Haitian rum
50 College sports org.
51 "___ my brother's keeper?"
52 What priest in the Bible is mentioned as having no mother or father?
59 Daughters of the Amer. Rev.
60 In addition
61 One of Aaron's priestly sons
62 Before, of yore
63 Disencumbers
64 *The Thinker* creator

DOWN

1 Commandments container
2 ___mate: chess
3 K-O connection
4 Pentecostal denom.
5 Haggai's role when sent to encourage the rebuilding of the temple under the priest Joshua
6 Architect ___ van der Rohe
7 *Faerie Queen* heroine
8 Soho sleuth
9 What is the only book of the Bible named after a priest besides Ezra?
10 Whom did King Ahaz order to make a copy of a pagan altar he had seen in Damascus?
11 Kingdom
12 Yuletide visitor
17 Pot-au-___ (meat and vegetable dish)
18 Norm
22 Lockman Foundation's Bible version: Abbr.
23 Kleenex competitor
24 Old-womanish
25 What did two priests (Aaron's

sons) offer to the Lord that caused their death?
26 Beginning of Michelangelo's workplace
27 For vinegar and oil
28 Made tracks
30 Former Argentinian newsmaker
32 Arrived breathlessly
34 Heavy lifter
35 Bhutan and Bangladesh neighbor
37 To be, to Brutus
38 Apost follower
40 Another priestly son of Aaron
41 What priest was the first head of the Levites?
43 Prefix with center
45 Geological period of time
46 Daughter of David
47 Educ. site
48 "Bali ___"
50 Sgt., for example
53 What priest received the boy Samuel as a servant?
54 Illegal drug, familiarly
55 Nigerian
56 Accomplished
57 Grandson of Jacob
58 Hungarian Communist leader Bela

The Company of Apostles (Part 1)

ACROSS
1 Who was the apostle to the Gentiles?
5 By what other name was Matthew known?
9 Serving meth.
13 Spanish angel's instrument
14 Pope John Paul II's real first name
15 Potpourri
16 Who is identified with Bartholomew, mentioned in John 1:45?
19 Central American tree
20 Feet forms
21 Having a backing fabric
22 Wallace, of *Reader's Digest*
23 Morgue tag
24 Who is supposed to have been executed by being cut apart? (place on answer in 65-Across)
31 Drifting
32 Skillful
33 "___ is me": Isaiah
35 ___ Bator: capital of Mongolia
36 Fetch
38 Fifth bk. of Moses
39 Cover
40 Horse with a gray-sprinkled coat
41 Waffle brand
42 Who was with Jesus at the Transfiguration?
47 Bandage brand
48 Cartoon light bulb
49 Refine, as metal
52 *Pagliacci* soprano
54 African Meth. Episcopal Church letters
57 Who brought Greeks to Jesus?
60 Invitation word
61 Blue dyes
62 Double-reed woodwind
63 Gathered cong.
64 Who, according to tradition, preached in Persia and died a martyr there?
65 One answer from 24-Across

DOWN
1 Windex target
2 Yasir Arafat is one
3 Doing, so to speak
4 ___-di-dah
5 Father of Mareshah
6 "Able was I ___ saw Elba": palindrome
7 Pts. of a set
8 UN agency
9 Party
10 Ex-senator Cranston
11 Speeder's penalty
12 Warty-skinned amphibian
14 Used a prie-dieu
17 An exemplar of neatness
18 Root beer concoction
22 Home equity is one
23 Four after cee
24 What was Paul's original name?
25 Long Island locale
26 Gettysburg general
27 Patsy's pal on *Absolutely Fabulous*
28 Eastern discipline
29 Town near Binghamton
30 Hard
34 English prince's school
36 Brought forth
37 British rule in India
38 ___ vu

40 Straight starter
43 Christian artist Kirk
44 Center
45 Old Norse collections
46 Actors Connery and Penn
49 Org. that safeguards pets
50 Conductance units
51 Navigator leader/author Leroy
52 Disney's *World's Greatest Athlete*
53 City in Oklahoma
54 ___ kanfoth (Jewish garment)
55 Cat's call
56 Gershwin biographer David
58 Petroleum Assn. of Japan
59 Windows forerunner

Speaking of Churches (Part 1)

ACROSS

1 Dr. Luke's church history book
5 ". . . baked in ___"
9 Paul was driven out of the Iconium church by unbelieving ___
13 Horse trot
14 ". . . ___ bell"
16 Motion supporters
17 Gillette product
18 Town, in Scotland
19 Swerve
20 At what church was Paul accused of turning the world upside down?
23 *Ah, Wilderness!* mother
24 Spanish gold
25 Gibr., for one
28 Notebook divider
31 What church had fallen prey to the legalistic Judaizers?
33 What church was neither hot nor cold?
38 German artist of the Renaissance
39 Fish-eating bird
40 Tennis term
43 Method of learning
44 Water retention
46 What church tolerated the heresy of the Nicolaitans?
48 What church had Crispus, a synagogue leader, as a member?
51 Flower necklace
52 Made of mins.
53 "Happy ___ the merciful"
54 Four-time Grammy Award–winner Lou
59 What is the most commended church in Revelation?
63 Who told an Asian church to buy white clothing to hide its nakedness?
66 ". . . partridge in ___ tree"
67 Confined
68 Shoe insert
69 City Paul visited on first and third missionary journeys
70 Neck of the woods
71 Outermost Aleutian
72 Presidential candidate Perot
73 Jack Sprat's diet

DOWN

1 Multicolored marble
2 Notre Dame & Chartres: Abbr.
3 Radials
4 Former E. German secret police
5 Hebron, of olde
6 Who founded the church at Antioch of Pisidia?
7 Japanese equivalent of a purse
8 Holiday drink
9 Cawfee
10 Hurricane center
11 Itty-bitty
12 Pre-Yeltsin Russ.
15 Biblical census taker
21 Pharaoh after Rameses I
22 Unresponsive
25 Senator Thurmond
26 Connect with
27 Rises, as a horse
29 Certain elec. outlets
30 Nectar gatherer
32 Glow
33 Sucker
34 Zeal
35 Humdingers

36 ___tasse coffee
37 Dadaist Jean ___
41 Ancient writing mat.
42 Poetic palindrome
45 Esau's in-law
47 Kind of Scout
49 Threesome
50 Assistant
55 Horrify
56 Traveler's query
57 Top of a form to be filled out
58 The church at Smyrna suffered because of the "synagogue of ___"
59 Before matic
60 Plane beginning
61 Pats gently
62 "___ TV" (1974 hit)
63 Jordan Trade Assn.
64 Uneaten morsels
65 Highly excited, with up

Horns of the Altar (Part 2)

ACROSS

1 What god's priests danced around the altar while they cut themselves with knives and daggers?
6 Foxy
10 What evil king of Judah built an altar modeled on the altars of Syria?
14 Gasoline or Tin Pan
15 Edmonton's prov.
16 Dry prefix?
17 What book of the Bible mentions a talking altar?
19 Feminine suffix
20 Biblical giants' patriarch
21 Cal. units
22 ____-El (Superman's real name)
24 Barbie's partner
25 Gr. Lake
26 Hammerstein or Wilde
30 Mess hall "slaves," for short
32 Col. deg.
34 Actress Thurman
35 Enlarged, of olde
38 What military leader was killed while holding on to the horns of the altar?
40 What God promised Sarah and Abraham
41 Who rebuilt the Jerusalem altar when the exiles returned to Israel?
44 Jazz trumpeter Al ___
45 Holland, for short
46 4-H activities
47 Card
48 Doctors' bd.
49 Scotland's major river
50 Who built an altar and called it "The Lord is my banner"?
52 Tobacco giant's initials
54 Chiropractor's work, for short
57 Very, to Jose
59 Orbiting astron. observatory
60 Word in a magician's phrase
61 What king of Israel built a Baal altar to please his pagan wife?
64 What was the altar in the tabernacle made of?
67 Miami's county
68 Derelict
69 Dig into
70 Radio-active trucker?
71 Lockman Foundation's Bible version letters
72 Parcels, with "out"

DOWN

1 Biblical military leader
2 Coeur d'___, Idaho
3 U.S. astronomer Clark
4 Onion's kin
5 Wd. fragment
6 Williams title start
7 Santa keeps one
8 Pontiac of the '60s
9 Pull quickly
10 Skaters' jumps
11 Rooster's mate
12 Prince Valiant's son
13 Playwright Akins
18 Who had a vision of the Lord standing beside the altar?
23 Aeronautical angle, in brief
27 Prophet Zephaniah's father
28 Love, in Lourdes
29 Hindu princes
30 Didn't part with

31 Drug compendium: Abbr.
32 Turkish, e.g.
33 Presidential monogram
35 Hebrews' wilderness campsite
36 A Marx
37 Toast start
38 Army vehicle
39 Opening: Med.
40 Have ____ in the matter
42 Corporate appendage
43 *Death ____ Salesman*
48 Tempe sch.
49 Picard subordinate
51 Glowing log
52 Chestnut equines
53 Who built an altar and named it for El, the God of Israel?
54 Like ____ from the blue
55 Pushed ahead
56 Light green colors
58 Hang open
60 Bide-___
61 Minors' govt. support
62 O.T. minor prophet, for short
63 Humorist George ___
65 Richard Helms's agcy.
66 Fleet cmdr.

A Bevy of Priests (Part 2)

ACROSS

1 Norse thunder god
5 "You ___?" (butler's response)
9 Wad
13 Discourteous
14 Love lyric of Provence
15 ". . . ___ perfumed sea"
16 What are the only books of the Bible named after priests?
19 "It's ___ sordid"
20 Persians' allies
21 Mu ___ (mushroom)
24 Nobel author Andric
25 In the past
27 Old English letter
28 What is the only parable of Jesus to have a priest as a character?
32 Strong point
33 Trig. function
34 Loyal, in the Highlands
35 Broad tie
37 Sibs, e.g.
41 Burton of *Star Trek: TNG*
43 Grass spike bract
44 What priests—two of Aaron's sons—were killed because they offered "strange fire" to the Lord?
47 Antique car
49 Exposure index
50 German oil
51 Be under the weather
52 Dine at home
54 Nearsighted Mr.
56 What were the names of the two stones worn in the high priest's breastplate and used to determine God's will?
61 North Carolina campus
62 Damage, with up
63 Longest river in Switzerland
64 Letterman's rival
65 "Now I see!"
66 Muddy, as the water

DOWN

1 *Uno, due,* ___
2 Son of Nahor and Milcah
3 Czech river
4 One who sees it as it is
5 Rescue payment
6 Fashion designer Gucci
7 Compass dir.
8 Atlas name locator, for short
9 Furnace fuel
10 Speed skater Eric
11 Slim as ___
12 Football Hall of Famer Bill
17 A as in Edison?
18 Overact
21 It's all the same to moi
22 Stocking
23 Santa ___, California
25 Buck ending
26 Central idea
29 TV's angel Reese
30 Capital of Ghana
31 One fiddler
35 Gardner and namesakes
36 Former Cincinnati Red Chris
38 Aka Charles Lamb
39 Mormon leader to America
40 What king ordered the execution of Ahimelech and other priests because they had conspired with David?
42 Minneapolis suburb

43 Mount ____ Observatory
44 Vague idea
45 "___ into the ark"
46 SA rodent
47 What priest of Midian taught Moses how to administer justice among the Hebrews?
48 *College Bowl* host Robert
53 Mae West's ___ *Angel*
54 Rocky, for short
55 Hawaiian thrush
57 Scottie Pippen's org.
58 "Any fool knows that!"
59 Son of Bela
60 Ott or Gibson

1
2
3
4
5
6
7
8
9
10
11
12
13
14
15
16
17
18
19
20
21
22
23
24
25
26
27
28
29
30
31
32
33
34
35
36
37
38
39
40
41
42
43
44
45
46
47
48
49
50
51
52
53
54
55
56
57
58
59
60
61
62
63
64
65
66

The Company of Apostles (Part 2)

ACROSS

1 In ____ (pickle)
5 Sarai's husband
10 Wt. meas.
14 Doozy
15 She played Thelma in *Thelma & Louise*
16 Saint Philip ____ (Renaissance figure)
17 Mine access
18 Arrive at, as a solution
19 Boring affair
20 Who did Jesus say he would make into fishers of men?
23 Japanese national park
24 Honest ___
25 Biggest weapon
29 Rangers' org.
32 Christian children's clubs
36 Jericho inn?
38 Faithful lead-in
40 German cathedral
41 Who brought Greeks to Jesus?
45 Bone doctors' org.
46 Blest be the one that binds
47 Gaines rival
48 Pert
51 Newspaper initials
53 Starter's alert
54 Letters of credit
56 Certain model railroads
58 Who is supposed to have been executed by being sawn in pieces?
66 Curse
67 Central Minnesota town
68 Utah city
69 Osso ___ (Italian veal)
70 Trans-Jordan city Moses conquered
71 Scandinavian name
72 Spanish custard dessert
73 Some Canadian fliers
74 Removes the squeak

DOWN

1 Gain ___ on
2 Who, according to tradition, preached in Assyria and Persia and died a martyr in Persia?
3 Settled
4 Silent
5 Titled Turks
6 Know about
7 Taken back, in brief
8 Wild ox of Celebes
9 Bread from heaven
10 Which apostle, originally a disciple of John the Baptist, was supposed to have been crucified on an X-shaped cross?
11 Irish poet Aubrey Thomas de ___
12 Command in a western
13 What Prodigal Son fed
21 What disciples called Jesus
22 Aka for a business
25 Italian harps
26 Brazilian state
27 Buckeye state's
28 Last Old Testament bk.
30 Dearest
31 Degree for DA
33 Paul sailed the ___tic Sea
34 Eternal
35 Home products company
37 San Francisco is one: Abbr.
39 Drop bait lightly
42 French river
43 Florence Nightingale, e.g.

44 Dr. of rap
49 Devout man who held Jesus
50 Hoo starter
52 "____ no business like . . ."
55 Let loose
57 Harriet's husband
58 What was Paul's original name?
59 Andean of old
60 *Crimson* ___: movie thriller
61 "____ I stand": Martin Luther
62 Moreover
63 By what other name was Matthew known?
64 Zerubbabel's son
65 Cookie containers
66 Baptist Bible Fellowship org.

Speaking of Churches (Part 2)

ACROSS

1 "Love ___ Wonderful Thing" (Bolton hit)
4 Round rods
10 Snow runners
14 Writer Anais
15 Mrs. Walton of *The Waltons*
16 Verve
17 ___ *York* (Gary Cooper movie)
18 With whose wood did Solomon build the temple?
19 Singer Vallee
20 What is the most commended church in Revelation?
23 Goal of mountaineering is to be here
24 Wool source
28 ___ B. DeMille
30 Vegas starter
33 Bishop of old TV
34 Old English crossed d
35 Christie of mystery
38 "___, old chap . . ."
39 What was the first church to appoint deacons?
41 Gingko tree
44 Secondary sports event
45 Canadian Cattlemen's Assoc.
48 *Speed* name
50 Bran source
51 In what church did Paul raise up Eutychus, who had fallen to his death out of a window?
53 Mesh
55 Large coffeepots
56 At what church was Paul accused of turning the world upside down?
62 Tableware
65 Actresses Dern and Hutton
66 Opposite of alt
67 Marsh bird
68 Show clearly
69 Hiking path, for short
70 Trash thief, perhaps
71 Obligations
72 Presidential initials

DOWN

1 Where one is weightless
2 Ornithologist's log entry
3 At what church were believers first called Christians?
4 Capital of Qatar
5 Smelly
6 Telegram
7 Weigh, for short
8 Flaccid
9 Russian-born violinist Schneider, informally
10 Order of angels
11 Part of KKK
12 Start of the Christian Era
13 Like a wallflower
21 Det. amt. of text on a printed page
22 Parisian pronoun
25 Loser to D.D.E.
26 Council of Econ. Advisors
27 Not a picky specification
29 New Guinea port
30 Cruise ship *Achille* ___
31 *Victory* ___ (1954 film)
32 Commandment word
36 Specially strenghtened, pliable substance, for short
37 Boxer Muhammad
39 David's best friend

40 C.P.R. giver, perhaps
41 Mamie's husband
42 100 yrs.
43 Battle-ax: slang
45 What church had Crispus, a synagogue leader, as a member?
46 Some tumors
47 Battery's companion
49 Charlie Brown's exclamation
52 Score, on the diamond
54 Caught congers
57 Sea near Timor
58 Clubs or diamonds
59 Buffalo
60 Queen Anne's plant
61 Sugars suffix
62 US Army medal
63 Celsius steam point
64 Box-office letters

1
2
3
4
5
6
7
8
9
10
11
12
13
14
15
16
17
18
19
20
21
22
23
24
25
26
27
28
29
30
31
32
33
34
35
36
37
38
39
40
41
42
43
44
45
46
47
48
49
50
51
52
53
54
55
56
57
58
59
60
61
62
63
64
65
66
67
68
69
70
71
72

Encounters with Angels

ACROSS

1 How many angels rescued Lot and his family from the doomed city of Sodom?
4 Gargantuan
11 *Mr.* ___ (Michael Keaton movie)
14 "Well, well, well!"
15 Fuel additive
16 Natl. news service
17 According to Jesus, what causes the angels to rejoice?
20 Teaching English as a 2nd lang.
21 Picnic pest
22 A spinning ___
23 Junior's boy
25 NYC theater district, familiarly
27 Whose parents were told by an angel that the angel's name was a secret?
31 Delightful declaration
32 Front man, for short
35 Provo resident
36 Periods of mil. service
38 Out of town
39 Upstate New York city
40 U.S.D.A. power agcy.
41 Do some logrolling
42 Touches lightly, as with a hanky
43 Disputed Mideast strip
44 Southwest England area
45 This, in Barcelona
46 Dinner dipper
47 Busybody
49 In accompaniment
50 Suffix with drunk or tank
51 Monopoly purchase
54 In demand
56 Sulfur and bauxite
60 What person did Philip encounter after the angel of the Lord instructed him to go to Gaza?
64 Law, in Lyon
65 Person in a cast
66 ___ Lanka
67 ___ Moines
68 Followers of Zedong
69 "___-up!" (guide dog command)

DOWN

1 Civil offense
2 Coaster rider's cry
3 Butterfingers' exclamation
4 Angels came to Abram in the form of ___
5 Reach
6 Tai Long
7 Start of some Italian church names
8 Abbr. on a bank statement
9 Inter vi___: law
10 What prophet was fed two meals by an angel?
11 Horace or Thomas
12 Store sign
13 Who was told by an angel she was blessed among women?
18 Whose master was taken to Heaven in a whirlwind?
19 One of Napoleon's marshals
24 Water softener exchange
25 What prophet could not see the Lord's angel, but his donkey could?
26 Existed
27 "Blue ___ Shoes"
28 Globe guide
29 Fast ballroom dance

30 What kind of angel did Isaiah see in the temple praising God?
32 Slop
33 Chili con ___
34 Polk's predecessor
37 Cyrano's nose
38 What is the name of the evil angel of the abyss in Revelation?
43 Acquired
44 Commander, for short
46 At what pool did an angel stir the waters periodically?
48 "In the day that thou ___ thereof thou shalt surely die" (Gen. 2:17)
49 Several North China dynasties
51 Restrained
52 Plains Indian
53 "___ is a test. . ."
54 Spy Mata ___
55 Washington bills
57 "High priority!"
58 Light tan color
59 On what was Paul riding when an angel assured him that he would be tried before Caesar?
61 Presbyterian Church in Amer.
62 Trial judge Lance
63 Carrier letters

1
2
3
4
5
6
7
8
9
10
11
12
13
14
15
16
17
18
19
20
21
22
23
24
25
26
27
28
29
30
31
32
33
34
35
36
37
38
39
40
41
42
43
44
45
46
47
48
49
50
51
52
53
54
55
56
57
58
59
60
61
62
63
64
65
66
67
68
69

Wonders of Elijah and Elisha

ACROSS
1 What feature of Elisha's head caused children to make fun of him?
5 Who did Elijah miraculously outrun on the way to Jezreel?
9 Grill maker
14 Iowa State site
15 Moses' mountain lookout
16 Allan-___ (Sherwood Forest figure)
17 What did Elisha throw into some bitter water to purify it?
20 *The Spanish Tragedy* dramatist
21 Elijah prayed to the ___ to take his life
22 Prepared an orange for eating
23 *Wheel of Fortune* request
24 Form ringlets
25 What attacked those who ridiculed Elisha?
29 *Bonanza* role
30 Best-selling Bible paraphrase initials
33 Canaanite city
34 A few
35 Mars: Prefix
36 Who was healed of leprosy when he followed Elisha's instructions?
39 Wise ___ (smart aleck)
40 When the French go en vacances
41 Your, in Paris
42 Ford's former luxury line
43 Sanka rival
44 Perfect places
45 Round: Abbr.
46 Three strikes
48 Appalachian range
51 Once, once
52 "Lord, is ___?"
55 Who did Elijah supply meal and oil for through miraculous means?
58 Exasperated
59 Soft white cheese
60 Tonsorial creation
61 Duma votes
62 Advertiser Francis Wayland ___
63 College disease

DOWN
1 Support
2 Chinese seaport
3 Advance, as money
4 August hrs.
5 One negatively-charged atom
6 Painter Matisse or Rousseau
7 Tucked in
8 Part of N.Y.C.
9 Communion items
10 Ford's folly?
11 What false god was Elijah up against when fire from the Lord burned up a sacrifice and the water around the altar?
12 Fashion magazine
13 Taken back, in brief
18 Where Nome is home
19 Compositions
24 Hale-Bopp, e.g.
25 Highly hackneyed
26 Solar-year excess
27 "___ Day's Night"
28 Hoarfrost
29 Blah
30 Lacking freshness
31 Live's partner
32 What belonging to Elisha brought a dead man back to life?

34 Greek fatalist
35 Spare this to spoil a child
37 Constricted
38 Actress Mimieux
43 Two-legged supports
45 Officer-to-be
46 Do-___
47 Wedding attendant
48 Precipitation
49 Off kilter
50 Lapel item, sometimes
51 Liza's mentor, to Liza
52 Golfer Aoki
53 Result of 25-Across (with "apart")
54 Fascinated by, in a way
56 Atty.'s organization
57 33 or 45, e.g.

Miracles of Jesus

ACROSS

1 What did two blind men ask of Jesus?
5 La ___ opera house
10 Which Gospel records the miraculous catch of fish after Jesus' resurrection?
14 Netman Nastase
15 Less convincing, as an excuse
16 Neck and neck
17 Happened to temple veil when Jesus died
18 ___ a time
19 What Jesus restored to Lazarus
20 Who announced Jesus' conception to Mary?
23 New Zealand native
24 Made a tax valuation: Abbr.
25 ___ alai: speedy sport
28 Confidence man's game
31 Man and teen ending
33 A Khan
36 Who appeared with Jesus at his miraculous transfiguration?
40 Consequently
42 Soap substitute in the Southwest
43 South African Peace Nobelist
44 Completion of 4-Down
47 Catch on
48 "___ as the hills"
49 Chopped cabbage
51 Crash investigation bd.
52 Uniform
56 Plane seating choice
60 What miracle in Jesus' life is mentioned most in the New Testament?
63 How many loaves did Jesus use to feed thousands of people?
66 Margarine fat
67 Into what did Jesus send the demons he drove out of the Gadarene demoniacs?
68 Secondhand
69 Guides
70 Suffix with differ
71 Jesus, through miraculous means, saw a future disciple sitting under a ___
72 "Live free ___": New Hampshire motto
73 South African assembly

DOWN

1 King of Tyre
2 Jimmy Dorsey's "Maria ___"
3 Shoptalk
4 What woman got up and started doing household chores after Jesus healed her of a fever?
5 Work hard
6 Where did Jesus work his first miracle?
7 Algae eater
8 Corporate jets
9 Hoopster Gilmore
10 Set
11 Prefix meaning egg
12 Nickname in magazine publishing
13 Compass direction (about 1 o'clock)
21 Dog parasites
22 Dutch cheese
25 Who miraculously escaped from a crowd that was going to push him off a cliff?
26 Mountain ridge
27 Her ___ of blood stopped when a woman touched the hem of Jesus' garment
29 Winglike
30 Entertainers Rogers or Benzell
32 Was infected with

33 Hindu world soul
34 When the disciples saw Jesus walking on the water, what did they think he was?
35 Traffic jammers
37 Provost of TV's *Lassie*
38 Start of a Bard title
39 What Jesus did to ten lepers
41 Hard cover, in brief
45 Move sideways
46 WWII mil. lady
50 Jesus cursed a figless vine, causing it to ___
53 Brownings' Italian home
54 Nicodemus was a ___ of the Jews
55 What Jesus multiplied to feed the multitudes
57 Saint Catherine's birthplace
58 Spanish poet Federico Garcia ___
59 Stopped
60 Advice of yore
61 ___, *Pagliaccio* (aria)
62 Massachusetts motto word
63 By-and-by, in brief
64 Tel-Aviv res.
65 Churchill's sign

Miracles of Paul and Peter

ACROSS

1 Star in Perseus
6 Drunkards
10 Sketch
14 Marie Antoinette, e.g.
15 "You're the ___ Care For" (1930 song)
16 String tie
17 What miraculous occurrence delivered 54-Across from prison in Philippi?
19 Grad.
20 Plants
21 Hebrides island
23 NASA's overseas counterpart
24 What two apostles placed their hands on the believers at Samaria?
27 Socioeconomic status, in brief
30 John Brown's dog
31 Akkadian god
32 Valentine's Day cherub
34 Granite
37 Who twice delivered Simon from prison?
41 What dangerous creature did not affect Paul when it bit him?
43 Classic Japanese theater
44 Lena or Marilyn
45 Centric starter
46 Produce a young goat
48 Mailed
49 Follows bah or dior
51 Frontiersman Carson
53 Past tense
54 What two missionaries were miraculously delivered from prison in Philippi?
60 B'nai B'rith org.
61 Laura, of song
62 Resort port in Israel
65 Film director Wertmuller
67 What the believers at Samaria received when 24-Across placed their hands on them
70 Navy diver
71 ___ even keel
72 Crusader ___ Bryant
73 Turkish "tent"
74 *The Way We* ___ (Streisand film)
75 Marsh, of mystery

DOWN

1 Is for two
2 Autumn dropping
3 Paul exorcised a spirit from a possessed ___, whose owners became furious
4 "___ of Old Smoky"
5 MacNeil's news partner
6 Toward Antarctica, for short
7 Walking ___
8 Amos's home
9 Yellowish brown
10 Sole prop. alias
11 Logrolling contest
12 Drunkard description
13 Dorcas, whom Peter raised from the dead, was one
18 Neighbor of Saudi Arabia
22 Commander in King Jehosaphat's army
25 Black
26 Belonging to the queen of the Olympian gods
27 Spare
28 Radiate

29 Before a jr.
33 Kidney-related
35 Cedar Rapids campus
36 Uniform cloth
38 Increased
39 Sicilian resort
40 Allows
42 Empire of the apostles
47 White and Blue rivers
50 Whatever else one may say
52 Great merchant in China
54 Peter healed Aeneas of long-term ___
55 Good-bye
56 Forearm bone related
57 Hum
58 Kind of flare or system
59 David's weapon against Goliath
63 Operatic vocal solo
64 Small, reddish monkey
66 Elev.
68 Chem. suffix
69 Confucian path

The Very Devil

ACROSS

1 Hebrew letter
6 Invoke divine favor
11 Contains
14 Gospel singer Mrs. Waters
15 Mountain range in Utah
16 Halloween mo.
17 What animal does I Peter compare Satan to?
19 U.N. agency
20 Humiliate
21 Fond du ___, Wisconsin
22 Good angel in Peretti's books
23 According to the parable of the sower, who snatches from the heart the word of the kingdom that was heard and not understood?
27 Record speed, in brief
30 There was much of this in Shakespeare
31 He's jumbled?
32 Acorns' homes
34 Realtor's sign
37 Pert. to the iris
41 Endor's most famous inhabitant
43 Dit's companion
44 Remarkable
45 Seaweed
46 Anti-leaker?
48 What, according to the New Testament, is the final place for Satan?
49 Status of some srs.
51 Tour vehicle
53 Cruces or Palmas
54 What does Satan masquerade as in the present world?
60 *Knots Landing* actress Park Lincoln
61 Gun gp.
62 Weaver and Warren
65 Psalm 23 starter
66 A king of Israel had court prophets who had been the agents of a ___
69 Diamond decision
70 Witch-trial locale
71 Formal jackets
72 Wee, to Burns
73 Elizabethan employ
74 Good judgment

DOWN

1 Three times: phar.
2 Portico for Plato
3 King in 66-Across who sold himself to the devil
4 Emulate the Pied Piper
5 Biblical miracle worker
6 Computer program glitch
7 Actress Palmer
8 Early computer
9 Wall Street purchases
10 Before Jose or Francisco
11 Instruction manual
12 Hebrew thief
13 Mink wrap
18 Must-haves
24 Golf clubs
25 First Hebrew judge
26 Belial
27 Up-front theater locale
28 Item for Jack and Jill
29 Adv. and distr. dept.
33 Close call
35 New Guinea port
36 Abu ___
38 Ben-Gurion carrier

39 ___-Seltzer
40 Caustic solutions
42 Achilles' vulnerable spot
47 Toboggans
50 Skater Harding and others
52 Circles and such
54 Choir members
55 Old Testament book
56 Garbo or Gustafson
57 Living the life o___y
58 Ocean routes
59 Played out
63 "Dianetics" author ___ Hubbard
64 Breaks a commandment
66 Baton Rouge Tigers sch.
67 Time's std.
68 It's on the tip of the Tung?

A Gallery of Gods (Part 1)

ACROSS

1 Informal attempt
5 Master's follower, maybe
8 Become limp, like lettuce
12 Natural res.
13 Non-clergy
16 "I came, ___, . . ."
17 Perry Mason's occ., e.g.
18 Open-eyed
19 Type of second
20 In Paul's speech to the men of Athens, he mentions the altar of a god. What is the altar's inscription?
23 Trumpets
24 Valuable resource
25 Self-help author LeShan
27 Holy book
31 To what idol did the Israelites in the wilderness bring offerings?
36 *Peer Gynt* character
38 Rat Island resident
39 Econ. Coop. Admin.
40 Idol Hebrews made at Mount Sinai
45 Mr. Spanish speaker
46 Tint
47 Crippled
51 Racer Allison or boxer Moore
55 What horrible practice was part of worshipping the gods of the Moabites and Ammonites?
59 Et ___ (and others)
60 Musical transition
61 Weaver's tool
62 *The Sound and the Fury* director
63 The gold of the conquistadors
64 *Vogue* rival
65 King Saul's father
66 Sega rival, for short
67 Seized, in Scotland

DOWN

1 Scythe handle
2 Call to quarters: Var.
3 Oil of roses
4 Yul
5 Marshall, for one
6 Sell on the street
7 Goddess of Ephesus
8 Shoe style
9 Golfer Aoki
10 Dry ground
11 Duo
14 Boxer's stat
15 Some evergreens
21 Cabinet dept.
22 Colo. neighbor
26 Place near Jerusalem
28 Complaint
29 Fleet off.
30 Pilot's ann.
31 "___ there; done that"
32 Days of yore: Archaic
33 Once known as
34 It rises at dawn
35 Impress deeply
36 Amer. Temperance Soc.
37 Haggard classic
41 Biblical giant
42 Evangelist Roberts
43 German car maker
44 Tract
48 Gds.
49 Dresden donkey
50 Fish-shaped god of the Philistines
52 String quartet instrument

53 Paris's ___-de-Medecine
54 Oman neighbor
55 152 in Rome
56 Broadway successes
57 Remedy
58 Early autos
59 The presence of this caused 50-Down to be broken into pieces

1 2 3 4 5 6 7 8 9 10 11
12 13 14 15 16
17 18 19
20 21 22
23 24
25 26 27 28 29 30
31 32 33 34 35
36 37 38 39
40 41 42 43 44
45 46
47 48 49 50 51 52 53 54
55 56 57 58
59 60 61
62 63 64
65 66 67

A Gallery of Gods (Part 2)

ACROSS

1 What fertility god of Canaan is mentioned more than any other foreign deity in the Bible?
5 Seoul carrier initials
8 Musical note
13 Napoleon's empire of 1814–15
14 "___ and a-two"
15 Day to save for
16 What gods did the Avites worship?
19 Wonders
20 Con's preoccupation
21 Backwards brew?
22 112, in Rome
23 Type of surgery
27 Coin's reverse
28 Pesticide
31 Divisions politiques
32 Oil price council
33 Syrup maker
34 What is the inscription of an alter Paul mentions in a speech to the men of Athens?
37 Lesage's Gil
38 Hands over, in Glasgow
39 California Indian: var.
40 Poet's dusk
41 Preserves for winter
42 No, in pig latin
43 Use a strop
44 Tigers' pl.
46 "There's ____ on the horizon"
49 Handpicks
53 What was Nehushtan?
56 Japanese aborigines: Var.
57 Pull an all-nighter
58 Jai follower
59 Old hat
60 Summertime?
61 Mint plant

DOWN

1 London's big one
2 One amt.
3 Statesman Eban
4 *The Wizard of Oz* actor
5 Australian tree-dweller
6 Landers and Jillian
7 Showed the way
8 Salvador's country, to Salvadorans
9 Stuffed
10 Grammy-winning Ford
11 Take ____ (siesta)
12 Youngster
14 Ishmael's relative
17 Disinclined
18 Big refiner
22 French limestone
23 Do not disturb
24 One painted metalwork:
25 The god of this world
26 Biblical verb enders
27 Toll rds., usually
28 What fish-shaped god of the Philistines was disgraced when his statue was broken by the presence of the ark of the covenant?
29 Words before hint or line
30 Morning TV show
32 Cat-___-tails
33 Fort ___ (gold depository site)
35 Kampala's country
36 "___ than snow"
41 Raceway
43 Wanderers, sometimes
44 Found another chair

45 Gr. K–6
46 "___ on the shoulder"
47 ___ Pet (novelty item)
48 Contact, perhaps
49 Sov. states
50 Ernst & Young staff
51 Weblike tissue
52 Hitch or glitch
54 Advanced deg.
55 Precursor to a playoff

1 2 3 4 5 6 7 8 9 10 11 12
13 14 15
16 17 18
19 20
21 22
23 24 25 26 27 28 29 30
31 32 33
34 35 36
37 38 39
40 41 42
43 44 45
46 47 48 49 50 51 52
53 54 55
56 57 58
59 60 61

So Many Versions (Part 1)

ACROSS

1 Choice of sizes: Abbr.
4 Couple or so
7 Persian or Siamese
10 Nickname for Coverdale's 1535 edition of Scripture, due to an unusual translation for Psalm 91:5
13 Tee follower
14 Hospital addition
15 Arabian garment
16 Plurality of being
17 Start of MGM's motto
18 Scandinavian salmon
20 Rep.
21 Nickname for an 1806 edition of Scripture that mistranslated 1 Timothy 5:21
24 ___ a time (single file)
25 Manila hemp
26 Going downhill
27 Lotion ingredients
31 Nickname for the Bishops' edition of Scripture due to its rendering of Jeremiah 8:22
37 Econ. Coop. Admin.
40 Computer corr.
41 Command to dog
42 Nickname for "An American Translation" (1931) by Goodspeed, Smith, and others
47 ___-Rudman Act
48 Mexican tribe Cortes met
52 Sound result
56 Star of *It Had To Be You*
57 Nickname for an 1801 edition of Scripture that contained a misprint of Jude 16
61 Baby boy
62 Subject of Newton's first law
63 MPH aloft
64 Currently popular
65 Cable network
66 Frequent end to business letter
67 British islet
68 Rock pioneer Brian
69 Club or drug
70 Measure
71 Hems and haws

DOWN

1 Dark follower
2 Spanish wool
3 Smaller
4 Tyson is one
5 Old Testament author
6 Wash's partner
7 Joshua's fellow spy
8 Addis ___
9 Checker or Yellow
10 Ancient Phoenician idol
11 Drive
12 Procure
19 Comp. monitor type
22 Bone holder
23 Indonesian island near Java
28 Out of date, for short
29 Inventor Whitney
30 Put
32 Brain wave test
33 ___ amas amat
34 Truck driver's "home"
35 Year in Claudius's reign
36 Bends before ow
37 Heart rhythm strip
38 Follower of Jesus, for short
39 Builders' body, in brief?

43 Nav. officer
44 Witch
45 World literacy father Frank
46 King David's estate manager
49 Leg bones
50 Chocolate confection
51 Safekeeping sites
53 Tubular pasta
54 Radial feature
55 Every other hurricane
57 Tide regulator
58 Do ___ others . . .
59 Numbered hwys.
60 Burning bush loc. (Acts 7:30, KJV)
61 Pronoun for a ship

1 2 3 4 5 6 7 8 9 10 11 12
13 14 15 16
17 18 19 20
21 22 23
24 25
26 27 28 29 30
31 32 33 34 35 36
37 38 39 40 41
42 43 44 45 46
47 48 49 50 51
52 53 54 55 56
57 58 59 60
61 62 63
64 65 66 67
68 69 70 71

Who Said That? (Part I)

ACROSS

1 Who said, "I was no prophet, neither was I a prophet's son; but I was a herdman, and a gatherer of sycamore fruit"?
5 Robed church musicians
10 Mediator's skill
14 Gospel author
15 Mr. Ed
16 Peek-___
17 Deborah and Barak sang, "___ for the avenging of Israel, when the people willingly offered themselves"
20 Cardinals' cap initials
21 Marksman of Swiss legend
22 Complied
23 Roll call answer
24 Belonging to Michael Jordan's org.
25 Dangerous, colloquially
27 Word in a promise
28 Fashionable resort
31 Marten's kin
32 Vegetable
33 Uncle Sam's c.
34 David said, "___, and my fortress, and my deliverer"
37 Consumes
38 Shoe width
39 Orchestra horns
40 Letter addendum
41 Dr. Luke's church history book
42 Pumps
43 Reclines
44 Milk givers
45 Twins on high
48 Like a streaker
49 Airline to Karachi
52 David said, "___, O ye gates"
55 Legal-memo starter
56 Clipped
57 Lather
58 Harry's wife
59 Product of Bethlehem
60 Coin entry

DOWN

1 Current meas.
2 Trade center
3 Evangelist Roberts
4 Water runner
5 In good spirits
6 Game expert Edmond
7 Baseball great Hershiser
8 Start of enumerated list
9 King Solomon's son-successor
10 Chaucer's *Canterbury* ___
11 Johnny Cash's "___ Named Sue"
12 Apple center
13 One first lady's maiden name
18 Sound system
19 Israeli statesman Abba
23 Alive with the sound of music
24 Scandinavians
25 Laugh track sounds
26 Encourages
27 The Friendly ___
28 Dealt a deadly blow
29 River to the Rio Grande
30 Torah holders
31 Walk start
32 "Golden Boy" dramatist
33 Guthrie and others
35 Paid proofs
36 Hebrew God
41 Japanese aborigine
42 Horse color

43 Lower-calorie versions
44 Reason
45 Flippant
46 One, to Wilhelm
47 Makers
48 Carried
49 Who said, "Why should it be thought a thing incredible with you, that God should raise the dead?"
50 King Solomon's biographer
51 Supv.'s helper
53 However
54 Slalom run

What Gets Quoted Most?

ACROSS

1 Chinese emperor ___ Tsu
6 Off. of Mgt. and Budget
9 Loony
14 Grown larvae
15 Cadence count
16 Uncover, in Pennsylvania
17 Greek capital residents
19 Fort ___, Florida
20 Creamy white
21 Wild river of Borneo
22 Louisiana town
26 What long book of prophecy ranks sixth with 141 references?
30 Son of Gad
31 Almond flavor, as coffee
32 ___ Epistle to the Romans
33 Rackets
34 Greek letter
35 Tolkien's treefolk
36 Scorch
38 Nickname for the Cowboys' hometown
39 Bigger than med.
40 Southeast Kansas town
41 Student
42 What book by one of the later prophets ranks eighth with 125 references?
44 Cake decorators
45 Obscure stuff
46 Pemaquid chief
48 Teachers' org.
49 Joan of art
50 Squirrel's snack
52 What book, probably one of the least read of Old Testament books, ranks ninth with 107 references?
57 Sleep prefix
58 Experimental Aircraft Assoc.
59 Exaggerated advertisings
60 "The best ___ to come"
61 Some emergency rm. cases
62 School cheers

DOWN

1 Qualified num. cruncher
2 Shack
3 N.T. book
4 Protestant church org.
5 What book, part of the Torah, ranks third with 260 references?
6 Scarlett, in *Gone With the Wind*
7 What's cooking
8 Bits per sec.
9 What book, mostly history and part law, ranks tenth with 73 references?
10 Release oxen
11 What group of people told Abraham that they would not refuse him burial in their tombs?
12 Type of weapon: Abbr.
13 Photo ___ (pol.'s news events)
18 Suffix with gymnast
22 Town near Billings
23 What a juggler may practice with
24 What book, more law than history, ranks fifth with 208 references?
25 Right-angle joints
26 Pioneer: Abbr.
27 Western writer Grey
28 Open-shelved cabinet
29 Most garish
31 Deserter from Saul to David
36 Evening abroad

37 "Now ___ me down . . ."
38 Osso ___ (Italian veal)
40 "Don't play with me!"
41 New Testament pastor
43 Nev'r-ending
46 City in central Turkey
47 Actress Meyers
49 Drink for Robin Hood
50 "Unaccustomed ___ . . ."
51 Fortune 500 orgs.
52 Papal name
53 ___abarim: Hebrews' wilderness site
54 Mil. rank
55 Sam and Mig finisher
56 It's got your no.

Everyday Phrases from the Bible

ACROSS

1 Conservative Cong. Chr. Conf.
5 Single-celled prefix
9 Computer magazine
13 Great help
14 Tempo
15 Amazing interjections?
16 Everyday phrase from Isaiah 40:15
19 Surgeons' beams
20 Comedienne Prentiss
21 Pertaining to bees: Prefix
23 Type of whale
24 Dyer's need
26 Many heads but no brains
27 Everyday phrase from Job 14:10
31 Mr. Haley's
32 ___ in the right direction
33 Rockefeller Center muralist
34 Attention-getting sounds
36 "___ example . . ."
40 Synthetic fiber
42 Don Marquis character
43 Everyday phrase from Isaiah 65:5
47 Junkyard canine
48 ___ King Cole
49 Saudi Arabia founder ___ Saud
50 Pause fillers
51 Crisis, in brief: Var.
53 Clay pigeons
55 Everyday phrase from Matthew 5:13
59 Handle: Fr.
60 Eggs, in Emden
61 In ___ of
62 *Cheers* actor Roger
63 Anacondas
64 Gather on a surface, chemically

DOWN

1 Bookstore org.
2 Grandma's medicine oil
3 Mrs. Dithers
4 Crete's Minoan capital
5 Third Person of the Trinity
6 Pots' partners
7 Wood sorrel
8 Confed. soldier
9 ___ Raton, Florida
10 "Li'l Abner" characters
11 Everything
12 Cornerstone abbr.
17 Coop cry
18 ___ *Down Staircase*
21 "That's ___!"
22 Carpet surface
24 Part of a three-piece suit
25 Ins. workers
28 Praise
29 Lacks, briefly
30 Design technique
34 Bargain
35 Do postal work
37 Simon's partner
38 Pause tones
39 Belongs to Empire State's col.
41 Beatle Starr
42 Tempers
43 Animal society
44 Ultimatum words
45 Backpackers, often

46 Standard for busyness
47 Actor Romero
52 Roads: Abbr.
53 Singer George Beverly ___
54 The Stooges make one
56 Valentine's Day mo.
57 Tijuana uncle
58 Spoke holder

The Old Testament in the New

ACROSS

1 "Like a ___ dumb before a shearer, so opened he not his mouth" (Acts 8:32)
5 Private eyes
10 Lucy's husband
14 Phone code
15 ___ Arenas (world's southernmost city)
16 English architect Christopher ___
17 "Thou shalt love the Lord thy God ___" (Matt. 4:10)
20 Easy reply method, in brief
21 Venus de ___
22 Wedding site
23 Without, in Nice
24 Comp. "modifier" key
26 Chocolate giant
29 Put into piles
30 Entrepreneurs' govt. agcy.
33 Take off a cravat
34 "But thou art the ___, and thy years shall not fail" (Heb. 1:12)
35 Swedish auto
36 What everyday phrase from the Bible is in Ecclesiastes 8:15?
39 Round ender
40 *Portrait of a Lady* painter
41 "One day is with the Lord as a thousand ___" (2 Pet. 3:8)
42 Moose
43 Mother of our Lord
44 Past vogues
45 Kemo ___
46 Not amateurs
47 Stages
50 Old Testament mountain
51 Existed
54 "Behold, now is ___" (2 Cor. 6:2)
58 Thanksgiving meat request
59 Where Joan of Arc died
60 "As I live, saith the Lord, every ___ shall bow to me, and every tongue shall confess to God" (Rom. 14:11)
61 Eye sore
62 Like some gases
63 Cultivate

DOWN

1 "I will put my ___ into their mind, and write them in their hearts" (Heb. 8:10)
2 Soprano's solo
3 Dole out
4 "___, humbug!" (Scrooge)
5 Slat
6 Draws
7 "___ each life . . ."
8 Biblical verb ender
9 For example
10 "Let his habitation be desolate, and let no man ___ therein" (Acts 1:20)
11 The E in QED
12 Que ___, ___
13 Complete verb: Abbr.
18 Hebrews' Old Testament enemy
19 "B.C." cartoonist
23 "O death, where is thy ___? O grave, where is thy victory?" (1 Cor. 15:55)
24 Hair arrangers
25 "Cursed is everyone one that hangeth on a ___" (Gal. 3:13)
26 Gentle push
27 Register, as a student
28 Perform lousily

29 Unhappily
30 Abram's wife
31 Wilkes-___, Pennsylvania
32 Bottomless pit
34 Drum or noose
35 Tree starters
37 Moby Dick pursuer
38 "The Lord said to ___, 'Sit thou on my right hand'" (Acts 2:34)
43 Not fem.
44 Point in the right direction
45 Said of old
46 The Big Fisherman
47 Specs.
48 What this isn't
49 Uncanny
50 Cast forth
51 Beverage color
52 Prayer ender
53 Sesame product
55 Sommes shout
56 Vast length of time
57 Entr. pass

Who Said That? (Part 2)

ACROSS

1 Butchers' offerings
6 Earlier than, for short
9 What David watched as a youth
14 Start
15 61 in Rome
16 Forest, to Fabius
17 The Lord said, "___ is mine; I will repay" (Rom. 12:19)
19 Error partner
20 Chemical compounds
21 Years ago, years ago
23 Sponsors' times
24 Bible quote
28 Author of Bible quote, for short
31 "The Star-Spangled Banner" preposition
32 Govt. agency
33 "___ Rhythm": Gershwin
35 Mt. Rushmore site
38 Frome or Allen
42 Chaucer's *Canterbury* ___
44 East or west end
45 Abu ___
46 Pyramid place
47 Rod's companion
49 Recipient of Bible quote
50 Opposite of fast
52 ___ *Miserables*
54 Fem. saint
55 Bible quote continued
61 Dad's girl, for short
62 British mil. decoration
63 Sneaker brand
67 Circled
70 Bible quote concluded
72 Father of Leah and Rachel
73 A bustling about
74 Washington, for one
75 Pottery piece
76 Fashion designer's monogram
77 Start of Jesus' cry from the cross

DOWN

1 Cupid's province
2 Individuals
3 "Money ___ everything"
4 Palestinian desert
5 Family room feature
6 Bet. million and trillion
7 Microsoft's spreadsheet
8 Farmer's workplace
9 Concorde, e.g.
10 Sute starter
11 David's older brother
12 Dodge
13 Shaking
18 Sackcloth companion
22 Withdrawal syndrome letters
25 Court demand
26 Biblical son of Ruth
27 Solemn promises
28 Where it's at
29 Amalekite king
30 Fastener type
34 Red Cloud's residence
36 Is for two
37 Assumed prayer posture
39 Actor Lukas of *Witness*
40 Lie adjacent
41 Aswan Dam's river
43 Immediately, in the E.R.
48 *Merry Widow* composer
51 Phone for the deaf: Abbr.
53 Extreme cruelty
55 Some statues

56 Old Testament matriarch
57 Good ole boy
58 Theme paper
59 Highways
60 Swell
64 Corner to corner, for short
65 Deed in Madrid
66 Burpee's bit
68 Play by ___
69 Popular adventure game's initials
71 Newspaper seg.

So Many Versions (Part 2)

ACROSS

1 The Pentateuch
6 Arrow shooter
9 Sprinkle
14 Purplish blue
15 Reverence
16 Papal cape
17 God's Word
19 Pass twice
20 Double to get two
21 Some deer
22 Bible's longest book
23 Always, in verse
24 Right angle
25 Half of alternating sound
26 USAir rival
27 Le Havre hubby
28 Minute pts.
31 Maze choices
34 Christians' sacred book
36 Biblical barterer
37 Driver directives
38 Group, as cattle
39 Classic English Bible
41 Hymn part
42 Arctic resident, for short
43 Reveler's cry at Bacchanalia
44 Shade
45 Buddhist sect
46 Last Old Testament bk.
47 WWII Greek org.
50 Intercession
54 Warner's partner
55 Chairman Tse-tung
56 Woman of Jericho
57 Old or New
59 ___ *of Two Cities*
60 ___ *Haw*
61 Evening, in Avila
62 *The Pirates of Penzance* heroine
63 Printer's measures
64 Cairo's land

DOWN

1 Lake ___, Nevada
2 Atmospheric layer
3 Straightedge
4 Mission end
5 Bible book
6 Place of confusion
7 Big-eyed night birds
8 Barely visible
9 Church service
10 Vicinity
11 Six-foot or more
12 Ancient Persia
13 Congressmen, for short
18 Allen, Kansas, county seat
22 Where the Eiffel Tower is
25 Cautions
26 Vicious criminal
27 *Fibber ___ and Molly*
28 Plaintiff
29 Goofs
30 Grant, as a point
31 Short Chinese dog?
32 Sale condition
33 Military vehicle
34 Peter's alias
35 "With this ring I ___ wed"
37 One interested in interest
40 Wicked Israelite queen
41 Jerome's Latin Bible
44 Male deer
46 Hebrew Bible author
47 Polishing medium

48 Grocery name since 1869
49 Palestrina piece
50 British baby buggy
51 Pro ___
52 Husband of 40-Down
53 Ivy League college
54 "Where have you ___?"
57 "___ Lord is my Shepherd"
58 Alloy rim

Beginning at the End

ACROSS

1 Miraculous sustenance
6 Polite address
11 Hundredweight, for short
14 Small porch
15 "___ That Will Not Let Me Go" (hymn)
16 Rio de ___
17 What Bible book ends with "Make haste, my beloved, and be thou like a roe or to a young hart upon the mountains of spices"?
19 Nancy's husband
20 Large quantity
21 Slug, old-style
23 Augusta is Maine's
27 Was king
29 Sinful
30 Mold again
31 Hog
32 German power-tool maker
33 Word on a towel
36 Good friends
37 Moses' father-in-law
38 Broad
39 Hindu honorific
40 Overcooked
41 Author Mark ___
42 Repeatedly beaten
44 Thick-skinned mammals
45 John the ___
47 What Isaiah said to his horse?
48 Thai or Laotian
49 Robert ___ Chorale
50 Moniker intro
51 What Bible book ends with "And in all that mighty land, and in all the great terror which Moses showed in the sight of all Israel"?
58 Bernstein, to pals
59 "Come in!"
60 Cowboys' exhibition
61 '60s campus grp.
62 Plow inventor
63 Night vision

DOWN

1 What eds. edit
2 From ___ Z
3 Part of NCO
4 Yuletide beverage
5 Mark, for one
6 Trier's river
7 "That's ___ blow!"
8 Mr. Juan
9 Mean, for short
10 Handel oratorio
11 What "First" Bible book ends with "My love be with you all in Christ Jesus. Amen"?
12 Penned
13 ___ down: Muted
18 Execution method
22 Brit. sports cars
23 Crown points
24 President Sadat
25 What Bible book ends with "The grace of our Lord Jesus Christ be with you all. Amen"?
26 Products of gamma rays
27 Bowling alley button
28 What Bible bk. ends with "For God shall bring every work into judgment, with every secret thing, whether it be good, or whether it be evil"?
30 Spherical
32 Special Forces cap

34 Manner of speaking
35 Horse or common
37 Sticking places
38 V-J Day ended it
40 Dazzled
41 Jesus
43 Pilot's announcement, for short
44 Niagara Falls' sound
45 Canaanite idols
46 Inquired
47 Traveler's query
49 Trick ending?
52 Compass direction (about 1 o'clock)
53 Cousin of a Comanche
54 Partner of neither
55 Poem of praise
56 ___ culpa
57 Day, to Dayan

1 2 3 4 5 6 7 8 9 10 11 12 13
14 15 16
17 18 19
20 21 22
23 24 25 26 27 28
29 30
31 32 33 34 35
36 37 38
39 40 41
42 43 44
45 46 47
48 49
50 51 52 53 54 55 56 57
58 59 60
61 62 63

Between the Testaments (Part 1)

ACROSS

1 Mail, as a letter
5 Exchanges
10 Glided
14 Zone
15 Main circulatory trunk
16 Fill the hold
17 A book of wise sayings attributed to a king of Israel
20 Fish trap
21 Small deer
22 "The Boot"
23 Polygraph flunker
24 Pre follower in subdivisions
26 Delegate
29 Handle problems
30 Dir. or indir.
33 Teacher in a turban
34 Mistake
35 Historic introduction?
36 A shortened form of a five-volume historical work by Jason of Cyrene containing letters to the Jews in Egypt
39 ___-leaf cluster
40 Greet the day
41 Angler's needs
42 Blvds.
43 Plenty
44 Long angry speech
45 Cook's meas.
46 Slothful
47 Pong maker
50 Beverage color
51 *Much ___ about Nothing*
54 A tale of Babylonian idol worship and some conniving priests
58 Earned run averages
59 Singer Pat
60 Alike
61 Whip
62 Sudden contraction
63 Matures

DOWN

1 According to tradition, how Simon the Zealot died
2 Old eastern railroad
3 Egg holder
4 Male parent, informally
5 Polynesian
6 Tempter
7 Rover's remarks?
8 Basketball scores, in brief
9 Paulo's predecessor
10 Openings for coins
11 Mongolian monk
12 Worship object
13 Say it ain't so
18 Adam's legacy
19 Reform advocate
23 Chauffeur-driven vehicle
24 Baseball play
25 Intertestamental bks.
26 Place on Paul's journeys
27 Exertion excretion
28 Plunders
29 Coarse
30 *Don Giovanni,* for one
31 Animal variety
32 David's father
34 Sends forth
37 It hangs from a faucet
38 What squirrels do with nuts
44 Bicycle for two
45 Refuse
46 Property securities

47 Biblical victim
48 Trillion prefix
49 "Woe is me!"
50 Horse's halter?
51 Amalekite king
52 Jerusalem's ___ of the Rock
53 Change for a five
55 Dir. broadcast sat.
56 Spinner
57 Simile phrase

Who Said That? (Part 3)

ACROSS
1 President George
5 Short way in
9 Wrong
14 Where China is
15 Rome's fiddler emperor
16 Sticks' partner
17 Bible quote (answer continued in 66-Across)
20 Boston party
21 China's gift to Nixon
22 ___ de coeur
24 E.R. devices
27 Vietnam Veterans Memorial designer Maya
28 Ecology guardian org.
31 Youth speaker Hutchcraft
32 Jamaica's Ocho ___
34 Bundles of fibers
36 Eastern philosophy
38 Capital of Okinawa
40 "Pride ___ before a fall"
41 Source of 17-Across
44 Tenth-century German emperor
47 And ___ bed: Pepys
48 Long fish
52 "Woe is me, for I am ___!": Isaiah
54 Very German?
56 After Ginnie but before West
57 The "I" in T.G.I.F.
58 R.N.'s specialty
60 Genetic trait carrier
61 "___ for ___, tooth for tooth"
62 O'Neill's ___ *for the Misbegotten*
64 Just scratch the surface
66 17-Across, continued
73 At full speed
74 Baseball great Slaughter
75 Pop singer Brickell
76 Synod site
77 "___ good, and not evil, that ye may live": Amos
78 WWII landing crafts

DOWN
1 Amt. due
2 Kind of tax
3 Before Bull or duck
4 "Thou shalt love thy neighbor, and ___ thine enemy"
5 From S.F. to Wyo.
6 Air Music composer Rorem
7 Animal catcher?
8 Kingly
9 Fiery furnace survivor
10 Adriatic wind
11 Cycle start
12 Standard deviations, in brief
13 ___col, source of giant grapes
18 Stylist's concern
19 1957 Nabokov novel
22 *War* ___ (Salvation Army paper)
23 Down Under critter, informally
25 Chianti, e.g.
26 Penetrates
28 Who said, "The serpent beguiled me, and I did eat"?
29 Bird or basset, e.g.
30 First Wednesday of Lent
33 Chases away
35 Kimono
37 Peek follower
39 In the wake of
42 Salve
43 Author of fourth Gospel
44 "Mais ___!"

45 Cable letters
46 N.F.L. scores
49 Biblical boils
50 "Now I ___ me down to sleep"
51 Bishop's district
53 *The Time Machine* race
55 Trans World Dome team
59 Ice cream holders
62 Bone-dry
63 Short round, for Woods
65 Who said, "Am I my brother's keeper?"
66 Gummy mass
67 Ins. plan
68 Cup part
69 Distress
70 "___, and ye shall receive"
71 Dye maker
72 Nintendo's Super ___

Between the Testaments (Part 2)

ACROSS

1 Command to Fido
5 Varieties
10 Cast a ballot
14 "___ sweet ___"
15 World War I vessel
16 "Able was ___ . . ."
17 Who predicted the birth of Jesus to Joseph and Mary?
20 Earth's star
21 Slacken
22 Rubbernecks
23 Unvarnished
24 Prefix with scope or meter
26 Hologram producers
29 Written agreement
33 In the past, in the past
34 Head for the hills
35 Lodge letters
36 Like some keys
37 "Just as ___" (hymn)
38 Jousts
39 Subdivision of land
40 Pivot point
41 Upright
42 Heavenly worshippers
44 Al ___ (Arafat followers)
45 Great achievement
46 "To ___ his own"
47 Unyielding
50 Land of Lima
51 E.P.A. rating
54 Who helped the son of a pious Jew in the Book of Tobit?
58 Three, in Germany
59 "This is ___!" (police cry)
60 Boy or girl lead-in
61 Took to court
62 Math functions
63 God's Word planted

DOWN

1 Ream pts.
2 ___bohu (chaos)
3 Hymn ending
4 Verily
5 Cane and confectioners
6 Fat
7 Part to play
8 Mark
9 Bus depot: Abbr.
10 Jesus' unique entrance to earth
11 Trompe l'___ (optical illusion)
12 Something only God can make
13 Electric fish
18 More on target
19 Brought forth
23 "Fear not!"
24 They could be verse
25 Mother of all living
26 Light providers
27 Limber
28 Sub detector
29 One can stake it or file it
30 Cop ___ (convict's negotiation)
31 Cut
32 They're held for questioning
34 Repair request
38 Mad Hatter item
40 Palindromic cry
43 Colonist William
44 Fs
46 Ominous
47 Specs
48 Drive-___ window
49 Shoe width

50 Blueprint
51 Check chaser
52 Rozelle or Rose
53 Plant with spikes of flowers
55 Neither solid nor liquid
56 Renato's aria "___ Tu"
57 Possesses

Some Amazing Animals

ACROSS

1 What venomous creature bit Paul on the hand but did not harm him?
7 Big name in crackers
14 ___ McDonald
15 Draws
16 Park in Maine
17 When children laughed at a prophet for his baldness, what appeared that mauled the children?
18 Luncheonette lists
19 Ike's WWII command
20 Into what did Jesus send the legion of unclean spirits he had cast out of a man?
28 *Independence Day* attackers, for short
31 It may take some hops
32 Grandmas
33 Vassal in Middle Ages
35 Lumber
38 Kill by mob action
39 "Woe ___!"
40 Sight user
42 Nick and ___ Charles
43 For what sulking prophet did God send a worm to destroy the vine that shaded him?
45 One of the four creatures God sent as plagues upon the Egyptians
46 Without end
47 Where lions met Christians
48 "___ Can It Be?" (hymn)
50 Egyptian snake
51 What miraculous animals parted Elijah and Elisha as Elijah was taken by a whirlwind into heaven?
56 Wash-up site
57 One of David's chiefs
61 Sears & Roebuck's original specialty
66 What foreign prophet had a talking donkey to ride on?
67 What did Jesus use to feed the five thousand?
68 Accurately
69 Hollywood hopeful
70 Boxer Mike's

DOWN

1 Ancient Syria
2 Viva ___
3 ___ uproar
4 *The Taming of the Shrew* locale
5 Prophet in 17-Across
6 Vitamin stat.
7 "I'm ___ this area"
8 Distant
9 Baby's spill-catcher
10 Hard water?
11 Temple assistant
12 Mid.
13 C.I.A. forerunner
17 Kennedy or Turner
21 Liberian Christian station
22 Try to stop a squeak again
23 Variety show since 1975, briefly
24 Mad Anthony
25 Canon computer model
26 Mother-of-pearls
27 F, musically
28 What prophet was fed by ravens in his solitude by the brook Cherith?
29 Cache in the Sierra Madre
30 Rocker Sting's surname
34 They're in control of their faculties
36 Japan's largest lake

37 Regular alternative
41 Italian painter Guido ___
44 "Some ___ meat and canna eat": Burns
49 Overcast
52 Follows cru or schi
53 Should
54 Shipper's statements, for short
55 Immigrants' Island
58 Othello's thorn in the side
59 Ghengis ___
60 Qtys.
61 Pennies, for short
62 One mass, e.g.
63 Dedicatory phrase
64 Kenya's cont.
65 Al Capp's "___ Abner"
66 In the law, what mammal is classified as an unclean bird?

Snakes and Other Creepy Things

ACROSS

1 Defense excuse
6 Austen heroine
10 Woodcutters
14 Natural depression
15 Corporate jet maker
16 Aleutian island
17 Egyptian sun god's
18 What Moses raised a pole image to heal
20 The great serpent's name in Revelation
22 Mexican holiday ___ de Mayo
23 English entertainer Laine
24 Prophet whose vine was eaten by a worm
25 Whitney's engine partner
28 Break a commandment
29 Animals from the Nile that plagued Egypt
30 Destructive creature in prophet Joel's vision
36 Tunnel cutter
37 Express disapproval of
38 ___ buco (veal dish)
39 What a loveless father would give a child asking for an egg
41 Amherst sch.
42 Georgia city code
43 Swarming pests that plagued the Egyptians
44 1954 Oscar-winning composer
47 Work detail, for short
49 Horn tap
50 Blood-sucking creature that can't be satisfied
55 Judahites' name for the bronze serpent in the temple
58 Cosmetologist Lauder
59 "What's ___ for me?"
60 Toward
61 In any respect
62 Insect devouring treasures stored up on earth
63 Plant part
64 Land rover?

DOWN

1 Mammal classified as 41-Down in the Law
2 Plaster base
3 Words of enlightenment
4 Hard spot
5 Bugs
6 Beast of Borden?
7 Edison's Park
8 Ewe's sound
9 Zoological boat
10 Polio vaccine developer
11 One of David's heroes
12 Time piece
13 Shetland Islands shed
19 ___-class (airplane section)
21 Very light turbulence: Abbr.
24 Leave in the lurch
25 Short method?
26 Hershey candy
27 Finish for teen or golden
28 Dead and Caspian are two
29 Some radios
30 Hammer or sickle
31 Spouse name
32 Unresponsive state
33 Triathlete's org.
34 Kettle sound
35 ___ and fros

37 What Amos said a man who rested his hand on the wall of his own house would receive (with "a")
40 Trousers
41 Inedible creatures per Leviticus
43 Acceleration measure
44 Shorthand writer
45 Not to miss
46 4-H participant
47 Declare
48 Part of Cambodia's capital
49 City of Judah
51 "What's this, Pedro?"
52 Rock where Samson was captured
53 Spanish novelist who won a 1989 Nobel
54 Restrained
56 His
57 Dynamite

1 2 3 4 5 6 7 8 9 10 11 12 13
14 15 16
17 18 19
20 21 22
23 24
25 26 27 28
29 30 31 32 33 34 35
36 37 38
39 40 41
42 43
44 45 46 47 48
49 50 51 52 53 54
55 56 57 58
59 60 61
62 63 64

The Lion's Den

ACROSS

1 He saw a lionlike creature near the throne of God
5 Disobeyed a zoo sign?
8 Key of Beethoven's Symphony No. 7
12 Rectangular pier
13 Groucho Marx symbol
15 "And away ___!"
16 French ladies, for short
17 "___ at the office"
18 Together, musically
19 Brave soldier in David's army who went into a pit on a snowy day and killed a lion
21 Prophet who had a vision of a creature with a lion's face on one of its four sides
23 Sherwood's Forest site, in brief
25 Beauty preceder?
26 Electrical unit
30 ___ Na Na of rock
32 Pesky insects
36 Ancient Asia Minor
38 MacDonald's last words
40 "___ sport . . ."
41 Father and son David said were stronger than lions
45 Lightweight pullover
46 Wallace of *E.T.*
47 Caller's complaint
48 MS enclosures
51 Opp. of rev.
53 European evergreen
54 French 101 word
56 Loudness measure
58 Whose vision included a lion with eagle's wings?
62 Who had a throne with lion statues beside it?
67 Soldiers' social sites letters
68 According to 1 Peter, what person is like a ravenous lion?
70 Corn bread
71 Winnie's one
72 "Haste makes waste," e.g.
73 NBA's Nick Van ___
74 Soprano Berger
75 Game cube
76 Gear teeth

DOWN

1 Window side
2 "The joke's ___!"
3 Coordinate in the game Battleship
4 US rocket launcher
5 Battles
6 Computer display type
7 Humorist Barry
8 Come to
9 Care starter
10 Tropical fever
11 Bible book speaking of the Lion of the Tribe of Judah
13 "See you," in Sorrento
14 Shah Mohammed Pahlavi
20 *Gandhi* setting
22 Hen's product
24 God's chosen people
26 Religious rituals
27 Circe's island
28 Rakes
29 The works
31 Bone doctors' org.
33 Detest
34 Pond dwellers

35 Horse racing Hall of Famer Earl
37 Common joiner
39 Singer Yoko
42 Meaning, for short
43 Heavenly helper
44 Notwithstanding, briefly
49 Biblical miracle worker
50 *Curly* ___ (movie)
52 Drug dole
55 Ingrid's *Casablanca* role
57 Zippo
58 Put one over on
59 Hebrew lyre
60 Midday
61 Youth movement
63 Arab league
64 Bolivian Indian
65 Blood type, in brief
66 Scandinavian name
69 Mai ___

1
2
3
4
5
6
7
8
9
10
11
12
13
14
15
16
17
18
19
20
21
22
23
24
25
26
27
28
29
30
31
32
33
34
35
36
37
38
39
40
41
42
43
44
45
46
47
48
49
50
51
52
53
54
55
56
57
58
59
60
61
62
63
64
65
66
67
68
69
70
71
72
73
74
75
76

Shepherds and Sheep

ACROSS

1 Number of lost sheep in parable
4 Ten, in Caesar's time
9 What almost-slaughtered son asked his father, "Where is the lamb for a burnt offering?"
14 Animator's unit
15 "___ a minute"
16 Mea ___ (my fault)
17 To whom did Jesus say, "I send you forth as sheep in the midst of wolves"?
20 Plain text files
21 Cable network, briefly
22 Baby danger, in brief
23 Commander in King Jehosaphat's army
26 Own, to Burns
28 Pope's church's initials
31 Religious bookstore gr.
33 Who was out shearing his sheep when David's servants called on him?
37 Psalm that says, "We are his people and the sheep of his pasture"
40 Stone pillars
42 Mogul empire founder
43 Toss a grenade
45 Bagnold and Markey
46 Prophet who spoke of a wolf dwelling with a lamb
48 Festival from the Egyptian exodus when a lamb is slaughtered
50 *The Untouchables* composer Morricone
51 Tit for ___
52 Pueblo pronoun
53 Society column word
55 Political satirist Mort
58 Banished baseball legend
62 Ours, to Wilhelm
64 Recesses at church
68 Foreign traveler reading about the Messiah being a sheep for the slaughter
72 Israeli politico Moshe ___
73 Martian
74 Environmental intro
75 Shepherd girl Zipporah's husband
76 Founder of a French dynasty
77 Grass-covered soil

DOWN

1 Hepta follower
2 CNN feature
3 Amps and volts' subj.
4 Former shepherd who wrote, "The Lord is my shepherd"
5 Scottish uncle
6 Spanish hero, with El
7 New Haven collegians
8 ___ Stele, aka the Moabite Stone
9 Here, in Montreal
10 Has dinner
11 "___ want for Christmas is . . ."
12 Mimicked
13 Elliot of The Mamas and the Papas
18 Debussy heroine
19 Lost in a parable series with sheep
24 Cash register maker
25 The first shepherd
27 Archibald and Thurmond
28 1944 Nobel physicist
29 Fox hunt, e.g.
30 Castro or Batista
32 Take and rear
34 Descendant of Merari
35 Wanted-poster word

36 Fills the hold
38 German's no
39 Sap
41 Being: Sp.
44 Sheep cries
47 Cultivate, as a garden
49 Amtrak stop, for short
54 First digital computer
56 Frequently visit
57 Hosp. worker
58 500 sheets
59 Another, south of the border
60 Females
61 Mozart's "___ Kleine Nachtmusik"
63 Reception room
65 Seeks redress
66 Behold, to Bellini
67 Did a blacksmith's job
69 Grp. in old spy novels
70 "___ it in the bud"
71 Ample shoe width

Biblical Bird Walk

ACROSS

1 What prophet asked, "Does a bird fall into a trap on the ground where no snare has been set?" (NIV)
5 What vultures swoop down on
9 Run, as ink
14 *Fame* star Irene ___
15 Platonic ideas
16 First bird released from the ark
17 Liberal lobby
18 Cities in Holland and Nigeria
19 New York city
20 Who called his companion "My dove, my perfect one"? (cont. in 48-Across)
23 Thompson of *The Beverly Hillbillies*
24 Vienna's co.
25 North Pole-like
29 Latin 101 verb
31 "Just say, '___' has sent me"
34 Indira's son/successor
35 Guinness or Baldwin
36 Taro root
37 Two birds Abram sacrificed to God
40 Opposite of "yes, she"
41 Iraqi military missile
42 What nation's women did Isaiah compare to fluttering birds?
43 Turner's network
44 Female deer
45 Talks back
46 Frying, for one
47 Bird honoring God for providing streams in the desert
48 Conclusion of 20-Across
55 Daggers, in printing
57 Mute swan
58 Inflict on
59 In Revelation, what bird went about crying, "Woe! Woe!"?
60 Heaven's pavement
61 Wee bit
62 Cleaner/disinfectant brand
63 Monkeys' kin
64 Palestine's ancient neighbor

DOWN

1 Parakeet's foe
2 Speed relative to sound
3 Heraldic border
4 What king searching for his rival is compared to looking for a partridge in the mountains?
5 Vexed
6 "___ cock horse to . . ."
7 River of southern Germany
8 "___ am he" (response)
9 Assassin of Julius Caesar
10 Plaster supports
11 Christian musician Tornquist
12 Common Market abbreviation
13 Chromosome chain letters
21 Kind of leaf a bird brought back to the ark
22 Civil rights org.
25 It's spent on the Riviera
26 Unwanted home gas
27 New Testament book
28 Present
29 Italian printer Manutius
30 Margaret ___, US anthropologist
31 Concepts
32 PageMaker maker
33 Belonging to a Frenchman
35 Ending for attend
36 Ids

38 Bird's call
39 "___ ears"
44 Who had a vision of a lion with bird's wings?
45 Dueling devices
46 Mexican chicken
47 "___ Mio"
48 Grapefruit pieces
49 Model railroad scale
50 Broadway bomb
51 Garfield's canine friend
52 Pervading tone
53 Director Preminger
54 Linguist Chomsky
55 Oil, in Frankfurt
56 ___ of Pigs

The Lowly Donkey

ACROSS

1 Catholic service
5 Genealogy
9 Legal wrongs
14 "What's ___ you?"
15 Collector's suffix
16 Brilliantly colored fish
17 Who sent her servant on a donkey to inform Elisha that her son had died?
19 Conclusion of 17-Across
20 Gen. Pershing's cmd.
21 Foreign: Prefix
22 Knights' titles
23 Continuous arrival
25 The only Gospel recording Jesus' riding on a donkey
28 Electromagnetic amplifier
29 Sheep
30 Mrs. Chaplin
31 What future wife of David rode out to meet him on a donkey when she was pleading for her husband's life?
34 Rembrandt van ___
35 Donkey trail
38 *Saturday Night Live* creator
39 Donkey's pest
40 "___ *bin ein Berliner*"
41 Pseudo fat
43 Hard precipitation
45 Grandfather of King Saul
46 Top Boy Scout rank
50 Who used a donkey to carry the wood he would sacrifice his son on?
52 Prophet of Moab with a talking donkey
53 Burns out
54 Company CEO
56 Michael Jordan's status, for short
57 Watergate coconspirator
59 Who predicted the Messiah would enter Jerusalem on a donkey?
61 Find ___ for (pair with)
62 Story line
63 Country superstar McEntyre
64 Chief city official
65 Cotton de-seeders
66 Some B'way shows

DOWN

1 Be off the target
2 Parthenon sculpture
3 What a taxidermist does
4 Junior
5 Watch word
6 Kind of check
7 Inner, in combinations
8 Ext. arith. element
9 Namely
10 Portuguese port
11 Donkey caller?
12 Fourth letter of Arabic alphabet
13 Common ID
18 Part of a metro region
22 Young fish
24 Jacob's first wife
25 Pipelines
26 "Orinoco Flow" singer
27 Poverty
29 Less common
32 Actress Massey and others
33 Robot of Jewish legend
35 ___-hiroth, where Pharaoh overtook the Israelites
36 Hail ___
37 When in creation God made plants

39 Insurrectionist Abimelech defeated
42 *How to ___ Book*: Adler & Van Doren
44 ___ rest (obituary item)
47 Wilder tasting
48 Wall planter
49 Stress starter before "is"
51 English popular novelist
52 Thailand money
54 Prefix with port
55 Subj. for an M.B.A.
57 Jeremiah's second bk.
58 "___ b-a-a-d boy!": Costello
59 Census rept., perhaps
60 Southern Pacific et al.

1
2
3
4
5
6
7
8
9
10
11
12
13
14
15
16
17
18
19
20
21
22
23
24
25
26
27
28
29
30
31
32
33
34
35
36
37
38
39
40
41
42
43
44
45
46
47
48
49
50
51
52
53
54
55
56
57
58
59
60
61
62
63
64
65
66

Horses and Horsemen

ACROSS

1 Son of Abraham and Sarah
6 Andy's radio partner
10 Restaurant
14 Offset printing
15 Tom, Dick, or Harry
16 Huxtable et al.
17 Who had a vision of the hills filled with horses and chariots of fire?
20 Work on hides
21 Kayak's relative
22 Who had a vision of an angel on a red horse?
28 Sweetsops
29 Suffix with buck
30 Currycombs comb them
32 Go down, as a computer
34 Devil worshiper
39 Whirlpool site
41 Prophet to David
43 Paid attention
47 Port-au-Prince's country
48 Actress Blakley
50 Rumor source, often
51 Directly confronted
56 In Revelation, what horse represents Death?
58 ___ the good: so much the better
59 One ___ million
60 Who ordered seventy horsemen to accompany Paul out of Jerusalem?
67 Spelling of *Beverly Hills 90210*
68 Any of the Galapagos
69 Furniture woods
71 Sp. ladies
72 Field for an engr.
73 Belgian violinist

DOWN

1 Chicago's st.
2 *"Sprechen ___ Deutsch?"*
3 Georgia city code
4 Buz clan leader
5 Before Mesa in California
6 Biblical liar
7 Barker and Kettle, e.g.
8 Mantras
9 Get it?
10 Ulster county
11 *A Bell for ___*
12 Maniple
13 ___ Park, Colorado
18 Injure
19 His Master's Voice co.
22 John the Baptist's father, to friends
23 Flynn of film
24 Raccoon's relative
25 Party throwers
26 Anecdotal collection
27 Angry, with up
31 ___ Diego
33 Quarterback's cry
35 Slangy refusal
36 "Cosmicomics" author Calvino
37 Not as outgoing
38 British good-byes
40 Before eave or wick
42 Running shoe name
44 Queue before Q
45 Disney deer
46 Samson's girlfriend
49 Start of a count
51 Almanac tidbits
52 ___ nothing
53 Barton or Bow
54 Small needle cases

55 Govt. mil. agcy.
57 Be wasteful?
61 998 in Rome
62 Function
63 Jesse Jackson's org.
64 Plural suffix
65 S & P's highest bond rating
66 Plane's place
70 Compass direction

The Biblical Greenhouse

ACROSS

1 Ghost star
7 Steadied
13 Most favorable
15 Mascara target
16 What tree's fruit was symbolically represented on the clothing of Israel's high priest?
18 Spanish aunts
19 Stein
20 Letters after Gov. Jeanne Shaheen's name
21 Digital communication?: Abbr.
22 San ___: Italian resort
23 Spots, biblically
26 ___ Fein
28 Tithable pungent plant in Bible
29 Vessel associates
34 ___ a dozen
36 What massive trees were brought to make the beams and pillars in the Jerusalem temple?
38 Battery terminal
39 Hush, as in forest
40 No value
41 Yields
42 Emulate Mr. Chips
45 Lodge members
47 Type of sleep
50 Fourth letter of Arabic alphabet
51 Longing
52 Father of King Menahem
53 On what did the exiled Jews hang their harps?
58 High-drama competition?
59 African flies
60 Most like Solomon
61 Looms

DOWN

1 Terra ___
2 Garden pest
3 Baseball action
4 Dice features
5 Funnyman Philips
6 Pirate's drink
7 Saxophonist Don
8 Tears
9 One narrow passage
10 Henry VIII's last
11 Chin end
12 Certain BB batters
14 Souvenirs
15 Beginning of a conclusion
17 Sticky stuff
22 Transfer and messenger materials
24 Ring heavyweights
25 13 to 19
26 Miner's nail
27 Hungarian poet Madach
29 Paltry
30 Skater Sonja
31 Second Commandment breakers
32 Newt, but not Gingrich
33 Noose
34 Competently
35 Aykroyd et al.
37 High notes
43 Beloved, in Brest
44 Cantina beans
45 Brontë's Jane
46 About 2 cents, in Albania

47 Pay hike
48 Lawn trimmer
49 Young lady's property
52 Long Civil War movie, for short
53 Marble shooter
54 Venetian canals
55 Congressional passage
56 Q-U connection
57 Auto racer Fabi

1
2
3
4
5
6
7
8
9
10
11
12
13
14
15
16
17
18
19
20
21
22
23
24
25
26
27
28
29
30
31
32
33
34
35
36
37
38
39
40
41
42
43
44
45
46
47
48
49
50
51
52
53
54
55
56
57
58
59
60
61

Some Earthquakes

ACROSS

1 Head plague?
5 Practices boxing
10 An earthquake during King Uzziah's reign was so remarkable that this Hebrew prophet dates his book "two years before the earthquake"
14 Buddhist sacred mountain
15 What famous mountain smoked like a furnace and quaked greatly?
16 Hollywood corner
17 Chinese politico Li
18 Drinking vessel
19 Intestinal parts
20 An earthquake occurred when Jesus died on the cross. What other spectacular event occurred at that time in Jerusalem?
23 Dixieland
25 Watcher
26 Clinic workers, for short
27 Lew Wallace's Ben
28 Bad prefix
31 British motorists' org.
33 When some lunch hours start
34 Hosiery purchase
37 Puccini opera
41 Spectacular event from 61-Across concluded
45 Caruso was one
46 Like Rioja wine
47 Estonian river
48 Copy, in brief
50 Chiang ___-shek
52 Morning hrs.
53 Dallas football team letters
56 Biblical daughter-in-law
59 Soft drinks
61 Spectacular event from 20-Across continued
65 General Robert ___
66 Missouri city
67 Book of the RC Bible
70 An earthquake at Philippi eventually led to the release of two Christians, Silas and ___, from prison there
71 Super bargain
72 Greek mountain
73 Classify, as blood
74 Nervous
75 Magi's guide

DOWN

1 Snip
2 Harrison's ___ *Mine*
3 At Jesus' crucifixion, who said, "Truly, this was the son of God"?
4 Ice skating figure
5 An NCO
6 Heap
7 What's in ___?
8 Grating
9 George, of Hall of Fame
10 Part of Israel's capital
11 Type of racer
12 This comes before a million
13 Playful mammals
21 Nat. Safety Council org.
22 Poetry Muse
23 Mine opening
24 Outlandish
29 Military address
30 Toy "bullets"
32 Army bed
35 Resident ending
36 Plymouth landmark

38 Unwavering
39 Semicolon's cousin
40 Gather
42 Stylish
43 Cape Cod resort town
44 Coiling snake
49 Most virtuous
51 O.T. prophet
53 Like most airliner wings
54 Asian peninsula
55 Deplete
57 Certain investment, informally
58 Biblical City of Refuge
60 *Stand and Deliver* star Edward James ___
62 Boob tube, in Britain: Var.
63 Actor Peeples et al.
64 Sound in health
68 Jefferson Davis was its pres.
69 Elevator

Rivers, Brooks, Lakes, Seas

ACROSS
1 Elevator stop
6 Laze in the tub
10 Drumbeat
14 Set itinerary
15 *To Live and Die* ___: 1985 flick
16 Czech river
17 *The Lady* ___ *Tiger?*
18 Aircraft landing apparatus
19 Author Janette and family
20 What was the Sea of Galilee called in Old Testament times?
23 Children's game
24 T-man's org.
25 Fly
26 Surveying instrument
29 Taylor University president Jay
30 Has substance
34 ___ Hillary Clinton
35 By what lake did Jesus appear to his disciples after the Resurrection?
40 Tyrannosaurus ___
41 Congressman Thomas J. ___ (D; NY)
42 Encrypt
46 ___ Beach on Delaware Bay
50 Son of Arphaxad
51 Pro's partner
53 U.S.N. division
54 In John's vision, what happened to the sea when the second angel poured out his bowl on it?
58 Taro-root dishes
59 The Rome of Hungary
60 Other: Fr.
61 Sea eagle
62 Film maker
63 Slopes occupant
64 NCOs
65 Collies and spaniels
66 Parties

DOWN
1 Famed snowman
2 Makeup maker
3 Power off
4 First-century Roman emperor
5 Great Barrier, e.g.
6 Part of a gun
7 "___ by land . . ."
8 Economist Greenspan
9 Luxor temple
10 Iowa town
11 Ohio recreational area
12 Aiders
13 Interlockers
21 Sacramento's st.
22 Between day and night
27 Vt. Educ. Assn.
28 Bible's second bk.
31 Seminary deg.
32 Maria, for one
33 So. Bapt. Network
35 Jesse Helms and Strom Thurmond
36 Thrilling
37 People: Prefix
38 "Vive le ___!"
39 Participle ending
40 Chef's collection
43 Burdens
44 Patriotic org.
45 Group of nine
47 Flub a grounder

48 South Carolina whitewater site
49 Ducks for down
51 *B* followers
52 Others: Sp.
55 Frozen waffle brand
56 Tape maker
57 Skywalker

Builders of Cities

ACROSS

1 Hezbollah stronghold: ___ Valley
6 Undergrad deg.
9 Charitable donations
13 Beery and Webster
14 Court cry
16 Water pipe
17 Filmdom's Andrews and Wynters
18 Bargain spread
19 "Green Gables" girl
20 Who rebuilt Babylon on a grand scale?
23 None in the inn in Bethlehem
24 Smallest amount
25 What king of Israel built Penuel?
28 "There ___ crooked man . . ."
31 Not all
32 ___ *Kapital*
35 Novelist Hesse
39 Domestic aide
41 W. hemisphere org.
42 Philistine city
44 European or Chinese lead-in
45 What king of Judah built up the defenses of Bethlehem?
49 The L of AWOL
53 Cows' home
54 City Nimrod built
60 Gehrig and Rawls
61 Girl's casual slacks
62 Mary was one
64 Overture follower
65 Correct: prefix
66 "Remember the ___"
67 Stimulate
68 That muchacha
69 Nauru's island capital

DOWN

1 Germany's natl. intelligence serv.
2 Of the dawn
3 Orson Welles's film *Citizen* ___
4 Hiel rebuilt Jericho during the reign of King ___
5 Guarantee
6 Cry
7 What Jesus told Peter to feed
8 How Woods got the ball off
9 Dumbfound
10 Opera's Mario
11 Nova Scotia basin and channel
12 Hagar the Horrible's dog
15 Part of the Holy Trinity
21 Two N.T. letters
22 ___ Gantry
25 Toast spread
26 Agents like Bond
27 Black denom.
28 The one that
29 Actors' org.
30 AARP concern
32 King Jeroboam erected golden calves in ___ and Bethel
33 Common connector
34 I stand: Lat.
36 Be of one mind
37 Protestant church org.
38 Power raiser?
40 Vigor
43 Creatures coined by J. R. R. Tolkien
46 Who rebuilt Ramah in order to keep people from entering or leaving Judah?
47 Heavenly body
48 At all
49 Four-time Emmy-winning series

50 City Cain built east of Eden
51 Critical
52 Stopover
55 Army staff rank
56 Wheat field weed
57 Gwen in *Damn Yankees*
58 ___ Khayyam
59 Moniker
63 Absent prefix?

Cities Great and Small (Part 1)

ACROSS

1 Property title
5 The *Constitution,* e.g.
9 Thyatira, the home of Lydia, was an ___ city
14 Jazzy Fitzgerald
15 Issuer of a famous report
16 Where did Peter cure Aeneas?
17 Estuaries
18 Dessert specialist
19 Courtier of King Josiah
20 Site of Jacob's famous dream
22 Air-to-gnd. missile
24 "For ___ jolly . . ."
25 Israeli prime minister Levi ___kol
26 Negating word
28 Opera by Verdi
30 Western resort lake
32 What city was the fifth of the seven churches mentioned by John?
36 Jezebel's Phoenician home city
39 A.M. meal
41 Dockworkers' org
42 Close
43 In what city did Silas and Timothy stay while Paul went to Athens?
44 Where did Jesus raise a widow's son from the dead?
45 Ashes holder
46 Popular travel guide author
47 Hebrew Bible author
48 At what town was Saul publicly proclaimed king?
50 Consumers' champion
52 Roman highway
54 Start for Alamos or Angeles
55 Johnnie Cochran's org.
58 Ancient kingdom in Jordan
61 Soak up the sun
63 What city was Paul's hometown?
65 "Waves of grain" color
67 Ho Chi of Vietnam
69 Gets by, with "out"
70 City destroyed by God for its wickedness
71 Epithet of Athena
72 Pause prefix
73 Metal monies
74 Shaped by chopping
75 They're exchanged at the altar

DOWN

1 What city did Paul visit on his first and third missionary journeys?
2 Writer Wiesel and others
3 Ezion-Geber, Solomon's seaport, was at the head of the Gulf of ___
4 Track event
5 What city was home to the tabernacle after the Israelites conquered Canaan?
6 Precedes cough or cup
7 Virginia willow
8 Where were Paul and Barnabas deserted by Mark?
9 Pie ___ mode
10 In what Samaritan town did Jesus meet the woman at the well?
11 "___ delighted!"
12 Big deals
13 Japanese religious center
21 Father of Naphtali leader Ahira
23 Beethoven's ___ *Solemnis*
27 "And so ___ . . .": Pepys
29 High-tech recording med.
30 Windswept spot

31 What Philistine city worshiped the god Baal-zebub?
33 "Buenos ___"
34 "Would ___?" (sleazeball's question)
35 ___ serif typeface
36 Like contented bugs
37 Pietro's yesterday
38 Frontiersman Boone, to pals
40 Untamed
43 Classical pianist Jorge
44 Neither go-with
46 The 2 percent of 2%
47 City near Phoenix
49 Where did Solomon have a dream when he asked for wisdom?
51 Where did Elisha strike Syrian soldiers with blindness?
53 Where was Samuel buried?
55 Sought information
56 Good, in Madrid
57 What seaport in Asia did Paul walk to from Troas?
58 Not fem. or neut.
59 South Seas adventure story
60 Grandfather of King Saul
62 Cairo's river
64 Do followers
66 Apartment ad abbr.
68 According to Revelation, there be no night in the ___ Jerusalem

Palatial Living

ACROSS

1 R's four followers
5 Ebenezer's partner
10 Newsmag of note
14 M. Hulot's creator
15 Cow stomachs
16 Prepaid ins. plans
17 Ardor
18 Organize
19 Drip site
20 Who served as a cupbearer in Persia's royal palace?
22 Tower of London's river
24 Kwai
25 Stadium feature
26 Water sound
29 What Judean king took Babylon's envoys on a tour of his palace?
33 "Ta-da!"
34 Having divided windows
35 Charlemagne's dom.
36 Peel
37 Domesticated
38 Ooh ender
39 The O of O.T.
40 Basic Halloween costume
41 Like wartime messages
42 Stately
44 Belonging to the very devil
45 Scandinavian goddess
46 Harasses for money
47 Theater lines
50 What king was assassinated in his palace by Pekah?
54 What country had a palace carved from rock?
55 Azel's brother
57 What Israeli king built Samaria as his royal city?
58 Mater preceder
59 The gold of the conquistadors
60 Volcanic landform
61 Pet bird, familiarly
62 Music for nine
63 Ancient slave

DOWN

1 British carbine
2 *Peter Rabbit,* for one
3 Great Salt Lake site
4 Naboth had a coveted ___ close to Israel's royal palace
5 Judean royal reformer
6 "If I ever do ___ action . . .": Sterne
7 Bishop's church: Abbr.
8 Buckeyes' sch.
9 Immersed, for some
10 Sacred Hebrew chest
11 The Ayatollah, for one
12 Traffic cop's order
13 Suffixes relating to nationality
21 Ponder
23 Be guided by
25 Basic belief
26 Razor sharpener
27 Pa. hub
28 Ivan of tennis
29 *Hill Street Blues* star
30 "___ little pony . . ."
31 "I Love a Parade" composer
32 ___ or tails?
34 Song of praise
37 Solomon took ___ years to build his palace
38 Where angels stayed in Sodom

40 Octagonal sign word
41 Biblical wedding site
43 Twenty Questions category
44 Jewish Feast of Tabernacles
46 Tractor man John
47 Restaurant spot
48 A year in the life of Attila
49 City of Caesar's palace
50 Study of speech sounds, for short
51 "___ corny as Kansas . . ."
52 Islands near Ireland
53 Add to the payroll
56 Irish county Sligo: Abbr.

1 2 3 4 5 6 7 8 9 10 11 12 13
14 15 16
17 18 19
20 21 22 23
24 25
26 27 28 29 30 31 32
33 34 35
36 37 38
39 40 41
42 43 44
45 46
47 48 49 50 51 52 53
54 55 56 57
58 59 60
61 62 63

Up Against the Wall

ACROSS

1 Reporter's query
5 Protestant synod letters
8 What rebel against David was beheaded, with his head thrown over the wall of Abel to Joab?
13 Nimbus
14 Insect's sense organ
15 Abram's Mesopotamian home
16 Benjamin's grandson's
17 Personal-articles case
18 Floating flavor
19 Who sacrificed his son on the city wall when he was losing the battle to Israel?
22 Big ___ theory
23 Teletypesetter, in brief
24 What city was famous for its fallen walls?
28 Ballet step
29 *My Gal* ___
32 High priest's vesture
33 Benefitting
34 Personal protection item
35 What perfectly square city is described as having walls made of jasper?
39 Art philanthropist Sir Henry
40 Possessed
41 Japanese dog or seaport
42 ___ Research (computer maker)
43 Not well
44 Who built the walls of Jerusalem?
46 Part of FWIW
47 Q string
48 What warrior, the victim of a king's scheming, was killed when shot by arrows from the wall of Rabbah?
56 Sheriff's band
57 Pertaining to an outpatient fac.
58 Auth. unknown
59 Victoria's Secret fabric
60 Spanish leader
61 C.S. Lewis's ___ *Christianity*
62 Belonging to the herdsman prophet
63 Wager
64 Social equal

DOWN

1 Forcible impact
2 Legendary race loser
3 Loc. legislators
4 Baloney
5 Barrio resident
6 Hung on
7 Fat as ___
8 Elevator passages
9 Injures
10 Switch or smack ender
11 Crimson Tide, for short
12 Canaanite city of giants
14 King of Israel who besieged Judah
20 Alphabet's first quintet
21 Japan's ___ Bay
24 Volkswagen model
25 Ancient Hebrew measures
26 He had Scarlett fever
27 *The Last Days of Pompeii* heroine
28 For: Sp.
29 Town near Jordan River
30 Vinegar, in combinations
31 Lake of Geneva
33 Disobeyed a zoo sign?
34 Shark
36 Early form of bridge
37 Narita's national carrier

38 "Cheers!" in Cherbourg
43 Greek capital
44 It's not automatic trans.
45 Chocolate drink for short
46 Pathological cause: Suf.
47 U. S. Grant's opponent
48 ___-daisey
49 Travel far and wide
50 Ratio words
51 Voice of the Andes (call letters)
52 Pack down
53 Arrow poison
54 Ripped
55 Year starter, in Spain

1
2
3
4
5
6
7
8
9
10
11
12
13
14
15
16
17
18
19
20
21
22
23
24
25
26
27
28
29
30
31
32
33
34
35
36
37
38
39
40
41
42
43
44
45
46
47
48
49
50
51
52
53
54
55
56
57
58
59
60
61
62
63
64

Cities Great and Small (Part 2)

ACROSS

1 City of Jesus' first miracle
5 Fast-buck artist's ploy
9 #2 on the phone
12 Thin as ___
14 Have to
15 Crossing
17 Hide-and-seek word
18 What city was home to the man who gave Jesus a burial place?
20 In what Syrian city did Paul have his sight restored at the hands of Ananias?
22 Perceive, per King James
23 Shoe-touting bulldog
24 The city of Beersheba is usually mentioned as the southern limit of ___
25 Classify
29 Before chow in Chinese city
30 Zahlah is the largest city in this valley
31 What city is often referred to simply as Zion?
37 "I smell ___!"
38 Australian aquatic plant
39 Thirteenth cent. Persian poet
40 What city was the birthplace of both David and Jesus?
42 What Phoenician city was home to evil Jezebel?
43 Poet's dusk
44 Movie theater
45 Military personnel
49 Aircraft acronym
51 Volleyball start
52 What city was home to Philemon?
57 Where did Jesus stay when John the Baptist was in prison?
60 Periodic radio signal
61 Sun product
62 Variety of lettuce
63 Craze
64 Sighs of relief
65 Juneau's st.
66 Copy, briefly

DOWN

1 Christian singer Michael
2 Length x width
3 Son of Caleb
4 Opera set in the time of the Pharaohs
5 Character in Tolkien's *The Hobbit*
6 Opposite of bless
7 "___ was saying . . ."
8 Engineering deg.
9 In the wake of
10 A black tea
11 Iraklion is the largest city on this island
13 Where was Paul mistaken for the god Hermes?
16 *James and the Giant Peach* author Roald
19 What seaport in Asia did Paul walk to from Troas?
21 Op. ___ (thesis ref.)
24 Paper promises
25 Rhyme scheme
26 Dried up
27 Three-player card game
28 Scout recitation
29 Gift tag word
31 ___ said the city of Pergamos had "Satan's seat"
32 Summer, on the Seine

33 "Z ___ zebra"
34 Stow cargo
35 Amos cursed the Philistine city of Gaza for its slave trade with ___
36 "Dracula" miss
38 Wine sediment
41 One returned to thank Jesus
42 What tower, mentioned by Jesus, killed eighteen people when it collapsed?
44 Oliver North's mil. rank
45 Toxic Substances Control Act of 1976: Abbr.
46 Lariat
47 Naomi's other duaghter-in-law
48 Hot spots?
49 Aqualung
50 Graves
53 Timetable listings: Abbr.
54 E-mailed
55 Philadelphia receives the most praise of all the seven cities of ___
56 Coup d'___
58 Bulls and Celtics org.
59 Be sick

1 2 3 4 5 6 7 8 9 10 11
12 13 14 15 16
17 18 19
20 21 22
23 24
25 26 27 28 29
30 31 32 33 34 35 36
37 38 39
40 41 42
43 44
45 46 47 48 49 50
51 52 53 54 55 56
57 58 59 60
61 62 63
64 65 66

Wells, Cisterns, and Other Large Containers

ACROSS

1 Esek, Sitnah, Rehoboth, and Beersheba are all names of ___
6 Applause
10 Da Vinci's Mona
14 "I can't believe I __ much!"
15 "Like peas in ___"
16 Tolkien tree creatures
17 Suez, for example
18 Who promised the citizens of Jerusalem that they could be free to drink from their own cisterns if they would surrender to Assyria?
20 Aged
21 October gem
23 Cop ___ (negotiate for a lighter sentence)
24 Greek consonants
25 Joseph nearly perished after being thrown into a ___ by his brothers
27 Mather and gin
31 Rent out
32 Kind of renewal
33 What prophet was imprisoned in a water reservoir?
38 Rosary aid
39 Housetops
41 Largest continent
42 Whose servant found a wife for Isaac at the well of Nahor?
44 Fire station sound
45 "___ we there yet?"
46 Sticks to
48 Chicago Bears' Field
52 Vowel sequence
53 Judas's pos. among the apostles
54 Silo occupant, in brief
55 Author Rand
58 Who tried to take the well of Beersheba away from Abraham?
61 ___-Detoo, *Star Wars* android
63 Bridal shower?
64 Peace-prize winner Wiesel
65 "Read all ___ it!"
66 Sorority letters
67 "Realize how kind the Lord has ___ to you" (1 Pet. 2:2)
68 King of Israel for only seven days

DOWN

1 Site of Baylor University
2 Catchall abbr.
3 Trust one for
4 Law Sch. Admission
5 What king ordered the construction of the Sea, the great basin in the temple court?
6 Pester
7 Be ___ to (help out)
8 San Francisco's ___ Hill
9 Driller's deg.
10 Jumped
11 Hint at
12 Head for the ranch?
13 Town assigned to tribe of Simeon
19 Waste maker
22 Bit of paronomasia
25 Musical sign
26 Cloth ends
27 Castro's country
28 Midianite general
29 Vail conveyor
30 Joni Eareckson ___
33 Nigerian city
34 Father or son
35 Danube tributary

36 After concession or million
37 Unskilled actors who overact
39 Steak order
40 Two-quart manna container
43 *Apollo 13* astronaut Fred
44 Who besides Jonathan escaped from Absalom's men by hiding in a well?
46 German coronation city in Middle Ages
47 Society inductee, for short
48 Look and look and look
49 Mir's path
50 Nikon rival
51 Actresses Anderson and Whitty
54 Intl. Conf. for Itinerant Evangelists
55 Fermi's fascination
56 "At ___ service"
57 Little Red Hen retort
59 Beruit's c.
60 Engineer's course, in brief
62 Slugger's stat

Gates, Doors, and Other Openings

ACROSS

1 India's Taj
6 Mediterranean, for one
9 "God ___ refuge" (Psa. 46)
14 "___ lead on a new job"
15 *Beauty ___ the Beast*
16 ___-cotta, as tile
17 What entrance into Jerusalem was rebuilt under Nehemiah's leadership?
19 ___ one's ways
20 Italian tenor Enrico
21 *Xanadu* rock grp.
23 Vietnamese coin
24 Who healed a lame man at the temple's Beautiful Gate?
28 Whom did God speak to about the "gates of death"?
31 Clerical error?
32 Help wanted abbr.
33 Continent between Europe and Pacific
35 Swiped
38 "The voice is Jacob's, but the hands are ___" (Gen. 27:22)
42 Chinese emperor ___ Tsu
44 Emergency meas.
45 Highest, in honors
46 Milne creature
47 Home, to Hans
49 CEOs establish these
50 O.T. bk. with visions of dry bones
52 ___ Bernina, central Alps' highest peak
54 Church altar inscription
55 In Revelation, which of the seven churches in Asia had set before it an open door that no man could shut?
61 End of statement, for short
62 Before Cat or cone
63 Most senior
67 Hebrew tribe
70 According to Moses, on what were God's words to be written?
72 Tally again
73 City of Faith sch.
74 More or less vertical
75 At the first Passover, what kind of blood were the Israelites told to apply to their entryways?
76 Follower of the Pied Piper
77 Cattle clusters

DOWN

1 Catchall file label, in brief
2 ___ Khan
3 Cultivator
4 Thoroughly enjoyed
5 Oversights
6 South Africa Airways letters
7 "The door's open!"
8 Journalist Rogers St. Johns
9 "___ a girl!"
10 Look
11 Lawn products brand
12 What faithful soldier slept in front of the king's palace instead of going home to his wife?
13 Talked continuously
18 "I have the answer!"
22 How many doors did Noah's ark have?
25 Father of Methuselah
26 Executes
27 The Messiah
28 Item in a trunk
29 Workers' protection org.
30 Well, to Pierre
34 Who rolled back the stone from Jesus' tomb?

36 ___-Locka, Florida
37 Big name in German steel and armaments
39 Mine, on the Moselle
40 Expression of disbelief
41 Talk back
43 From what city's gate did Samson remove the massive doors and carry them to a hill at Hebron?
48 Southwestern Canaanite town
51 Wynn and Sullivan
53 Leah's handmaid
55 What are the gates of the New Jerusalem made of?
56 Prophet married to a prostitute
57 Bandleader Jones
58 *Star Wars* planet
59 Irish lullaby syllables
60 Muhammad Ali's "rope-___"
64 Danish weight
65 African village
66 Contempt expressions
68 Teacher's deg.
69 Aves.
71 Umpire's call

Portable Places to Dwell

ACROSS

1 So. Hemisphere constellation
4 Arafat's gr.
7 Fed's purchasing dept.
10 Medicare org.
13 Tombstone letters
14 Ireland's ___ Lingus
15 Words of surprise
16 Swiss river
17 Keystone character
18 Potato chip brand
20 Einstein's birthplace
21 What, in the dream of a Midianite soldier, tumbled into the Midianite camp and flattened a tent?
24 Singer/comedian Sherman
26 Son of Micah
27 Iranian coin
28 Customer
30 ___ Darya (Central Asian river)
33 Protestant denom.
34 "___ I cared!"
35 "___ Fire" (Springsteen hit)
36 Who plundered the tents of the Syrians after the army fled their camp?
40 The Emerald Isle
41 What did the famous ship captain Noah live in?
42 Small amount
44 Newsman Rather
45 "I understand now"
46 Accounting prin.
47 Union rate
50 Florida Congressman ___ Hastings
51 What was the tent that was made according to God's specifications?
56 "It ___ to Be You"
57 Giveth rise to
58 Counterpart of long.
61 "___ out a living"
62 Telecommunications letters
63 ___ long way
64 Grads of O.T.S.
65 "___ at work" (road sign)
66 Distaff Masonic org.
67 Disobey God
68 Timber tree

DOWN

1 What did David pitch a tent in Jerusalem to house?
2 Precedes Grande in Texas
3 Region of Tennessee and Kentucky
4 Hebrews' temporary wilderness "home"
5 Blood disease: Abbr.
6 Golden carp
7 Played eighteen
8 What rebel against David said, "Every man to his tents, O Israel"?
9 Very, to Verdi
10 Damascus Road convert
11 Shopper's delight
12 Part of *M*A*S*H*
19 Ancestors
22 Orioles' Ripken
23 Brother of Nimrod
24 In current existence (pl.)
25 Picked up
28 "Born in the ___"
29 ___ City: computer game
31 Jefferson's home
32 Perilous
34 Enzyme suffix
35 Sheraton's parent org.
37 Modern painter Max
38 Abbr. next to a phone number

39 Daughter of Cadmus
43 Famous signature John ___
45 Certain Eskimos
46 Breastfeeding org.
48 Kind of bean
49 Relieve taxes
50 Who took spoils from the fallen Jericho and buried them inside his tent?
51 "___ There Eyes": 1930 song
52 Cod relative
53 Adam's first home
54 Photo films, briefly
55 Yours, in Tours
59 *One Day ___ Time*
60 Sound of disapproval

Makers of Music

ACROSS

1 King David, who was also a ___ and musician, embarrassed his wife by dancing in the streets
5 Jubal is the father of those who play the ___ and ___ (place one answer in 10-Across)
10 One answer from 5-Across
14 Short story–writer?
15 66 is one
16 Nondairy spread
17 Autocratic leader
18 Painter and fashion designer Delaunay
19 Reclined
20 King ___ wrote over a thousand ___ (place one answer in 75-Across)
22 David's ___ caused Saul's "evil spirit" to leave him
24 Harpooner's response to Mr. Land: Jules Verne
26 Ranch follower
27 Place for a mower
29 Taster's response
31 Saul and Ahab
35 Freer
37 Night flyer
39 Composer Edouard or Schifrin
40 Have
41 When the foundation for the second temple was laid, the ___ played ___ (place one answer in 59-Across)
44 Tic-tac-toe goal
45 *Cheers* actor Roger
47 Scooby ___
48 Sampras, for one
50 ___ dust
52 A bk. of Moses
54 "___ a New High" (1937 Lily Pons song)
55 Earlier than, for short
57 Common ending
59 One answer from 41-Across
63 The prophetess Miriam played a ___ and led the women of Israel in a victory song after the ___ Sea incident (place one answer in 36-Down)
67 Darth's daughter
68 "Imprisoned in every fat man ___ one is wildly signalling to be let out": Cyril Connolly
70 Greasy
71 It's right on the map
72 Concorde is one
73 General Bradley
74 Correct: Prefix
75 One answer from 20-Across
76 Reid or Smith

DOWN

1 DC arm-twisters
2 Aniseed liqueur
3 Etc. alternative
4 Sovereigns' seats
5 Welles of *Citizen Kane*
6 "Didja ever wonder . . . ?" humorist
7 Saturday night special
8 Server's desire
9 1959–60 Wimbledon winner Fraser
10 Priest's "tool"
11 Jai ___ (game)
12 Bit attachment
13 Ping-___
21 Fashion figure
23 Boat Noah built
25 Not convinced

27 Seeder
28 Sweetheart
30 "Welcome" bearer
32 Ruth's mother-in-law
33 Revel in self-satisfaction
34 Before long
35 King David had 4,000 musicians who praised the ___ with instruments he had made
36 One answer from 63-Across
38 Hamilton bill
42 ___ Trapps: *The Sound of Music* family
43 Earthshaking event
46 Jewish weekly holy day
49 An edition of *The Living Bible*
51 Baltic or Black
53 Measuring, of olde
56 Wing parts
58 WXY phone buttons
59 Marc Antony's love, briefly
60 Decade division
61 Haze
62 Normandy battle site
64 Abel's *Green Mansions* love
65 Israeli seaport
66 Unreliable musical instrument?
69 Chinese people in general

Artsy, Craftsy Types

ACROSS

1 Researcher George
6 Noah built a ___ ___ of gopherwood (place one answer in 29-Down)
10 ___ alone (fly solo)
14 Hebrew king
15 Scarlett's plantation
16 ___ Fitzgerald
17 Offset printing
18 Which coppersmith had, according to Paul, done him great harm?
20 What Israelite, a worker in gold, silver, brass, stone, and wood, had responsibility for furnishing the tabernacle?
22 Sandwich need
23 Chicago's st.
24 Beat
26 Evangelist Billy
30 Philosopher David
31 Edit a soundtrack
32 Who was the first metal craftsman in the Bible?
37 Puzzle type: Abbr.
38 Packing a piece
39 VIII
40 What notorious opponent of Paul was a silversmith in Ephesus?
42 Went astray
43 Knocks
44 Creators
45 Bible book recording making of the tabernacle
49 Wirehaired terr___
50 *Henry & June* character
51 Money maker?
56 ___, son of a ___, was involved in rebuilding the walls of Jerusalem (place one answer in 5-Down)
59 More than miffed
60 Division of a shield, in heraldry
61 Tropical palm
62 Site of a Herculean feat
63 Young lady
64 Eight, in Bonn
65 Rubbernecker

DOWN

1 It's often screwed up
2 Auto racer Luyendyk
3 Hotel or cracker name
4 Okinawan port
5 One answer from 56-Across
6 Madame de ___
7 Campus building
8 Part of Br. Isles
9 ___ Romana
10 Art category
11 Of yore
12 Of an intestine
13 Evening, in Avila
19 Egypt's Mr. Nasser
21 Dutch disease target
24 Board game set
25 *Diary of ___ Housewife*
26 Alumnus
27 Philosopher Descartes
28 Famous rib donor
29 One answer from 6-Across
30 Soil component
32 Comings and goings
33 Stopper
34 Farmland measure
35 Ancient road to Rome
36 Visual OKs

38 Sandarac tree
41 Head lock
42 Jewelry item
44 Marmee's eldest
45 Late actor Conrad
46 Shrub genus
47 Ice cream treats
48 Waits for
49 ___ water (facing trouble)
51 ___-A-Sketch (drawing toy)
52 Code word
53 Theda Bara, e.g.
54 Derby winner Lil ___
55 Desk admiral
57 Universal City studio
58 The Games org.

1
2
3
4
5
6
7
8
9
10
11
12
13
14
15
16
17
18
19
20
21
22
23
24
25
26
27
28
29
30
31
32
33
34
35
36
37
38
39
40
41
42
43
44
45
46
47
48
49
50
51
52
53
54
55
56
57
58
59
60
61
62
63
64
65

Glad Rags

ACROSS

1 What king of Israel is mentioned as wearing a crown and a gold bracelet?
5 Sty occupants
9 Check for ID
13 Freedom from care
14 Certain skirts
15 "As Long ___ Needs Me" (*Oliver!* song)
16 What people wore fine Egyptian linen and purple ___? (place one answer in 31-Across)
19 Charged particle
20 Cavern, in poetry
21 Anagram for steer
22 Director Lee of *Sense and Sensibility*
23 Half a deadly fly
24 Madrid Mrs.
25 Joseph, an Egyptian official, was given fine linen, the ___, and a gold chain for his neck
31 One answer from 16-Across
34 Miracle-___ (garden product)
35 "___, black sheep"
36 Words teachers like to hear
37 Plumbing tool
39 Riches alternative
40 The "S" in R.S.V.P.
41 Son of Benjamin
42 Severe
43 High priest ___ wore fine colored ___ with embroidered bells and ___, a breastplate with gold and precious stones, and a gold-studded hat (place one answer in 2-Down and another in 50-Down)
48 Research site
49 King Features competitor
50 Eye part
53 Offhand remark
56 Clamorous
58 Seine sight
59 John the Baptist wore a ___
62 Russian ruler
63 Autographs
64 Cauterize
65 Congressional VIPs
66 Decisive defeat
67 TV's Mr. Griffith

DOWN

1 Photo tint
2 One answer from 43-Across
3 Operating
4 Leonard's nickname
5 Nun
6 Fragrance
7 Eve was the first
8 Fast flyer's letters
9 Roman emperor
10 Off. helper
11 Korean president Syngman ___
12 Letter opener
14 The brainy bunch
17 Many churchgoers: Abbr.
18 The girl's
24 Comic crow
25 Footlike part
26 From the top
27 Where Mindy honeymooned, in 1981 TV
28 Supporting beam
29 Old horses
30 Bad cut
31 Carpentry tool
32 Buckeye State

33 Soothing ointment
37 Belgrade native
38 Shelter grp.
39 ___ Shamra tablets
42 "Love the Lord your God with all your ___"
44 Seniors
45 Scottish Highlander
46 Apply consecrated oil
47 Sadness signs
50 One answer from 43-Across
51 Homer's epic
52 Condemn
53 Dr. Luke's church history book
54 Encl. for a reply
55 "___ Old Cowhand"
56 Abinadab's son
57 Spaghetti sauce brand
60 Former Russian abbreviation
61 Cable network

So Many Children

ACROSS

1 What wicked king of Israel had 70 sons?
5 Home for *la familia*
9 Value of a share
14 Actress Maryam
15 Single unit
16 Lewis of children's TV
17 *East of Eden* brother
18 Paper currency
19 King of Germany called "The Child"
20 According to Deuteronomy, what was done to a rebellious son who would not submit to discipline?
22 "___ make a lovely corpse": Dickens
24 Miss, in Marseilles: Abbr.
25 Mama chick
26 Whereabouts, for short
28 Rock music's Ford
30 Diamond measure
32 Who was Jacob's favorite son?
36 What judge of Israel had 40 sons and 30 grandsons?
39 Millionaire
41 Pilot licensing org.
42 *Mission: Impossible* actress
43 What court prophet of David's had 14 sons and 3 daughters?
44 Kid
45 Goes with outs
46 Mama's mates
47 Moses' older brother
48 Who was adopted by Mordecai?
50 Parents
52 What prophet said he was neither a prophet nor a prophet's son?
54 6th c. date
55 Data transmission ck.
58 Slim gull-like bird
61 Decaliter, for short
63 What prophet spoke of a little child leading the wild beasts?
65 All together
67 Fuhrer's WWII partner
69 What little-known judge of Israel had 30 sons?
70 Birth related
71 Sacred image: Var.
72 Opposed stance
73 Fish dish
74 Brain scans, for short
75 Clever sayings

DOWN

1 A small amount
2 Creator of *Truthful James*
3 A blessing
4 Interim German capital
5 Honesty
6 "Is that a yes or ___?"
7 Who is the youngest son of Adam mentioned by name?
8 In a whirl
9 System of silent comm.
10 Which disciple was probably a twin?
11 Who advised young Christians to stop thinking like children?
12 Seed cover
13 Yeast's result
21 Sense of well-being
23 Mustard style
27 Punished in Bejing
29 Biblical city
30 Pull the wool over
31 Perez and Zerah were twin sons of Judah and ___
33 "You get an ___ effort"

34 El ___, Texas
35 German chemist Otto
36 Irish Rose's husband
37 Forbids
38 Space bet. two pts.
40 Headquartered
43 Gideon's campsite
44 N.T. book
46 Donkey's pty.
47 Onassis et al.
49 Who gave a coat to her son when she offered the annual sacrifice?
51 Little green men
53 Capp character
55 Mussolini's son-in-law/foreign minister
56 *Nick of Time* Grammy winner
57 Tennis champ ___ Evert
58 Earth tones
59 Which son was Isaac partial to?
60 Spoils
62 Which Gospel says that the child Jesus grew up strong?
64 In ___ (having trouble)
66 What priest was too indulgent toward his spoiled sons?
68 Mountain train

Food, Food, Food

ACROSS

1 Soak up
5 *Kon-Tiki* wood
10 It's this or on
13 Stretched Lincolns, perhaps
15 Weather forecast
16 Pigeon talk
17 What prized animal was killed for food when the Prodigal Son returned home?
19 "To ___ is human"
20 Concerning this
21 Mouths, anatomically
22 Shakespearean segment
23 Canaan is described as a land flowing with ___
27 Pork source
30 Store tomatoes
31 Bone cutter
32 First gardener
34 Mix salad
37 Sacred cow country
41 Tire layers
43 Affliction
44 Papyrus materials
45 Christian "rock" group
46 Kind of jerk?
48 X-ray units
49 Lung food?
51 Einstein's theoretical letters
53 Salt-pillar husband
54 What strange "food" tasted like honey to Ezekiel?
60 "___ the season to be jolly"
61 Popular card game
62 Ends
66 Drillers' assoc.
67 What Esau traded his birthright for
69 O. T. praise bk.
70 City in Kentucky, Ohio, and South Carolina
71 Grocery ___
72 List ender
73 Way in
74 White water

DOWN

1 Malaise
2 Never-ending sentence?
3 *Rubaiyat* author ___ Khayyam
4 Indian carving
5 Alphabet bite
6 Big name in aluminum
7 Discover
8 Caesar and Waldorf
9 Dog talk
10 Indian for one
11 Part of USAF
12 Number of years Hebrews ate manna
14 Passionless
18 Mozart's *Symphony No. 3 in ___ Major*
24 Is aware
25 It grows on you
26 Admitter
27 Founder of New York's Public Theater
28 Out of work
29 Canter or trot
33 King Saul's elder daughter
35 Jack of *Barney Miller*
36 Passover feast
38 Business agreement
39 King Solomon's biographer
40 Sec. in charge

42 Wind catcher
47 Refiner
50 Type of sandwich
52 G, F and C
54 Troop's encampment
55 Shakespearean verb with thou
56 Abraham's son
57 Sound from a horse
58 Crouch in fear
59 Shoe forms
63 Before long
64 ___-Disney
65 Gush out
67 "Honest" President
68 Nonclergy

1
2
3
4
5
6
7
8
9
10
11
12
13
14
15
16
17
18
19
20
21
22
23
24
25
26
27
28
29
30
31
32
33
34
35
36
37
38
39
40
41
42
43
44
45
46
47
48
49
50
51
52
53
54
55
56
57
58
59
60
61
62
63
64
65
66
67
68
69
70
71
72
73
74

Fasts and Breaking of Fasts (Part 1)

ACROSS

1 Meat/vegetable mixture
5 Food fish
9 Horned hopper
13 Gas company
14 Possessive
15 First sound in an M-G-M film
16 Who told the repentant people of Israel to go home and enjoy sweet drinks?
19 ___ volente
20 Bushy coif
21 Lacking skill
22 MacMurray or Waring
23 Even
25 Divvy up
28 Tap the ball
29 RAM-resident program
32 Old Testament city
33 Isn't on the street?
34 Moon prefix
35 What two apostles prayed and fasted as they chose elders for the churches?
38 Spruce up
39 Lampreys
40 Hip
41 Jean d'Arc, e.g.
42 ___ Canaveral
43 Racer Al or Bobby
44 Auditioner's aim
45 Porgy's beloved
47 Former Wheaton College pres. V. Raymond ___
50 Medicinal plant
51 Not yet disclosed
54 Whose deaths caused the people of Jabesh-Gilead to fast for seven days?
58 Can do
59 Vegetarian's staple
60 Goes with rave
61 Pre-owned
62 Cottage cheese lump
63 Zinfandel is one

DOWN

1 Kind of trap
2 Kilmer's symbol of beauty
3 Off-the-wall sound?
4 Sorrow
5 Archaeologist's puzzle piece
6 Freshwater salmon
7 Simile center
8 Daniel landed in one
9 General direction
10 Seep
11 Modern Maturity grp.
12 Fiddlesticks!
14 Eve was the first
17 First First Lady
18 Eating plan
22 In an appropriate manner
23 Bluefins and yellowfins
24 Short start?
25 Irish clans
26 Braid
27 Magna cum ___
28 Holy Scriptures
29 Humongous horns
30 Animal trap
31 Stair step
33 Proficient
34 Grassy places
36 Not far
37 Stomach sickness
42 Biblical wedding feast site

44 Went white
45 Towhead
46 Ages and ages
47 Biblical birthright barterer
48 Short light strokes
49 Stubborn beast
50 Food container, perhaps
51 Bangkok's language
52 Excommunication
53 Part of A.M.
55 News source
56 Fifth bk. of Moses
57 Communications giant

Spreading a Feast

ACROSS
1 Tobogganed
5 Trick
10 Door part
14 African ravine
15 Hardly a partygoer
16 By mouth
17 What wrote on the wall at Belshazzar's feast?
20 Abuse
21 British baby-sitter
22 Vow
23 Chooses
24 Vitamin C deficiency disease
27 Former Korean president
28 Towel monogram, perhaps
31 A rich cake
32 Restaurant spot
33 Eve's grandson
34 For whom did Lot have a special meal prepared in Sodom?
37 Water grass
38 Active one
39 Two-element semiconductor
40 Puncture sound
41 Receptacle for soup
42 Crystal-lined rocks
43 Take it easy
44 It's taken out at the seams
45 The rest
48 Lingo
52 Job's sons and daughters were so busy eating and drinking that they failed to notice that disaster was about to strike. What killed them?
54 Recess
55 Juliet's love
56 Biblical stew trader
57 Picnic pests
58 Desire greatly
59 Mends

DOWN
1 Traveled in water
2 Mongolian monk
3 Romantic interlude
4 Twisted, as truth
5 Like icy rain
6 It's the Law
7 Textbook division
8 New beginning?
9 At the dedication of Solomon's temple, 120 priests played what instruments?
10 ___ Gospel (fourth)
11 Western Romanian city
12 Lion's pride
13 Contractor, for short
18 Journey
19 Where it's at
23 Atheist Madalyn Murray
24 Night guides
25 Ice cream containers
26 Prods
27 Make merry
28 Headband
29 Motley crew
30 Satisfactory report marks
32 Glower
33 Pales from lacking light
35 Baal worship, e.g.
36 Colorful decorating periodical
41 Cold Adriatic wind
42 American actress Ruth ___
43 Onions' ally

44 One administering corporal punishment in Bejing
45 City of Jesus' first miracle
46 Last East German Communist party leader Krenz
47 Pony's gait
48 Variety of fine cotton
49 Olfactory organ
50 Animal stomach
51 120-pound Australians
53 "___ is me" (Isaiah)

Fasts and Breaking of Fasts (Part 2)

ACROSS

1 Leader, of retailing
5 Make-a-___ Foundation
9 World Court site, with "The"
14 Seven-year phenomenon
15 Gooey
16 Beautify
17 Length of Moses' fast on Mount Sinai
19 Article of food
20 "___ Close for Comfort" (Gorme song)
21 Top-rated
22 Meter maker?
23 Plumbing piece
24 Pt. of Canada
25 Vegetarian devourers
28 Actor Alain
30 French month
31 Three-player card game
32 Sense
35 Anger
36 Dessert
39 Skirt part
40 Television interference
41 "Chances ___"
42 Quaker's food
44 Open grasslands
46 Switch positions
47 Synagogue speaker
51 Abstinence from food
53 Not perm
55 Hosp. trauma areas
56 Pitch
57 More or less
58 Moo ___ gai pan
59 Lagoon locale
61 Where Jesus had a Passover meal with his followers
63 Transplant patient
64 One who prefers charges
65 ___ upon a time
66 Signs of future
67 Christian Science founder
68 Before *macht* for Hitler

DOWN

1 Deeply moved
2 *Lawrence of Arabia* star
3 Torah form
4 One page, in brief
5 Black spider
6 Pessimist's plea
7 Scottish island
8 TV/film director Averback et al.
9 Widespread destruction
10 Farewells
11 Type of leather
12 Ashes holder
13 Football position
18 Acropolis concert composer/pianist
22 Grosse ___, Michigan
25 Former pro footballer, briefly
26 Starchy root
27 Irish staple
29 Pindar's or Horace's type of poetry
30 Fulfills
33 Forks' companion
34 Trolley toot
36 Veal source
37 Length times width
38 Arch crown
40 Patty Hearst's kidnap grp.
43 Weapons provider
45 Like some kisses and bases
48 "Scram," to Shakespeare
49 Pinned ornament

50 Fraternal twin, in chemistry
52 Tropical getaways
53 Drank to excess
54 Nail file
57 Common tater
59 Hubbub
60 Turkey type
61 Purpose
62 Lineup

Fruit of the Vine

ACROSS

1 One bovine
5 ___ latte
10 Nutrition stats
14 Aquarium gunk
15 Squash type
16 Lawyer/writer Gardner
17 What did Paul recommend as a substitute for wine (with "the")?
19 Not very bright
20 In-flight attendant
21 Son of Dishon
23 Matter of fact introduction?
24 Sealy competitor
26 What was mingled with the wine Jesus was offered on the cross?
29 Three-step dance
30 Costa ___
33 *It's ___ . . . World*
34 What part of the body did Paul recommend wine for?
37 WWII personnel carrier
38 Abednego's Hebrew name
39 BBC's Italian counterpart
40 At what occasion did Jesus say he would drink wine again with his disciples when the kingdom had come?
42 Musical time out
43 Ancient capital of Lower Egypt
44 It's often pierced
45 *Soap* family
46 Posts letters
48 Street person
49 Precedes phyll
52 Go one better
56 Port-au-Prince ___i
57 Where was the one place the priest could not enter after drinking wine?
60 "I think I goofed"
61 ___-ski (post-skiing relaxation)
62 Soc. studies, once
63 Umpteen
64 Isaiah condemned drinkers who ___ early in the morning
65 Start of a cockney toast

DOWN

1 Oohs and ___
2 Blood block
3 Gawk
4 Prodigal
5 *It's a Wonderful Life* director Frank
6 Drug LSD
7 Pro
8 Workweek end, for short
9 Stage direction
10 Biblical giants
11 Lackluster
12 "It was ___ joke!"
13 Visualized
18 Miss America attire
22 Family name of Detroit brewery
24 Popular porters
25 Less strenuous
26 Shopper's paradise
27 Amer. hostels?
28 Former Soviet First Lady
29 Wedding site
31 Insertion mark
32 Make ___ for
34 Shih ___
35 Noah's ark sealant
36 Box office successes
38 Eden's location in Tel-___

41 To what pastor did Paul write that a church official must not be a wine drinker?
42 Violent disorder
45 Revolve
47 Tiny bits
48 What, according to Jesus, happens to old wineskins when new wine is put into them?
49 Pal
50 Laughter
51 King of the beasts
52 Wise one
53 Maple family
54 Gin flavor
55 Parts, in brief
58 Suitable
59 Swimsuit piece

Fasts and Breaking of Fasts (Part 3)

ACROSS

1 What king fasted all day and night while unsuccessfully inquiring of the Lord?
5 What meat was eaten at the Passover meal?
9 What prophet's preaching drove the people of Nineveh to fast?
14 Mexican money
15 Lead-in for gram or graph
16 Japanese eel
17 "Dear mother Ida, harken ___ die" (Tennyson refrain)
18 KP connectors
19 Pairs
20 What Roman official was fasting and praying when an angel told him to send for Peter?
22 Doves and hawks
23 Maya ___ (Vietnam Wall designer)
24 Vert.'s opp.
25 Comparative for a bird
29 Very, to Babette
31 Light between nights
34 Juan of Argentina
35 Weeder
36 Big name in Hawaii
37 What two apostles prayed and fasted as they chose elders for the churches?
40 Play to ___ (deadlock)
41 Floored
42 Ammonia-derived compound
43 Who prepared a meal for two angels in Sodom?
44 Expired
45 Grants Pass neighbor
46 Disobey God
47 Olympian, for short
48 Biblical patriarch
51 Whose father was angered when he unwittingly broke a fast while pursuing the Philistines?
57 Had ingested
58 Brain waves, in brief
59 Zoology suffix
60 What each star represents
61 Stimulate, as one's appetite
62 D-Day landers
63 Cry of delight
64 Just one
65 What did Jesus eat after his resurrection to prove he was not a mere phantom?

DOWN

1 Work-ord. detail
2 Space predecessor
3 Junky
4 Pork purchase
5 Actress Langtry
6 Mgmt.
7 Food selections
8 Shouts down
9 747s, e.g.
10 Walking ___ (elated)
11 Not artificial: Abbr.
12 Advanced in years
13 Spy Alger ___
21 Italy's last queen
24 Sir, in German
25 Shock
26 Former defense collective
27 What was the first sinful meal?
28 Actor's part
29 "And so ___ . . .": Pepys

30 "___ my lips": Bush
31 Zelda's heartthrob, in 60's TV
32 Bean and Bates
33 Some votes
35 Handyman's store, in brief
36 Condemn
38 Where Jesus resurrected a boy
39 Evening
44 Cartoonist Walt
45 ___ *of Honey*
46 Look after
47 Who brought food to the discouraged prophet Elijah?
48 Midrange
49 Vow
50 Grab with a fork
51 God's chosen people
52 ___ Rios, Jamaica
53 50 percent
54 Assoc. of Christian Schools Intl.
55 Takes home
56 Waist product

1
2
3
4
5
6
7
8
9
10
11
12
13
14
15
16
17
18
19
20
21
22
23
24
25
26
27
28
29
30
31
32
33
34
35
36
37
38
39
40
41
42
43
44
45
46
47
48
49
50
51
52
53
54
55
56
57
58
59
60
61
62
63
64
65

Seven Suicides

ACROSS

1 Armed conflict
4 Physicians' mag.
8 What king of Israel, who reigned only seven days, killed himself by burning down the palace with himself inside?
13 Common Market money of acct.
14 Persian Gulf entrance
15 Domestic helper, perhaps
16 Early Christian missionary
18 Pass
19 What judge of Israel had his armor bearer kill him so he would avoid the disgrace of being killed by a woman?
21 Who refused to obey the king's request to kill him, then followed the king in committing suicide? (answer continued in 36-Across)
24 Royal title: Abbr.
25 Truth in Lending org.
28 Tolstoy's Karenina
29 Kind of lie
32 What king killed himself by falling on his own sword?
33 Creator
34 Linguist Chomsky
35 Going, to Samuel Clemens
36 21-Across, continued
40 ___ *Is Born*
42 Building extensions to sides
43 Third bk. of Moses
46 Jericho's rebuilder
47 Which of Jesus' apostles committed suicide by hanging himself?
49 Blood: Prefix
50 "___ make a lovely corpse": Dickens
51 Fifth scale tone
52 Present action verb for thou
53 What friend of Absalom was so disgraced when Absalom did not follow his advice that he went and hanged himself?
57 What strong man killed himself along with a houseful of Philistines?
60 Trifling
64 Herring varieties
65 Genuine, in German
66 Bro or sis
67 Minds
68 ___ Hashanah
69 Col.'s superior

DOWN

1 Worldwide network
2 Camping gp.
3 Capek's android
4 Belonging to David's commander-in- chief
5 Both prefix
6 "Yes, ___"
7 Handle: Fr.
8 Nil
9 Babylonian district
10 Advanced deg.
11 KGB successor
12 After Benedict or glass
15 Middle English flank
17 *The Lion King* lion
20 Lord High Treasurer: abbr.
21 Start to collapse
22 Year, south of the border
23 Origination time unknown
25 Vermont vacation spot
26 Large container
27 Ohio city airline code
29 Romance

30 Start of a laugh
31 Lodge
32 Neighbor of Nor.
34 Diagnostic imaging initials
35 Jupiter feature, for short
37 "Too-Ra-Loo-Ra-Loo-___"
38 Guido's highest note
39 Capp and Capone
40 Lengthened expression
41 You, in Berlin
44 911 responder: abbr.
45 A large vessel
47 Unites
48 Nth, e.g.
49 Sacred
51 Some immunizations
52 End of life
53 ___ state of affairs
54 Phone button
55 ___ Bolivar (Venezuelan mountain)
56 Sec. sch.
57 Quiet!
58 Tailless primate
59 Church teacher's deg.
61 Bldg. materials maker
62 Germanic negative
63 Surveyor's dir.

1 2 3 4 5 6 7 8 9 10 11 12
13 14 15
16 17 18
19 20
21 22 23 24 25 26 27
28 29 30 31 32
33 34 35
36 37 38 39
40 41 42 43 44 45
46 47 48 49
50 51 52
53 54 55 56
57 58 59 60 61 62 63
64 65 66
67 68 69

People Getting Stoned

ACROSS

1 What Gospel mentions Jesus miraculously passing through a crowd that intended to stone him?
5 Dixit lead-in
9 Specific antibody against blood cells, etc.
14 Eyesight: Suffix
15 Kind of bag
16 State flower of New Mexico
17 Boys
18 Parisian ones
19 Single-masted vessel
20 Whose stones fell on the Amorites while Joshua led an attack on them?
22 View from Catania
23 Church summer sess.
24 River to the Rhine
25 Who pelted David and his men with stones while he accused David of being a violent man?
29 West Coast univ.
30 Opposite of ENE
33 Sharpener
34 Old Hebrew measure
35 Quadrillionfold prefix
36 Who fled from Iconium when they heard of a plot to stone them?
39 RC prelates
40 Stravinsky ballet
41 California city
42 Nautical chain
43 Opinion
44 Dark purplish red
45 Smooch
46 'eavenly 'eadwear
47 What owner of a vineyard was stoned after being falsely accused in front of Ahab?
50 Who was stoned by an irate mob while trying to carry out the orders of King Rehoboam?
55 Island near South America
56 *Crimes and Misdemeanors* actor
57 Peruvian city
58 1988 Olympics site
59 Antiaircraft fire
60 Take down ___
61 Major Leaguer Tom
62 Johnson and Johnson
63 Childish comeback

DOWN

1 Bump into
2 Colorful food fish
3 ___ and seek
4 Onetime athletic org.
5 Pianist/composer Jose ___
6 Cosmetics maker
7 Fr. holy women
8 Recipients' suffix
9 In what city did some Jews persuade the people to stone Paul?
10 Gateway to Amelia Island
11 Edinburgh resident
12 Small graphic image
13 California wine region
21 ___ barrel (in trouble)
22 Of the cheekbones
24 Who was stoned for holding back some of the loot from Jericho?
25 Cargo, for short
26 Submarine is one
27 Harden
28 Where Alice worked

29 Violin stroke
30 Grill maker
31 Plant supporter
32 Attended
34 Does some lawn work
35 Lead-in for graph
37 TV's Charlie Chan
38 Parachute material
43 San ___, Italy
44 Outer wraps
45 Alaskan river and park
46 Ancient Persian city
47 Author Ogden ___
48 One old Crown representative
49 "___ *giorno!*"
50 The works, in Wittenberg
51 One of David's famous warriors
52 Tears
53 Des Moines's neighbor
54 El ___ De Oz
56 Andrews, for one

All of These Diseases

ACROSS

1 What did Moses toss in the air to produce boils on the Egyptians?
6 Big brass
10 *Moby Dick* mariner
14 Words of agreement
15 Jewish cattle rustler
16 Hamstring sites
17 Woody
18 One of Columbus's trio
19 Old Phoenician capital
20 According to Revelation, what afflicts those who have the mark of the beast?
23 Sandpile
24 ___-mitzvah
25 No. cruncher
28 What righteous man suffered from boils?
31 Prefix with suction
33 What afflicted the Philistines when they captured the ark of the covenant?
35 "Whoso diggeth ___": Proverbs 26:27
37 Oreg. school assoc.
39 *The ___ Wars*
40 Vietnamese statesman Tho
42 Payment abbreviation
43 Sculptor's subject
44 Bridge bid, informally
45 Early-fall mos.
47 Political cartoonist Thomas ___
48 What apostle's mother-in-law had a fever?
50 Mobutu's middle name
52 Abnormal prefix: Lat.
53 Football-field divs.
54 Ill-wisher
56 Indian prince
58 In the parable of Lazarus and the rich man, what was Lazarus's affliction?
63 Jacob's twin
66 Hindu soul
67 Related maternally
68 Disney's *The ___ King*
69 Balsam
70 Turner and Louise
71 Minor encounter
72 Southern Judean city
73 Hebrew letter

DOWN

1 Quick
2 ___ *Scriptura!* (Reformation slogan)
3 Boundary city for Asher
4 Rectify a text
5 Wicked
6 Who is the greatest group Jesus healed at any one time of the same disease?
7 Submachine guns
8 Giant Ishbi-___
9 Noah's ark's mount
10 Rocky Mtn. highs?
11 "Watch it!"
12 Cabinet Dept.
13 Mad cow disease letters
21 Fresh-water mussel
22 Blow one's top
25 *Nostromo* author
26 Excessively fastidious
27 Scarves worn to the races
28 Old car
29 Spread
30 European bathroom fixtures
32 Nebraska natives
34 Particle of cosmic radiation

36 Pitch a piano
38 Where did Jesus encounter a woman who had had an unnatural flow of blood for many years?
41 Ionian isle
46 Heroin
49 Moonlight opus
51 Initiations
55 Insect prefix
57 Mount Helicon's district
58 Smallest of litter
59 Father of prophet Micaiah
60 Author Ayn
61 Greenland base
62 Former Zaire president Mobutu
63 Raised R.R.s
64 Taste liquid
65 Aeronautical angle: Abbr.

1 2 3 4 5 6 7 8 9 10 11 12 13
14 15 16
17 18 19
20 21 22
23 24 25 26 27
28 29 30 31 32 33 34
35 36 37 38 39
40 41 42 43
44 45 46 47
48 49 50 51 52
53 54 55 56 57
58 59 60 61 62
63 64 65 66 67
68 69 70
71 72 73

A Time to Weep

ACROSS

1 Lee that "nobody doesn't like"
5 Coinage catchwords
10 Place: Prefix
14 Once more
15 Pansy
16 Architect Ludwig Mies van der ___
17 What caused Nehemiah to weep? (answer continued in 57-Across)
20 Mississippi source
21 What's in ___?
22 Deodorant brand
23 Banners of socialism
28 Two of three men who wept when they saw Job's misery
32 Prison unit
34 City in northwest Kansas
35 Estonian river
36 FDR's pooch
37 "___ love!"
38 Vestment for the clergy
39 *Aunt ___ Cope Book*
44 Inca fortunes
45 57-Across, concluded
48 Counselor-at-law
49 Old horse
52 ___ Janeiro
55 Japanese naval base north of Nagasaki
57 17-Across, continued
62 Jack of '50s and '60s TV
63 Sour
64 Hebrew month
65 Monkshood variety
66 Musical staff sign
67 Some pens

DOWN

1 Master, in Calcutta
2 Pyrenees peak
3 Actress Ada
4 Takes one's breath away
5 Syria's neighbor
6 Pheasant brood
7 Astron. clock setting
8 Kosh's Wisconsin partner
9 Color changer
10 Clear, in brief
11 Alley Oop's girl
12 New Testament bk.
13 Lab wire
18 Biting
19 Prairie schooner
24 JFK predecessor
25 Craze
26 Mormons: Abbr.
27 Nitrogen: Prefix
28 Suntan spoiler
29 Blood: Comb. form
30 Novelist Kingsley
31 Dashed
32 Mickey's maker
33 Toulouse-Lautrec's hometown
36 Fourth scale degrees
37 Uncle Sam's collector
39 Church official
40 Mississippi, e.g.
41 L's three followers
42 Circular
43 Possessive Latin pronoun
44 Wee hour
46 Dock workers
47 The same
49 "___ say more?"
50 After bric

51 Leavers
52 Res. Officers' Pension Act
53 "___ first you don't succeed . . ."
54 Town near Santa Barbara
56 Wash the deck
58 Cal rival
59 Harvard Graphics producer
60 CompuServe's owner
61 Whopper

Rending the Garments

ACROSS

1 Who tore his clothes when he heard Joseph had been killed?
6 Delft product
10 Brand of power tools
14 Dazzling display
15 Harem rooms
16 Seed marks
17 What momentous finding caused King Josiah to tear his clothes?
20 Short emblem?
21 Bldg. materials maker
22 Actor Joslyn
23 Airwaves regulator
25 ___coke Island, North Carolina
27 Who tore their clothes when a "stolen" cup was found in Benjamin's sack?
35 ___ *Dei* (Lamb of God)
36 Biblical tares
37 Coll. course
38 Guide
39 Brazilian women of rank
40 Langston Hughes title
41 Amer. Missionary Fellowship
42 Greek sculptor (c. 450 B.C.)
43 Stop, at sea
44 Who tore their clothes when the people of Lystra began to worship them as gods?
47 Hydrocarbon suffixes
48 Fleet initials
49 *Melrose* ___
52 Sneaky laugh sound
54 ___ for apple
57 Who tore their clothes on seeing Job's pitiful condition?
62 Friend en francais
63 Escape action: Abbr.
64 Bovid's bag
65 Fourfront?
66 Bullfighter's cloak
67 Father-and-daughter Hollywood duo

DOWN

1 Super Bowl III champs
2 Feeling dull pain
3 Skelton's Kadiddlehopper
4 Best textbooks lists, in brief
5 '70s rock group, for short
6 Yan's pans
7 "It shouldn't happen to ___!"
8 Brit. flyers
9 Fla. or Del. winter time
10 Son of Judah
11 Hunter's take
12 "Now ___ me down . . ."
13 Mower's place
18 "That hurt!"
19 Stags
23 *Family* ___
24 Printer speed rating, in short
25 Illinois town
26 USPO terms
27 Vine-root resin
28 Highest town in Wisconsin
29 Mix-up
30 Personal weapons
31 Giant Ishbi-___
32 Cornerstone abbr.
33 Astronaut Edgar D. ___
34 Aberdonians
39 Unit of force
40 ___ the Terrible
42 Hebrew weight measure
43 Brief reply?

45 Hannibal ___ (*The Silence of the Lambs* character)
46 German river
49 Terrific, on the street
50 Lemon's relative
51 "___ was in the beginning . . ."
52 Clunker of a car
53 Lg. Protestant denomination
54 Man: Pref.
55 Short same?
56 Lith. and Azer., once
58 VCR button
59 Gabor of *Green Acres*
60 Birth control meth.
61 Dutch town

Grave Matters

ACROSS

1 Pkgs
5 Drop suddenly
9 Big dos
14 A Bull's target
15 Mississippi town
16 Scapula
17 Film director Kazan
18 Dear, in Dusseldorf
19 Rechargeable battery
20 In John's Gospel, who was the first person to see Jesus' empty tomb?
23 When some lunch hours end
24 Actor Carney
25 Undefiled
29 Common levels
31 Dawber or Shriver
34 Former President Mubarak
35 Lansbury role
36 Napoleon's exile site
37 Who buried Abraham?
40 Ribbed fabric: Var.
41 Who buried Moses? (with "the")
42 Like Pisa's tower
43 Expression of disgust
44 To drink excessively
45 Rightly
46 Not a beginner
47 "Alley ___"
48 What was placed over Achan's body after the Israelites stoned him?
55 Valuable violin
57 Turkish chamber
58 Manny, of the Dodgers
59 *Bolero* composer
60 Home of the Incas, today
61 Mil. units
62 Fort ___, Florida
63 Whale of a movie?
64 Dinesen who wrote *Out of Africa*

DOWN

1 Premed subj.
2 What judge of Israel was buried at Shamir?
3 Film ___ (bleak movie)
4 Neuter
5 According to Matthew, who ordered the guard at Jesus' tomb?
6 One of Nintendo's Mario Brothers
7 Approved
8 Sunscreen ingredient, often
9 Whose burial at Hebron caused the grief of David?
10 Fire-starting rock
11 Jewish or Gentile
12 Japanese medieval leader Nobunaga
13 But, to Nero
21 Suffix in camera names
22 Roman household gods
25 Feeder sound
26 What prophet, speaking the words of the Lord, said, "I will ransom them from the power of the grave"?
27 Author of many psalms
28 Take a photo
29 Chaplain
30 In among
31 Braid
32 Clear as ___
33 Beerlike
35 Bet. L and Q
36 Ambulance VIPs
38 Knock for ___
39 Main, in Frankfurt
44 Is behind

45 What leader was buried "in the border of his inheritance in Timnath-serah"?
46 In Luke's Gospel, who was the only apostle to actually investigate the empty tomb?
47 Joan ___
48 Own
49 Sleep: Prefix
50 Treaty of Versailles river
51 Who was the first king to be buried in Samaria?
52 Holiday drinks
53 Kett, of comics
54 Canadian prov.
55 Sleeve
56 Mother's Day month

1 2 3 4 5 6 7 8 9 10 11 12 13
14 15 16
17 18 19
20 21 22
23 24
25 26 27 28 29 30 31 32 33
34 35 36
37 38 39
40 41 42
43 44 45
46 47
48 49 50 51 52 53 54
55 56 57 58
59 60 61
62 63 64

Killed by the Beasts

ACROSS

1 What prophet saw two female bears devour the children who had made fun of his baldness?
7 William Shatner's ___ *War*
10 What animal devoured the foreigners who had moved into Israel?
14 Lumberjack
15 Elected, in Paris
16 Andean land: Abbr.
17 Eye covering
18 Sun. talk
19 "Oh, nuts!"
20 For what strange offense was a prophet killed by a lion? (answer continued in 51-Across)
23 It runs through trees
24 Cheesy
25 Costello's partner
29 Skater's jump
32 Brigham Young University site
33 Promise, e.g.
34 Radio type
38 Fit to be tried
39 Mixes
40 Actress Lenska
41 Town near Iloilo
42 Bird scare call
43 Private instructor
44 Seaport of Yemen
45 Which book mentions people being devoured by lions?
46 Antiseptic acid
50 Coal porter
51 20-Across, continued
58 Walter ___ Mare
59 Ref. electrode
60 Rock's ___ Brothers
62 Wormwood's companion
63 Lincoln or Ford
64 Takes in, for example
65 Mideast airline
66 One-room apt.
67 Signed over

DOWN

1 Sixth letters
2 Poland's Walesa
3 River in western France
4 Slave to detail
5 Start of a toast
6 Palestinian leader
7 Della Reese's angelic role
8 General Robert ___
9 Northern Iraqi
10 The king: Fr.
11 TWA's Carl
12 ___ left field
13 Ugly
21 Skyward
22 Mil. departure
25 Lhasa ___ (dog breed)
26 Dennis the Menace, at times
27 Singer-turned-politician Sonny
28 Where Hansel was headed
29 What animal killed a man for disobeying the old prophet of Bethel?
30 Dry: Prefix
31 Greek goddess of dawn
33 Will-___-wisp
34 ___ for one's money
35 Ricardo the Maestro
36 Large ice cube?
37 Crumbly soil

39 Religious deg.
43 Polliwog
44 Drat!, in Dresden
45 Trinket
46 Sheriff's star, e.g.
47 1995 NBA scoring leader
48 Missouri city
49 Let ___ hang out
50 Short 60 minutes?
52 Coal addition
53 Ottawa's flying org.
54 Tear line
55 Table d'___
56 Jonathan's son
57 Michelin is one
61 Bk. of the Apocrypha

Not to Be Taken Seriously (Part 1)

ACROSS

1 What a padlock may fasten
5 Church head
9 Wound marks
14 Phone code
15 Chilled
16 Fortuneteller's tool
17 Mammal's clothes?
18 Oral history
19 Fill with joy
20 How do we know Sarah's husband was smart?
23 Prom partner
24 Inflation rating
25 Look up to
28 Au ___ (served in its own gravy)
30 Son of Noah
34 Understanding
35 Mediocre
36 Ab ___ (from the beginning)
37 How do we know Hosea, Joel, Amos, Jonah, Nahum and Habakkuk were blind?
41 High school subj.
42 Touch down
43 Pound part
44 Spots
46 Nav. rank
47 Taxpayers' fears
48 Absorbed, as an expense
50 Artaxerxes' palace site
51 How is baseball mentioned in the Bible?
59 Conductor John Philip
60 Matted insulation
61 Not in use
62 Trapper John Jacob
63 Notability
64 Ancient Briton's collar
65 Underlings
66 Distance between supports
67 H.S. annual

DOWN

1 Double up with laughter?
2 Kuwaiti, for one
3 Old Testament mountain
4 What did God take away so Adam and Eve couldn't gamble?
5 What aviator is mentioned in the Bible?
6 "___, let us adore Him" (hymn)
7 Incidental benefit
8 First lady's home
9 Boils inside
10 French seaport
11 Large Russian sea
12 ___-Rooter
13 Manuscript mark
21 Entertainer Marx
22 Smelling salts
25 Infamous 1972 hurricane
26 Queen's mate
27 Dog's disease
28 Belonging to the "beloved apostle"
29 Pre-owned
31 Egyptian President Mubarak
32 Dislodge
33 Who broke all Ten Commandments at once?
35 Ball player Musial
38 Perry's command
39 What 45-Down brought down as the greatest speaker (with "the")
40 Boldness

45 He died from a minor affliction—fallen arches
47 "Pride and Prejudice" author
49 Ivan and Nicholas
50 Alabama city
51 Quickly, in memos
52 Medicine amount
53 Cougar or Jaguar
54 Show-___ (exhibitionists)
55 "Able to ___ tall buildings . . ."
56 Skunk's distinctive
57 Employees' advocate's acronym
58 What Noah sat on so they couldn't play cards on the ark (with "the")

Across the Biblical Spectrum

ACROSS

1 ". . . beauty is ___ forever"
5 According to Revelation, what color will the sun be when it became like sackcloth?
10 Before stick or happy
14 Mrs. Dithers
15 Reached in amount
16 Hindu pilgrimage center
17 Who sang a victory song that mentions white donkeys?
20 Ohio's main seaport: Abbr.
21 Affected manner
22 Feudal lord
23 Large coffeepots
24 Roman satyr
26 Purloin
29 Moon plain
30 Retailer's initials
33 "___ all, folks," (cartoon sign-off)
34 Silents star Negri
35 Composer Bartok
36 According to Proverbs, who thrives like a green leaf?
39 Part of Winnebago nation
40 Fork part
41 Astro follower
42 Footlike part
43 Breathe hard
44 An easy job
45 Carnival tune
46 Capital of Aisne, France
48 Narnia lion
51 Nickname for the Cowboys' hometown
52 Palooka of old comics
55 According to Joel, what fateful day would be a day of blackness?
59 Accused assassin James ___ Ray
60 Shadow
61 "You gotta be kidding!"
62 Rival for AMEX or NASDAQ
63 Argon and neon
64 Indian harvest festival

DOWN

1 Current choice
2 Who had a vision of ravenous locusts that devoured foliage and made the trees' branches white?
3 "Kill ___ killed"
4 Indigenous Tanzanians
5 Genius
6 Bert's folks
7 Collector's items
8 Box, in brief
9 Flattened opponent
10 Whence Columbus sailed
11 Tackle box item
12 Limp as ___
13 Wide toll road
18 Least common
19 What color was the cloth draped over the ark of the covenant?
23 ___ *Down Staircase*
24 What kind of teachers have a place of deep blackness reserved for them?
25 Give ___ (care)
26 Razor sharpener
27 In Revelation, what color do the armies of heaven wear?
28 Othello's villian's
29 Where was Jesus when his clothes became radiantly white?
30 Who warned his followers that they could not change the color of their hair by worrying?

31 Gingham, for one
32 Violet variety
34 Gist
35 Wernher von ___
37 Catchall abbr.
38 Use a cipher
43 ___ colada
45 Soup server
46 Petrol unit
47 Titled Turks
48 ___ o'clock scholar
49 Rural carriage
50 Irish and Brythonic gods of the sea
51 G.B. military radio
52 Who had a vision of horsemen with breastplates that were yellow like sulfur?
53 Trieste wine measure
54 Whose name means "red"?
56 Former Balkan st.
57 Nebraska city code
58 British bathroom

1 2 3 4 5 6 7 8 9 10 11 12 13
14 15 16
17 18 19
20 21 22
23 24 25
26 27 28 29 30 31 32
33 34 35
36 37 38
39 40 41
42 43 44
45 46 47
48 49 50 51 52 53 54
55 56 57 58
59 60 61
62 63 64

Going to Extremes (Part 1)

ACROSS
1 Loud laugh
5 Of a Hindu philosophy
10 Matched duo
14 Epithet of Athena
15 Sunshine State city
16 God's ___ (churchyard)
17 Grateful follower
18 Out-and-out
19 "With ___ ring . . ."
20 John the Baptist's workplace
22 Picture books widely used in the Middle Ages in place of the Bible by the illiterate were probably the ___ books to be printed
24 Heart ck.
25 Electrical letters
26 "Jesus wept" is the ___ verse in the Bible
31 No book in the Bible is ___ than Psalms
35 PC grouping
36 National anthem start
37 Fur piece
38 Grandparental
40 Branchlets
43 Drainage pit
44 Troikas
46 Christmas word
48 Sticky substance
49 Began a tennis game
51 *The ___ Story Ever Told* (1965 film)
53 Zeno's birthplace
55 Aspen activity
56 The ___ animal mentioned in the Bible is the gnat
60 Where to get fast service?
64 "Along ___ a spider"
65 Ind. Hall site
67 Cut into cubes
68 Altar vows
69 Recluse
70 High spirit
71 Glasgow land tax
72 Manasseh had the longest reign over Judah, for 55 ___
73 Flat rate?

DOWN
1 Mecca trek
2 Toast topper
3 Erode
4 Jacob's dream theme
5 The ___ king mentioned in the Bible is Joash, who began his reign at the age of seven
6 Columbus Day mo.
7 Airport exit
8 Of the small intestine
9 Study place
10 Job was the most successful physician in the Bible because he had the most ___
11 Deep yearning
12 Part of the eye
13 Take five
21 Deed, in Madrid
23 Durocher et al.
26 Venetian blind parts
27 Montana city
28 Studio sign
29 Tool with teeth
30 Binding
32 Nick
33 St. ___ fire
34 Indoor transplant

39 Sad marital state
41 Surprise expression, in Sussix
42 Take one on the chin
45 Brokerage order
47 Tahoe is one
50 Profoundly
52 Fire starter
54 ". . . old woman who lived in ___"
56 Univ. subjects
57 ___ in USA (label)
58 Andy's pal
59 One of the Sinatras
61 The longest river in the world
62 *Yes ___!*: S. Davis
63 Faxed
66 Irish sea god

Hugs and Kisses

ACROSS

1 Monopoly corner
5 Who had a tearful farewell, with many kisses, at the city of Miletus?
9 What aged father kissed one son, mistaking him for the other?
14 "Never ___ sentence with . . ."
15 "___ girl!"
16 "That doesn't ___ bell"
17 Carpenter's fastener
18 Secretion of sadness
19 Greek theater
20 Where was Jesus when the sinful woman kissed his feet and anointed him? (answer continued in 55-Across)
23 Riot-stopping gps.
24 *The Catcher in the ___*
25 Not artificial: Abbr.
26 Fuss over
28 Explorer Johnson
29 Aero. low visibility aid
30 Guard or tackle
33 NBA's Manute
34 First Bible bk.
35 Big Apple force
36 Mustard style
39 High-tech recording med.
40 What prophet talked about kissing calves?
41 Malay outrigger
42 Garment
43 Greek past tense: Abbr.
44 Rope support
46 Defense syst.
47 Top brass, in brief
50 Enzymes suffix
51 African fox
52 Visual aid, for short
53 Gangster's gun
55 20-Across, continued
58 Different
60 Colorado ski resort
61 Do-well intro
62 Whom did Joab murder while kissing?
63 "Tickle Me" doll
64 Church altar area
65 Salad bar implement
66 Joint
67 One of TV's Huxtables

DOWN

1 Who met Moses in the wilderness and kissed him?
2 Irritates
3 Name for Edom
4 Better than never?
5 Unexpected difficulty
6 Nuclear tryouts
7 British Airways's former partner's former name
8 Rouse, old style
9 Some decals
10 Entertainer Caesar
11 According to Proverbs, whose kisses are deceitful?
12 Wowed
13 Gives the boot
21 Tear-jerker in the kitchen
22 Viking deity
27 Pavarotti, e.g.
30 Rent
31 Orangutan
32 Dentists' org.
33 Tugs and ferries
34 Enforce secrecy
36 Agr. or Comm.

37 Anger
38 Who kissed David when he was fleeing from Saul?
39 Pug or boxer
40 Semilegendary Greek poet
42 *Entertainment Tonight* host
43 What rebel was so magnetic in personality that the men of Israel couldn't help kissing him?
45 Part of ancient red-rock city
46 Old Testament idol
47 When Jacob died, who wept over him and kissed him?
48 Smile trigger?
49 Audiophile's setup
51 ". . . and behold ___ horse . . ." (Rev. 6:8)
53 Annapolis mascot
54 Sphere starter
56 Times to call, in classifieds
57 ___ the finish
59 Empire State Games initials

1 2 3 4 5 6 7 8 9 10 11 12 13
14 15 16
17 18 19
20 21 22 23
24 25 26 27
28 29 30 31 32
33 34 35
36 37 38 39 40
41 42 43
44 45 46 47 48 49
50 51 52
53 54 55 56 57
58 59 60 61
62 63 64
65 66 67

Foot Coverings

ACROSS

1 Burt Reynolds movie ___ *End*
4 Which prophet accused the people of Israel of selling the poor people for a pair of sandals?
8 *Starsky and* ___
13 Hammer
14 Soil
15 Who told a king that he would not accept a gift of shoelaces?
16 Caesar, to Brutus
17 Hindu fire god
18 Moslem religion
19 Who ordered a pair of sandals for his son's feet? (cont. in 59-Across)
22 Eur. fast train
23 Freshly painted
24 Zebulon Pike's outpost site
29 University of Maine site
31 "___ Cassius has a lean and hungry look": Shakespeare
34 Mouthward
35 Hungarian liquid measure
37 New Guinea port
38 Roy Rogers's real surname
39 What were the best-made foot coverings in the Bible, since they lasted for forty years?
44 "___ fond farewell to . . ."
45 Education Auditing Institute: Abbr.
46 Fifth day of wk.
47 Florida reptile ending
48 Repugnance expression
50 Cry of frustration
54 Heavy silk fabric
56 Own, to Burns
58 Workers' org.
59 Repentant biblical bad boy
63 Twinge
67 Slovakian clergyman, 1887–1947
68 Sound system brand
69 Crystal-lined rock
70 It's unique
71 What book mentions the custom of giving a person one's shoe as a sign of transferring property?
72 Who was told by God to take his shoes off because he was standing on holy ground?
73 Gibraltar and Hormuz: Abbr.
74 Soc. of Physics Students

DOWN

1 Animal's restraint
2 Straight
3 Plenty: Var.
4 Booking
5 Powerful
6 French department or river
7 Mix around
8 Israeli seaport
9 United Bible Soc.
10 Oreg. was one
11 Early air-traffic gp.
12 Thoughtful expression
13 Mideast dollar?
20 Responded to the alarm
21 From furthest back
25 Who was told by the commander of the heavenly army to take off his shoes?
26 Woody Guthrie's son
27 Comedienne Martha
28 Lime coolers
30 One of David's heroes
32 Fatty acid

33 Slangy denial
36 Compliant one
39 TV listings
40 ___ roadblock
41 What nation did God toss his shoes upon?
42 Writer Santha Rama ___
43 Onetime *60 Minutes* journalist Alexander
49 Roll type
51 Take part in a rebellion
52 Crows
53 Inkling
55 Toll rds., usually
57 Stravinsky and Sikorsky
60 Sioux
61 Effort
62 Missives, in brief
63 "Unshackled" prod.
64 Vintage auto
65 Greek island
66 Bee string

Stones, Rolling and Nonrolling

ACROSS

1 Show surprise
5 Ground pine or bugle plant
10 Who had a vision of an angel casting an enormous stone into the sea?
14 Part of fiftieth state
15 Eminent Washington family
16 Altar word, sometimes
17 Mutt and Jeff et al.
18 Orient's
19 Curve or wave
20 Who did Jesus tell that the stones would cry out if the people were silenced?
23 Peleg's son
24 Brief repose
25 With pod, largest lizard
29 Hunky-dory
32 Rub the wrong way?
36 St. Francis slept here
38 Halloween shout
40 Social reformer Dorothea
41 What city is decorated with twelve precious stones?
45 Condensed, for short
46 Andean tuber
47 Shoot machine guns
48 Sour gum tree
51 Antonio's role in *Evita*
53 Seniors disparager
54 Short order?
56 502, in Rome
58 Who was Peter addressing when he spoke of Jesus as the cornerstone?
64 Not in Salman Rushdie's travel plans
65 Native of Natal
66 Greenwich mean time
69 Branch
70 Summed up
71 King of Norway
72 Gazelle
73 Challenges
74 Hightest reader's deg.?

DOWN

1 Who wrote on tablets of stone for Moses?
2 Org. for non-pros
3 Worn out
4 Shove
5 Open-mouthed
6 Who set up a commemorative stone after the Israelites covenanted to serve the Lord?
7 Murre genus
8 Backpack contents
9 Royal murder, for short
10 Who rolled the stone across the tomb when Jesus was buried?
11 Cousin of a Tony
12 Leghorns
13 Am. humorist Edgar ___
21 Irregular
22 Fluid-filled "bag"
25 Who suggested that stones could be turned to bread?
26 Hollywood's Hal
27 Consumers
28 ___-Tin-Tin
30 Voodoo relative
31 Hebrew homer
33 Mr. Stevenson
34 Feudal estates
35 Formerly in NYC opera?
37 ___ Jima

39 Suffix with libel
42 Merchants' org.
43 Flight component
44 Its cap. is Buenos Aires
49 Opener, of sorts
50 Early hrs.
52 Channel swimmer Gertrude
55 What shepherd boy went into battle with a bag of stones?
57 Rustic life poems
58 Handed down practice: Abbr.
59 Luxembourg town where George Patton is buried
60 "99 Luftballoons" singer
61 Consider, as in a high court
62 Shirt name
63 Invalid
64 Pension plan
67 Chou En-___
68 Educ. union

1 2 3 4 5 6 7 8 9 10 11 12 13
14 15 16
17 18 19
20 21 22
23 24
25 26 27 28 29 30 31 32 33 34 35
36 37 38 39 40
41 42 43 44
45 46 47
48 49 50 51 52 53
54 55 56 57
58 59 60 61 62 63
64 65 66 67 68
69 70 71
72 73 74

Going to Extremes (Part 2)

ACROSS

1 What king of Israel had the shortest reign?
6 Early word processor
10 What is the longest book in the New Testament?
14 "Let me repeat . . ."
15 Med or rad add-on
16 What makes blue eye blue
17 What is the shortest prayer in the Bible?
19 Gain
20 Clothed
21 Walker, in sign language
22 Film image: Infor.
24 Cardinal's covering
25 Mos. add up to them
26 Who was the youngest king mentioned in the Bible?
30 New Zealand parrot
31 Sympathetic sounds
32 WWII personnel carrier
33 Female prophet
36 French author ___ Prevost
38 One of five Norwegian kings
39 What is the longest chapter in the Bible?
42 River to the Seine
43 "___ ever so humble . . ."
44 Yorkshire city
45 Light line
46 Northumberland river
47 Table or chair part
48 What is the smallest animal mentioned in the Bible?
50 Wig's follower
51 Calls for quiet
54 Tolkien forest giant
55 An informal greeting
56 At the drop of ___
57 George Williams' org.
60 Free from moral blemish or impurity
63 Secure a ship
64 Rev. Roberts
65 Capp character
66 Mass officiants' robes
67 Archibald of basketball
68 Super hitter Tony

DOWN

1 Nil
2 Sicilia, for one
3 French Revolutionary Jean Paul
4 Before le to puzzle
5 Checks eligibility, slangily
6 Hillary and Tipper are two
7 Mastered
8 After Viet
9 Saskatchewan site
10 After hasta in Mexico
11 Charlottesville col.
12 Plop or plunk starter
13 Birth of a lamb
18 Guam's capital
23 Short queries
25 Town near Mt. Rainier
26 Front ruffle
27 TV's *Kate &* ___
28 Danish or Swedish, for short
29 Honey homes
30 Actor MacLachlan
33 Wear proudly
34 Basketball legend Thomas
35 Virginia
36 Concerning
37 Near, in Nuremberg

38 Rare blood type, for short
40 Religious offering
41 Grades K–6: Abbr.
46 Yearly rem.
47 Not of the cloth
49 Machine parts
50 What is the biggest animal mentioned in the Bible?
51 Questionable
52 ___ hand (humbly)
53 Dutch painter Jan ___
55 Love, in Latin I
56 "There oughta be ___!"
57 Singer Sumac
58 Sm. particle
59 Corn on the ___
61 Frank Buchman's peace gp.
62 Bldg. materials maker

1 2 3 4 5 6 7 8 9 10 11 12 13
14 15 16
17 18 19
20 21 22 23
24 25 26 27 28 29
30 31 32
33 34 35 36 37 38
39 40 41
42 43 44
45 46 47
48 49 50 51 52 53
54 55 56
57 58 59 60 61 62
63 64 65
66 67 68

Boats and Other Floating Things

ACROSS

1 Syrup flavor
6 Mutual agreement
10 Vamoose
14 With no hope left
15 Ancestor of Jesus
16 "Give it ___"
17 Who sent timber, in the form of rafts, to King Solomon?
20 Frozen Wasser
21 Scrooge, familiarly
22 Belongs to TV's Jack
23 *Peer Gynt* character
24 Intl. Luth. Hour
25 What was the only ship in the Bible mentioned by name?
34 Creme cookies
35 Ones voting yes
36 Tithable pungent plant in Bible
37 Domesticated
38 Native suffix
39 Have-___
40 ___ hunch
41 Air leak sound
42 Starbucks serving
43 Who joined with wicked King Ahaziah of Israel in building a navy to go to Tarshish?
47 Fishing need
48 Bambi's aunt
49 Sober-minded
51 Indiana lakeport
53 Originating co.
56 What two prophets predicted attacks from the warships of Chittim?
59 Crunch's rank
60 "Yikes!"
61 Syrian king
62 Greatly annoys
63 Planted seed
64 Portals

DOWN

1 Create
2 Et ___ (and others)
3 Flatlands, for short
4 Carry with effort
5 Home of Greek goddess Diana
6 Peel (an apple)
7 Muslim call to prayer
8 Fort front
9 Hot zones
10 Al ___ (Arafat followers)
11 A great stellar dist.
12 Makes a mistake
13 Needle hole
18 Mountain goat
19 Refrain syllables
23 Burn balm
25 *The Chosen* author Chaim
26 Algerian
27 Lake of Geneva
28 One salmon, e.g.
29 Untrue
30 Kind of code
31 Pledge of fidelity
32 "I'm ___ here!"
33 Spring forward or fall back
39 Wine county
41 Hawks
42 Nautical line
44 Cereal components
45 ___ de vivre
46 Political cartoonist Block
49 Rhineland river

50 Toll rd.
51 Nibble away
52 Subsequent, in brief
53 *Whiteoaks* author de la Roche
54 Inside the foul line
55 New Testament bk.
56 601, in old Rome
57 Back then
58 Best-selling author ___ F. Buscaglia

As a Reminder

ACROSS

1 Soft attention-getter
5 Noodles
10 Shpeak like thish
14 Stranded motorist's need
15 Toward the back
16 School subj.
17 Abnormal chest sound
18 ___about
19 Dingwall dialect
20 What ritual was to be a reminder of Christ's body and blood?
23 Some Balkanites
24 River to the Rhone
25 Billion years
27 Boring people
32 Depression-era inits.
35 What was given as a reminder that the world would never again be destroyed by a flood?
40 Maiden loved by Hercules
42 '50s drugstore refreshments
43 Ward of *Sisters*
44 What day of the week is a reminder of God's completed creation?
46 Apex
47 "Washington ___ Here"
48 Suffix for Japan
51 Tropical ferns
56 Milo of *Barbarella*
60 What reminds us that we serve a risen Lord?
64 ___-Cola
65 Texas city
66 ___ sapiens
67 Mit ___post (airmail from Bonn)
68 Ruby's partner
69 ___ out, as an existence
70 Tax-sheltered savings
71 Items often passed
72 Former Cub Sandberg

DOWN

1 Department at an auto shop
2 *60 Minutes* correspondent
3 Roman sandal
4 Number of memorial stones Joshua erected
5 TV entertainer Jack ___
6 Son of Gad
7 Theodore Giesel, a.k.a. Dr. ___
8 Cup of coffee, to Curie
9 Conductor Rodzinski
10 Nickname for a big dog
11 Italian currencies
12 Stalin's gov.
13 Travel plan, for short
21 ___ blanco (polar bear)
22 Prefix with cure
26 Crash-investigating org.
28 TLC providers
29 "Oh, right!"
30 English sport
31 Exchange
32 Mental faculties
33 Sci-fi writer Frederik
34 Sheltered from the wind
36 Nail type
37 Self-help author LeShan
38 Large rodent
39 Arthur, of the courts
41 Psychic's claim
45 Westernmost Aleutian
49 Chow-mein sauce
50 Feast of Purim honoree
52 Wide necktie

53 Further the function of
54 In ___ (untidy)
55 Sail spar
57 Truancy
58 Netherlands city
59 Igloo or teepee, e.g.
60 Soup du ___
61 Evang. Council on Fiscal Accountability
62 Hurdles for seniors
63 Little piggies
64 Caesar's 151

Not to Be Taken Seriously (Part 2)

ACROSS

1 Part of what God took from Adam and Eve so they couldn't gamble
5 Picture holder
10 They couldn't ___ cards on Noah's ark because Noah sat on the deck
14 Abnormal respiratory sound
15 Tiff
16 Eve was the first person to eat herself out of house and ___
17 Lawman Wyatt ___
18 Make bill law
19 Mary Kay competitor
20 Cain couldn't ___ God with his offering because he just wasn't Abel
22 There were newspaper reporters in Bible times because Zacchaeus couldn't see Jesus for ___
24 Adam never ___ or had parents, yet left two of them for his children
25 Ancient strongbox
26 Which days in Bible times passed by quickly?
31 Small porches
35 Admit as true, in brief
36 "Are we having fun ___?"
37 Pull along
38 End-time trouble per.
40 *Taming of the* ___
43 In ___ (naturally-positioned)
44 Belongs to Queen of the Olympian gods
46 Hero of *Exodus*
47 May 8, 1945 letters
48 Pippi Longstocking creator Lindgren
50 Hershiser and Ryan
53 ___ out a living
55 Owl's remark
56 Moses had to be hidden quickly as a baby because it was ___
60 What was on the side of Solomon's head?
64 Take the floor
65 Levi's *Christ Stopped at* ___
67 Statue in Piccadilly Circle
68 Actor Morales
69 Ticketed
70 Adam was the first person to have surgery when God removed one of his ___
71 Ankle-knee connector
72 Tickle response
73 Bob Hoskins's role in *Hook*

DOWN

1 Get ready
2 American Academy of Arts and Letters
3 Mozart's ___ *Pastore*
4 Banquet
5 "The Lord made every creeping thing" is the first mention of ___ in the Bible
6 Bank worry
7 Gray's subj.
8 Son of Mephibosheth
9 Records data
10 Tennis was played in the Bible when Joseph served in ___ court
11 How long did Samson ___ Delilah? (Until she bald him out)
12 "Famous" cookie man
13 Cravings
21 Glum
23 Poll amts.
26 Jazzman Earl ___ Hines

27 Classic speech "___ of Diamonds"
28 Avoid
29 Teen's agreement
30 Subway support
32 Popeye's sweetie
33 Who was the smallest man in the Bible?
34 Potatoes
39 What kind of fur did Adam and Eve wear?
41 Gad's son
42 How did God keep the oceans clean?
45 Golden Temple worshiper
49 Dishearten
51 Miler Sebastian
52 Numbers 11:32 mentions a baseball player who hit ten of these
54 Zelda's heartthrob, in '60s TV
56 Chemical suffixes
57 Diaper disease
58 Biblical river near Susa
59 Two out of two
61 Schoolmarmish
62 Earring locale
63 The better part of Jesse
66 Harper on the bookshelf

1 2 3 4 5 6 7 8 9 10 11 12 13
14 15 16
17 18 19
20 21 22 23
24 25
26 27 28 29 30 31 32 33 34
35 36 37
38 39 40 41 42 43
44 45 46 47
48 49 50 51 52
53 54 55
56 57 58 59 60 61 62 63
64 65 66 67
68 69 70
71 72 73

A Sign unto You (Part 1)

ACROSS

1 What nation suffered ten plagues that were signs of God's power?
6 Moms' gp.
10 High math.
14 Satchmo Armstrong
15 Goddess pictured in Egyptian tombs
16 "I cannot tell ____"
17 *Children of Crisis* author, Robert ___
18 What was given as a sign that the shepherds had found the baby Jesus?
20 Middle of month, of olde
21 Opium, for one
22 Intimidate
23 Genealogical abbr.
25 What king saw an altar broken as a sign that God was speaking through a prophet?
27 Mod. brake type
29 Prince Valiant's son
30 Hazards
33 ___ al Abyad (White Nile)
36 Replicate
39 What food was a sign of the Hebrews' deliverance from Egypt?
43 Shooting match
44 Followers: Suffix
45 Soup holders
46 Tot. parenteral nutrition
48 Lung disease initials
49 What prophet advised building a signal fire as a sign of the coming invasion of Babylon?
53 Josh Billings's Uncle
57 Dictation taker
59 Headstrong, for short
60 Actress Williams
61 According to Jesus, what sign of Jonah would be given to the unbelieving Jews?
63 Third wife of Augustus Caesar
65 Ripped
66 Self-governing
67 Crash
68 Network, for short
69 Ceiling coolers?
70 Money makers

DOWN

1 Charlton Heston epic
2 Former Philly mayor Wilson ___
3 Year-end holidays
4 Jack Horner's fare
5 Your, in Ypres
6 Bishop's hat
7 Assyrian war god
8 Part of Padres' name
9 Dist. sales mgr.
10 Land Joshua conquered
11 Wood for Hebrew temple pillars
12 Mortgage attachment
13 Proof of pur.
19 One June bug
21 Record players, familiarly
24 Lighted birthday sign
26 Troubadour
28 Youth troop gp.
30 Groove
31 Singer Kamoze
32 Camera type
33 Egyptian pleasure god
34 Carpenter, for one
35 "___ a jolly good fellow"
36 Morning moisture

37 Largest airline's corp.
38 Short planks?
40 Grape-producer
41 English network
42 Sign Rahab hung from her window
46 Flat taker
47 Not RC
48 Wife's degree? ("Putting Hubby Through")
49 Scoffs
50 Ballerina Shearer
51 *Peer Gynt* dramatist
52 Penance symbol
54 Perfect number
55 Royal decree
56 Canoes: Var.
57 Bilko and Preston, for short
58 Weight in gold
62 As loud as possible, in music
63 Low water mks.
64 Pensioner's payments

The Bible on Screen (Part I)

ACROSS

1 What 1976 film, part of a trilogy, was loosely based on biblical predictions about the Antichrist?
5 Spa amenity
10 Russian-built fighters
14 Lymph, for one
15 Recovery salts
16 Prepare to do laundry
17 On whose novel is the 1957 film *The Sun Also Rises* based, which also took its title from Ecclesiastes?
20 Dead or Red, e.g.
21 "And that's the way ___"
22 Tape deck option
23 Ran, as colors
24 Parody
26 Place for an ace?
29 Solid
30 Connected gr.
33 Join
34 Plane related
35 Fodder figure
36 What actor, known for his portrayals of gangsters, played the quarrelsome Dathan in *The Ten Commandments*?
39 Opposed, in Dogpatch
40 Heavy metal
41 Nary a soul
42 Stimpy's cartoon dog
43 Nourish
44 Polecats
45 Take advantage of
46 Barbecue accessory
47 Make amends (for)
51 Pronto
52 High-school subj.
55 Who starred as the lecherous king in the 1953 film *Salome*?
59 Legally it's wrong
60 Crannies' companions?
61 Fountain drink
62 Artaxerxes' palace site
63 Put out
64 Charlton Heston was one

DOWN

1 Singles
2 Encore!
3 ___ St. Vincent Milay
4 Born as
5 Backed wooden bench
6 Ladybug's food
7 Takes advantage of
8 __ de plume
9 French friend
10 Short Catholic official?
11 John Wayne's birthplace
12 Mardi ___
13 Pigpen
18 ___ screen (b&w film era)
19 Financial aid criterion
23 Started
24 Moses's brother
25 Math assign.
26 Daub
27 Overhang
28 Stu of old films
29 Role of 55-Across in 1953 film *Salome*
30 Badlands National Park sight
31 Dull impact sound
32 Gets an edge on
34 Concur
35 One end of a pig

37 Goes kaput
38 Signing, as a contract
43 Gas or wood
44 Marriage mate
46 Overcharges but good
47 Play parts
48 Holier than ___
49 Rowers
50 Natl. R. R. Trans. Auth.
51 Adagio
52 Film's box office receipts, e.g.
53 Pepsi is one
54 Beg.
56 Film's finale, with "the"
57 Great Lakes canals
58 British boat beginning

1
2
3
4
5
6
7
8
9
10
11
12
13
14
15
16
17
18
19
20
21
22
23
24
25
26
27
28
29
30
31
32
33
34
35
36
37
38
39
40
41
42
43
44
45
46
47
48
49
50
51
52
53
54
55
56
57
58
59
60
61
62
63
64

A Few Bits of Potpourri

ACROSS

1 Queen of the Greek gods
5 Missionary Junipero ___
10 Make an afghan
14 Settled, as on a perch
15 "That is to say . . ."
16 Hitler's party
17 You: Ger.
18 Main points
19 Scottish seaport
20 Who printed the first Bible?
23 Turndowns
24 Start of clusion
25 City in Nimrod's empire
28 PaperMate is one
29 Part of a Gilbert and Sullivan chorus
34 Humans' homes: slang
35 Liq. measures
36 Final letters
37 White-knuckled
39 Magi's homeland
40 California city
41 The law has a long one
42 Zwei follower
43 St. Patrick's people
44 Gershwin or Levin
45 Eden's location in Tel-___
46 Hebrews' wilderness oasis
48 Choose
49 What American president published an edition of the Gospels which left out all the supernatural elements?
57 Newman film
58 Mount Helicon's district
59 "I can't believe ___ the whole thing!"
60 Wk. at Mt. Palomar
61 Object
62 ___-dieu (prayer seat)
63 Part of Taiwan leader's name
64 Weave in and out
65 Disapproval sound

DOWN

1 Trip to Mecca
2 Chacon of the 1962 Mets
3 Wealthy
4 What Egyptian bishop was the first person to list the 27 New Testament books that we now have?
5 Autographs
6 Pioneer: Abbr.
7 Job-hunters' tools
8 Cane material
9 Photographer Adams
10 Door opener
11 Neighborhood theater
12 Long dress in the Middle East
13 Soft bell sound
21 Visual OK
22 "You've got the wrong guy!"
25 Old adders
26 Irish author/diplomat O'Brien
27 441 in Rome
28 Game-deciding stat
30 What material were the first manuscripts of the New Testament written on?
31 Lab gels
32 City of Crete
33 On the move
35 Sine ___ non
36 Electrical resistance
38 Character actress Tessie
39 Secretariat's org.
41 Country
44 New Testament book

45 Zoo attraction
47 Attorney-to-be's exams, in brief
48 Over 21
49 "___ the night before Christmas"
50 Quiet
51 Bone: Prefix
52 Which Gospel was, according to tradition, written first?
53 Stool pigeon
54 Pakistani woman's garment
55 Elevator maker
56 Social-page words

A Sign unto You (Part 2)

ACROSS

1 ___ apple
6 It's at one's fingertip
10 Mil. units
14 Pago Pago's region
15 Brother of Zaccur
16 "Dies ___" (hymn)
17 Trojan head
18 Somber
19 Janowitz who wrote *Slaves of New York*
20 Who bound King Zedekiah in chains and blinded him?
23 Miss Persia contest winner: abbr.
24 Australia's ___ Rock
25 Some phones
29 Car renter
32 Follows form or lamin
33 ___ en scene
34 Calendar mos.: Var.
37 Who put a golden chain around Joseph's neck?
41 Who made chains strung with pomegranates to decorate the temple?
43 Worship mtg.
44 Kind of chowder
46 Small child
47 *Crucifixion of St. Peter* painter Guido ___
48 Reverenced
50 Ind. Hall site
54 Two under Navy Capt.
56 Who dropped a scarlet cord from her window to aid the Israelite spies?
62 A son of Judah
63 Abominable snowman
64 *Fra Diavolo* composer
66 Being: Sp.
67 Who arrived in Rome bound by a chain?
68 College sports org. tournament
69 West, et al.
70 Although, to Ovid
71 Mississippi outlet

DOWN

1 Painkiller, for short
2 Mend
3 Parisian lady friend
4 Ancient kingdom in Jordan
5 Prophet to Saul and David
6 Evening
7 Father ___
8 Crocus or freesia
9 Paint
10 Posh
11 Just touch
12 Who gave birth to twins, one of whom had a scarlet thread tied around him by the midwife?
13 Famous Chicago Tower
21 Tech. sch. dept.
22 Flip chart site
25 Atlas features
26 Will-___-wisp
27 Tolerate
28 Tel-Aviv res.
30 Baron's sup.
31 100, 200, 400, etc.
34 Persian Gulf bigwig
35 Dawdle
36 Prune a Scotland yard
38 Oarsman's catch
39 *Giants in the Earth* author Rolvaag
40 Solo in space

42 Hiroshima's river
45 Place on Paul's journeys
48 Fed. health watchdog
49 Gofer's assignment
50 Introduction
51 ___-Barbera, "Tom and Jerry" animators
52 "___ it when that happens"
53 Bowling alleys
55 Kind of pepper
57 Kind
58 Warm up
59 Time founder
60 Son of Joktan
61 Ewe's feeder
65 Mandela's land: Abbr.

The Bible on Screen (Part 2)

ACROSS

1 Charlton Heston was one
5 Green garnishes
10 Hugging instruments?
14 Video
15 It is countered with "You must!"
16 Home for *la familia*
17 Anchorage's st.
18 *A Dog of Flanders* writer
19 Say for sure
20 Where to view *The Green Pastures*
22 Ahab and Ishmael's 1956 flick
24 Resident assistants, in brief
25 US Navy woman
26 Gaudy 1951 film based on a novel by Henryk Sienkiewicz, telling the story of the early Christians and their persecution under Nero
31 Actress Shirley
35 Stalemate
36 NY summer time
37 Lebanon's neighbor
38 ___ Aviv
39 Din
42 Out of date, for short
43 Sharp ridge
46 Negative prefix
47 Douay prophet
48 Follows Hillary
50 1973 musical, based on a stage play taken from the Gospel of Matthew and using old hymns set to new music, filmed in locations across Manhattan
52 This, in Barcelona
54 Pedal digit
55 *The Greatest Story* ___: Immensely popular 1965 movie with practically every name in Hollywood having a small role
59 Baseball division
63 Moses' mountain lookout
64 Tic
66 Graven image
67 Kind of bag
68 Papyrus, for one
69 Charles Laughton's part in *The Sign of the Cross* (1932 film)
70 Superman, for Christopher Reeve
71 Aides-de-camp: Abbr.
72 Umbrella, at Heathrow

DOWN

1 S.F.R.R. stops
2 After bath powder
3 On ___ with
4 Stand-by actor
5 Daniel's famous place
6 Post-op destination perhaps
7 Cripple
8 Underwrite
9 Make a ___ (try)
10 ___ Awards
11 Shankar of the sitar
12 Quick time meas.
13 Channel island
21 Oshkost fly-in sponsor
23 Designer Saint Laurent
26 Arabian emirate
27 In ___, to baby carrier
28 De-squeaked
29 Marriage vow
30 Iodine reaction
32 Style of writing
33 Defame
34 Artist's support

40 *Barney Miller* regular
41 Subject of prophecy films
44 What 1981 TV movie starred Anthony Hopkins and Robert Foxworth as two apostles?
45 Sunrise direction
47 Slot, for one
49 Peak of NE Greece
51 John Wayne's one-liner as the centurion at Jesus' crucifixion: "Truly, this was the ___ of God"
53 Swiss mountains, to the French
55 Locomotive op.
56 ___ Beach, Florida
57 Mount Gerizim's twin
58 Moms and ___
60 Mental picture
61 *Cheers* regular
62 Soft unappetizing food, on the street
65 ___ *York* (Gary Cooper movie)

1
2
3
4
5
6
7
8
9
10
11
12
13
14
15
16
17
18
19
20
21
22
23
24
25
26
27
28
29
30
31
32
33
34
35
36
37
38
39
40
41
42
43
44
45
46
47
48
49
50
51
52
53
54
55
56
57
58
59
60
61
62
63
64
65
66
67
68
69
70
71
72

. . . And Things Left Over

ACROSS

1 During the days of creation, the days weighed ___ than the nights
5 Las Vegas feature
10 Toxic Substances Control Act of 1976
14 An *Andy Griffith Show* role
15 Popular wedding gift
16 Old cars
17 How long did the shoes of the Hebrews who left Egypt last?
19 Braun and Gabor
20 Lumberjack's tool
21 Two in a million?
22 Begin, e.g.
24 What English translator died as a martyr before he could complete his translation of the Old Testament?
26 Memo starter
27 Sched. note
28 Slight advantage
30 Justice Dept. grp.
33 Spouse's
36 For whom did Rahab drop a scarlet cord from her window?
37 Cash sta.
38 What possession of Moses did God turn into a snake?
39 The Psalms of Solomon are eighteen ___ about the coming Messiah
40 Compass stabilizer
41 On the level: abbr.
42 In how many languages was the Bible originally written?
43 Who was told by God to take his shoes off because he was standing on holy ground?
44 S. Pole cont.
45 Has a snack
46 Campgd. chain
47 Johann Gutenberg printed the first Bible in the ___ 1456
49 Daniel said, "Prove thy servants, I beseech thee, ___; and let them give us pulse to eat and water to drink"
53 *Semper* ___: USMC motto
56 Maximilian's dom.
57 Sigma trailer
58 Greenspan or Shepard
59 God asked David, "Shall ___ of famine come unto thee in thy land?"
62 Florida vacation spot, with "the"
63 Finnish lake
64 Suitable for military service
65 A cinch
66 Car bomb?
67 Loretta, of country music

DOWN

1 Skim milk label
2 Adhesive resin
3 Lorelei
4 Hollywood workplace
5 Strait of Messina menace
6 "We hold ___ truths . . ."
7 Inlet
8 Letters from Calvary
9 Scripture selections
10 October handout
11 Shortest reign of any Hebrew king
12 Fossil fuel
13 Holly
18 Irish poet and Nobelist
23 Numbered hwys.
25 Legal paper
28 They're virtually pointless
29 Smallest American coin

31 Raison d'__

32 Which prophet accused Israel of selling the poor for a pair of sandals?

33 Town in Libya

34 What Old Testament character must have been as strong as steel?

35 How long did Moses fast on Mount Sinai?

36 Categorize

39 Religious leader in Jesus' day

40 Spur

42 Marsh duck

43 There was ___ on Noah's ark: The duck had a bill, the skunk had a scent, and the frog had a greenback

46 Essence

48 Ittsy-bitty

49 Fore or after leader

50 ___ rate

51 Capital of island of Nauru

52 Ms. B. Anthony

53 Imposter

54 Certain sections of the GI tracts

55 Fax button

60 Biological duct

61 End of line

1 2 3 4 5 6 7 8 9 10 11 12 13
14 15 16
17 18 19
20 21 22 23
24 25 26
27 28 29 30 31 32
33 34 35 36 37
38 39 40
41 42 43
44 45 46
47 48 49 50 51 52
53 54 55 56 57
58 59 60 61
62 63 64
65 66 67

The Naked Truth

page 3

S	E	L	A	H	■	S	A	L	P	■	N	O	A	H
A	M	O	C	O	■	T	W	E	E	■	A	W	L	S
G	E	T	H	S	E	M	A	N	E	■	D	E	D	E
E	S	T	E	E	M	■	R	A	R	A	A	■	■	■
■	■	■	■	A	B	B	■	■	E	B	B	I	N	G
P	A	S	S	■	R	E	M	A	D	E	■	P	A	U
A	T	K	A	■	Y	E	A	H	■	A	H	E	M	S
T	H	E	P	R	O	P	H	E	T	M	I	C	A	H
E	L	I	H	U	■	E	D	A	R	■	M	A	T	E
N	A	N	■	I	N	D	I	R	A	■	O	C	H	S
T	I	S	A	N	E	■	■	T	J	C	■	■	■	■
■	■	■	F	A	V	R	E	■	A	A	R	O	N	S
S	A	U	L	■	S	I	M	O	N	P	E	T	E	R
E	Y	R	A	■	K	E	E	P	■	A	L	T	A	I
L	E	E	T	■	I	L	U	S	■	C	Y	S	T	S

Laughers and Dancers

page 5

F	I	S	T	■	D	O	H	■	■	P	A	P	E	N
A	T	T	A	■	A	K	U	■	S	A	B	R	E	S
B	E	N	J	A	M	I	N	■	C	R	E	O	L	E
■	■	■	■	M	O	E	T	■	A	T	A	D	■	■
H	E	F	L	I	N	■	■	■	M	I	R	I	A	M
E	L	A	I	N	E	■	E	S	M	E	■	G	P	O
R	A	T	E	D	■	J	A	M	E	S	■	A	P	U
E	T	H	S	■	C	O	M	E	R	■	A	L	E	R
S	I	E	■	T	H	R	E	W	■	N	I	S	A	N
T	O	R	■	R	A	Y	S	■	S	E	T	O	S	E
O	N	O	N	E	S	■	■	■	E	I	S	N	E	R
■	■	F	O	N	T	■	O	R	I	G	■	■	■	■
R	A	T	I	T	E	■	H	E	Z	E	K	I	A	H
E	P	H	R	O	N	■	O	R	E	■	A	N	D	A
G	R	E	E	N	■	■	H	I	D	■	A	N	D	Y

They Did It First

page 7

E	N	O	C	H	■	A	B	I	■	■	S	I	M	I
L	A	N	A	I	■	L	O	G	■	B	E	Z	E	L
E	S	T	H	E	R	W	H	O	S	E	R	E	A	L
C	A	A	N	■	O	A	R	■	H	E	A	D	L	Y
T	S	P	■	I	M	Y	■	F	A	B	I	■	■	■
■	■	■	O	N	A	■	S	I	D	E	■	F	L	O
A	D	A	M	A	N	D	E	V	E	■	A	R	A	S
J	A	M	E	S	■	R	E	E	■	A	B	A	N	A
A	L	Y	S	■	S	I	M	O	N	P	E	T	E	R
X	E	S	■	S	P	E	E	■	O	E	L	■	■	■
■	■	■	E	P	I	S	■	H	E	X	■	C	B	C
A	W	O	M	A	N	■	T	O	N	■	E	B	R	O
N	A	M	E	W	A	S	H	A	D	A	S	S	A	H
G	R	E	E	N	■	I	R	R	■	U	P	T	H	E
E	M	I	R	■	■	G	O	D	■	R	A	V	E	N

Kings, Pharaohs, and Other Rulers

page 9

L	I	M	P	■	S	P	R	S	■	■	A	L	L	E
A	B	I	A	■	O	L	I	N	■	■	H	E	I	L
K	I	N	G	O	F	E	D	O	M	■	H	O	L	A
A	D	H	E	S	I	V	E	■	A	C	H	I	S	H
■	■	■	■	M	A	N	A	S	S	E	H	■	■	■
M	A	R	I	A	N	A	■	T	O	R	■	G	M	A
A	L	O	A	N	■	■	J	E	R	O	B	O	A	M
T	A	N	T	■	K	R	O	N	A	■	E	B	R	O
Z	E	D	E	K	I	A	H	■	■	J	A	B	I	N
O	D	O	■	L	P	N	■	G	O	O	D	I	N	G
■	■	■	H	A	N	D	F	U	L	S	■	■	■	■
C	O	T	E	N	U	■	I	N	D	E	B	T	E	D
A	M	O	R	■	K	I	N	G	O	F	A	R	A	D
K	I	L	O	■	■	L	A	H	R	■	M	A	T	A
E	T	U	D	■	■	S	L	O	T	■	A	D	A	Y

So Many Dreamers

page 11

A	M	I	S	H	■	T	B	A	R	S	■	B	B	S
N	E	C	R	O	■	O	R	B	I	T	■	A	I	L
A	L	I	O	N	A	B	E	A	R	A	■	R	D	A
■	■	■	■	A	L	E	R	T	E	R	■	L	E	B
F	A	M	I	N	E	S	■	■	■	E	B	E	N	S
I	R	O	N	■	■	■	P	I	D	D	L	Y	■	■
X	E	N	A	■	A	J	U	G	A	■	A	B	B	Y
I	N	S	■	■	C	O	R	E	S	■	■	R	E	A
T	A	T	S	■	T	E	E	T	H	■	N	E	E	S
■	■	E	T	O	I	L	E	■	■	■	F	A	B	I
P	A	R	A	N	■	■	■	S	M	O	L	D	E	R
E	B	W	■	S	H	O	O	T	E	R	■	■	■	■
T	O	I	■	L	E	O	P	A	R	D	A	N	D	A
E	L	T	■	O	R	G	E	T	■	E	V	I	A	N
R	T	H	■	W	E	A	L	S	■	R	A	B	B	I

What's in a Name?

page 13

J	U	D	E	■	S	M	I	T	H	■	T	G	I	F
E	L	I	Z	■	T	O	S	E	A	■	I	L	S	A
A	L	A	E	■	L	U	N	A	R	■	M	U	N	I
N	A	N	K	E	E	N	■	S	O	L	O	M	O	N
■	■	■	I	L	O	T	■	E	D	I	T	■	■	■
S	A	L	E	S	■	H	A	L	■	S	H	A	N	A
P	H	I	L	E	M	O	N	■	E	T	Y	M	O	N
A	O	K	■	■	T	R	O	M	P	■	■	B	H	A
T	R	U	M	A	N	■	N	E	H	E	M	I	A	H
S	A	D	A	T	■	D	O	R	■	M	A	T	T	S
■	■	■	L	A	T	E	■	C	A	P	T	■	■	■
L	A	Z	A	R	U	S	■	R	A	T	T	L	E	S
A	L	E	C	■	R	E	F	E	R	■	H	A	A	S
R	U	T	H	■	F	R	O	D	O	■	E	Z	R	A
A	R	A	I	■	S	T	E	I	N	■	W	E	S	T

The Runners

page 15

S	T	A	G		E	L	I	S	H	A		T	E	C
K	O	N	A		P	A	L	L	E	D		A	C	R
U	P	O	N	T	H	E	L	O	R	D		M	O	E
S	E	E	T	O			A	T	M			P	L	S
			T	H	E	Y	T	H	A	T	W	A	I	T
L	O	G		U	L	U			N	A	R			
E	L	A	T		B	K	G	D		B	E	A	D	S
A	L	L	W	E		O	E	R		L	A	B	A	N
D	A	V	I	D		N	E	A	T		K	I	W	I
			R	A	P			F	O	G		G	N	P
T	H	E	P	R	I	E	S	T	E	L	I			
E	A	P			L	A	O			A	L	C	O	A
M	B	I		M	A	R	Y	A	N	D	M	A	R	Y
P	I	C		A	T	E	A	S	E		E	L	E	E
O	T	S		R	E	D	S	K	Y		N	E	B	R

More Kings, Pharaohs, and Other Rulers

page 21

D	I	N	A	R		R	Y	A	S		A	H	A	B
I	C	O	M	E		E	A	T	A		R	O	L	L
J	E	H	O	I	A	C	H	I	N		M	C	C	I
O	N	A	N		H	A	O		T	T	Y			
N	I	T		D	A	B	O		A	E	S	O	P	S
			P	U	Z			L	A	G		N	O	I
O	H	A	R	A		A	R	E	N		H	I	L	O
M	E	R	O	D	A	C	H	B	A	L	A	D	A	N
A	R	A	G		N	E	C	O		T	Z	A	R	S
H	O	D		W	T	S			A	J	O			
A	D	O	R	E	E		J	A	R	G		P	B	A
			E	C	C		O	I	C		A	E	O	N
D	I	T	Z		E	S	A	R	H	A	D	D	O	N
O	M	R	I		D	U	S	E		C	E	R	T	E
P	E	I	N		E	D	H	S		C	R	O	S	S

Names Made in Heaven

page 17

F	I	S	T	S		S	A	E		I	N	C	A	S
A	M	A	S	A		O	D	D		S	A	B	L	E
L	O	R	U	H	A	M	A	H		A	B	N	E	R
S	U	A			T	A	M		A	I	S			
E	T	H	B	A	A	L		B	B	A		A	P	U
			L	H	T			R	A	H		D	O	N
A	T	R	E	E		B	E	A	N		F	A	L	C
T	H	E	A	N	G	E	L	G	A	B	R	I	E	L
W	E	I	R		R	E	Y	S		L	O	R	R	E
A	R	N		I	E	R			R	U	G			
R	M	S		S	Y	S		N	U	R	S	E	R	Y
			D	R	S		P	I	T			R	O	A
H	O	S	E	A		Z	A	C	H	A	R	I	A	S
C	L	O	S	E		A	S	A		I	R	A	N	I
R	A	T	E	L		G	A	D		A	S	N	E	R

Most Mentioned Men

page 23

S	A	U	L		J	A	C	O	B		A	N	A	D
O	H	R	E		A	R	G	U	E		N	O	S	E
S	E	B	A		B	R	A	I	D		K	N	E	W
	N	I	D	I				J	O	S	H	U	A	
			E	D	G	Y		A	G	I				
	A	B	R	A	H	A	M			D	A	V	I	D
C	A	I			I	G	O	R		S	L	A	T	E
O	R	E	M		J	E	S	U	S		P	S	I	S
N	O	H	O	W		R	E	N	A			C	O	T
E	N	L	A	I			S	O	L	O	M	O	N	
				V	S	S		N	E	C	O			
	J	O	S	E	P	H				C	S	O	S	
T	O	L	E		L	Y	C	E	E		T	R	I	P
C	I	A	S		A	E	S	O	P		L	E	L	Y
I	N	S	S		T	R	A	P	P		Y	O	D	A

Notable Women, and Some Less Notable (Part 1)

page 19

F	L	A	B		H	O	S	E	A		A	N	N	A
L	A	T	I		A	B	E	L	L		L	O	I	S
O	R	E	L		W	A	S	C	O		A	L	G	A
P	U	A	H	A	N	D	S	H	I	P	R	A	H	
S	E	R	A	L			A	O	N	E				
			H	E	I	N				C	H	L	O	E
S	O	V		P	R	E	F	A	B		C	E	E	S
T	H	E	C	H	U	R	C	H	A	T	R	O	M	E
A	N	E	T		N	A	A	M	A	H		V	S	S
M	E	R	A	B				E	N	R	Y			
				A	D	A	H			O	S	A	G	E
	H	E	B	R	E	W	M	I	D	W	I	V	E	S
J	A	E	L		A	N	O	L	E		D	A	T	S
A	L	K	A		R	E	N	E	E		R	I	M	E
G	E	S	T		E	D	G	A	R		O	L	E	N

Most Mentioned Women

page 25

M	E	S	S	I	L	Y		R	O	B	A	R	D	S
F	L	O	T	S	A	M		A	B	I	G	A	I	L
R	E	B	E	K	A	H		C	O	R	R	I	D	A
			N	E	R	A		H	T	S				
A	C	B	O	R				E	E	E		S	P	A
F	L	A	G		D	A	H	L	S		L	E	A	H
T	A	L		O	S	H	A			B	Y	A	R	S
	M	A	R	Y	M	A	G	D	A	L	E	N	E	
D	O	A	L	L			A	C	T	A		C	N	N
B	U	M	S		S	A	R	A	H		M	E	T	A
S	R	S		J	E	D				M	I	S	S	S
				I	R	U		I	G	O	R			
J	E	Z	E	B	E	L		T	I	D	I	E	S	T
R	A	I	M	E	N	T		E	L	E	A	N	O	R
S	U	T	U	R	E	S		M	A	M	M	A	R	Y

Still More Kings, Pharaohs, and Other Rulers
page 27

S	P	R	I	G	S	■	F	O	P	■	H	G	T	S
M	U	E	S	L	I	■	A	S	A	■	E	R	I	E
I	S	H	B	O	S	H	E	T	H	■	R	O	D	E
T	H	A	N	■	E	U	R	■	A	B	O	■	■	■
S	Y	N	■	T	R	A	Y	S	■	I	D	O	L	S
■	■	■	L	O	A	■	■	U	F	O	■	R	E	I
A	J	M	A	N	■	E	E	R	O	■	P	E	N	G
T	O	I	K	I	N	G	O	F	H	A	M	A	T	H
T	A	L	E	■	E	L	F	S	■	T	O	D	O	S
I	S	L	■	R	H	O	■	■	X	T	S	■	■	■
C	H	I	D	E	■	N	A	P	E	S	■	T	E	T
■	■	■	A	Y	S	■	P	E	R	■	P	O	G	O
M	E	R	V	■	A	R	T	A	X	E	R	X	E	S
I	G	N	I	■	U	A	E	■	E	L	O	I	S	E
D	O	D	D	■	L	D	R	■	S	T	A	C	T	E

A Herd of Prophets
page 29

A	H	I	J	A	H	■	N	A	B	■	S	A	P	S
J	E	R	O	M	E	■	D	P	I	■	I	L	E	T
A	M	I	N	O	R	■	U	R	B	■	L	O	C	O
R	P	S	■	E	R	A	■	A	B	R	A	H	A	M
■	S	H	E	B	E	A	R	■	■	A	S	A	N	A
■	■	■	H	A	N	A	N	I	A	H	■	■	■	■
F	R	A	U	■	■	■	D	I	N	A	■	I	T	D
L	E	A	D	S	I	N	■	M	A	L	A	C	H	I
A	M	B	■	C	O	N	G	■	■	■	S	A	U	L
■	■	■	■	U	S	E	A	T	A	P	E	■	■	■
J	E	S	U	S	■	■	D	E	B	O	R	A	H	■
O	B	A	D	I	A	H	■	V	I	C	■	L	O	P
N	O	R	D	■	Q	E	F	■	J	O	C	O	S	E
A	L	E	E	■	U	D	E	■	A	L	I	N	E	D
H	I	E	R	■	A	Y	R	■	H	A	G	G	A	I

Notable Women, and Some Less Notable (Part 2)
page 31

M	A	R	Y	■	A	C	A	G	E	■	K	R	O	C
O	X	O	N	■	D	O	N	O	R	■	L	O	D	E
W	I	S	E	W	O	M	A	N	O	F	A	B	E	L
N	S	A	■	O	N	E	B	■	■	A	T	B	A	T
■	■	■	O	F	I	T	■	P	A	R	C	■	■	■
J	A	I	R	U	S	S	D	A	U	G	H	T	E	R
A	R	N	E	L	■	■	I	S	N	O	■	R	A	E
N	I	O	S	■	R	U	N	A	T	■	L	I	T	T
E	E	N	■	M	A	S	A	■	■	R	E	A	T	A
T	H	E	W	I	T	C	H	O	F	E	N	D	O	R
■	■	■	A	L	E	G	■	N	A	N	A	■	■	■
S	U	C	R	E	■	■	P	E	R	E	■	E	P	A
T	H	E	B	A	H	U	R	I	M	W	O	M	A	N
P	U	B	L	■	T	S	A	D	E	■	E	M	U	S
S	H	U	E	■	S	A	M	A	R	■	D	A	L	E

They Heard Voices
page 33

I	S	A	A	C	■	A	W	O	L	■	D	E	L	E
M	A	R	I	E	■	I	I	I	I	■	A	G	A	S
T	H	E	L	O	R	D	S	S	E	R	V	A	N	T
H	E	N	S	■	A	E	C	■	■	O	I	N	K	S
E	L	A	■	I	I	S	■	R	E	A	D	■	■	■
■	■	■	O	C	S	■	J	E	A	N	■	A	Y	N
T	H	E	H	E	A	V	E	N	S	■	B	L	U	E
U	M	B	E	L	■	I	S	A	■	T	R	A	M	S
G	O	A	L	■	M	O	U	N	T	S	I	N	A	I
S	S	N	■	C	U	L	P	■	H	I	C	■	■	■
■	■	■	P	O	D	S	■	R	I	A	■	C	O	P
L	A	M	A	S	■	■	C	H	E	■	K	A	B	A
T	H	E	W	I	T	C	H	O	F	E	N	D	O	R
D	A	N	E	■	H	O	A	D	■	E	A	G	L	E
S	T	U	D	■	Y	O	D	A	■	K	R	E	S	S

Sleepers and Nonsleepers
page 35

A	D	D	E	R	■	A	O	G	■	E	S	S	E	■
H	I	N	D	U	■	D	R	E	■	R	E	O	S	■
I	T	H	E	S	S	A	L	O	N	I	A	N	S	■
■	■	■	■	T	O	G	A	■	E	A	R	N	E	D
T	Y	P	O	■	D	E	N	E	B	■	C	E	N	A
J	A	I	R	U	S	S	D	A	U	G	H	T	E	R
C	H	A	I	N	■	■	O	S	L	O	■	S	S	A
■	■	■	■	D	A	E	■	E	A	R	■	■	■	■
O	M	E	■	I	G	N	I	■	■	K	M	A	R	T
D	A	V	I	D	A	N	D	A	B	I	S	H	A	I
A	D	I	N	■	S	E	I	N	E	■	G	N	U	S
H	E	N	R	I	S	■	O	T	R	A	■	■	■	■
■	I	C	O	R	I	N	T	H	I	A	N	S	X	V
■	R	E	M	I	■	C	I	E	■	A	W	O	L	S
■	A	S	E	S	■	O	C	R	■	L	A	P	I	S

People in Exile
page 37

C	A	I	N	■	F	O	A	M	■	L	A	Z	E	D
A	R	N	A	■	E	A	R	T	■	A	N	E	L	E
M	A	R	Y	J	E	S	U	S	■	H	E	D	G	Y
B	R	O	■	A	L	E	M	■	E	T	T	E	■	■
I	A	M	■	C	A	S	■	G	N	I	■	K	U	M
O	T	E	R	O	■	■	B	O	A	■	O	I	L	S
■	■	■	A	B	S	A	L	O	M	■	L	A	N	G
G	I	G	I	■	H	E	A	P	O	■	P	H	A	R
A	C	E	D	■	A	S	S	Y	R	I	A	■	■	■
E	A	D	S	■	R	I	E	■	■	N	E	E	D	A
A	L	A	■	N	P	R	■	B	K	T	■	U	A	R
■	■	L	O	O	S	■	S	U	O	R	■	R	M	N
P	L	I	E	R	■	A	N	D	J	O	S	E	P	H
G	H	A	N	A	■	M	E	G	A	■	A	K	E	E
A	C	H	E	D	■	G	E	E	K	■	R	A	D	M

Violent People and Things

page 39

A	M	O	N	■	W	H	A	M	■	E	G	E	R	S
G	E	N	E	■	R	O	A	D	■	M	E	R	C	K
A	N	T	H	■	E	L	A	L	■	C	N	I	D	A
L	E	V	I	A	N	D	S	I	M	E	O	N	■	■
■	■	■	■	B	C	S	■	■	Y	E	A	■	■	■
M	A	T	Z	O	H	■	P	E	G	S	■	Y	A	M
E	T	A	I	N	■	O	E	N	O	■	P	O	R	E
A	T	W	O	E	D	G	E	D	D	A	G	G	E	R
T	E	N	N	■	E	R	T	E	■	D	A	I	L	Y
S	N	Y	■	G	L	E	E	■	F	O	S	S	I	L
■	■	■	B	O	H	■	■	D	R	L	■	■	■	■
■	■	O	U	T	I	N	T	H	E	F	I	E	L	D
O	R	B	I	C	■	A	R	O	E	■	A	L	U	I
T	O	R	C	H	■	D	E	L	L	■	N	E	A	L
O	S	A	K	A	■	A	K	E	Y	■	S	A	U	L

The Anointed Ones

page 45

P	A	U	L	■	F	L	E	A	S	■	R	A	S	A
A	C	R	O	■	R	I	N	S	E	■	E	T	E	S
T	H	E	C	H	U	R	C	H	E	L	D	E	R	S
S	E	A	■	A	G	R	E	E	■	I	O	N	I	A
■	■	■	D	E	A	■	■	S	C	E	N	T	E	D
M	I	R	A	C	L	E	S	■	A	N	E	■	■	■
T	H	E	Y	■	■	G	E	E	S	E	■	N	O	T
G	O	D	S	A	N	O	I	N	T	E	D	O	N	E
S	P	A	■	B	U	N	K	O	■	■	O	N	E	L
■	■	■	H	A	D	■	O	L	I	V	E	O	I	L
D	E	C	O	D	E	S	■	■	S	E	S	■	■	■
I	V	A	N	A	■	E	A	T	A	T	■	H	K	I
A	A	R	O	N	A	N	D	H	I	S	S	O	N	S
G	N	A	R	■	I	N	D	I	A	■	E	L	U	L
S	S	T	S	■	M	A	R	S	H	■	W	E	R	E

Taxes, Extortion, and Bribes

page 41

■	R	O	M	E	■	Z	E	E	■	A	V	E	N	■
■	T	R	I	B	■	U	P	C	■	M	E	T	O	■
■	H	I	S	B	I	R	T	H	R	I	G	H	T	■
■	■	■	■	S	D	I	■	■	U	R	G	I	N	G
T	P	K	S	■	A	C	T	U	P	■	I	C	I	E
A	H	A	L	F	S	H	E	K	E	L	E	A	C	H
N	I	N	E	R	■	■	E	E	E	E	■	L	E	T
■	■	■	■	E	G	A	■	R	S	O	■	■	■	■
M	S	T	■	S	U	R	F	■	■	N	O	E	A	R
T	H	E	C	H	I	E	F	P	R	I	E	S	T	S
G	A	R	R	■	N	O	V	A	S	■	D	O	P	A
S	C	R	A	P	E	■	■	S	T	D	■	■	■	■
■	K	I	N	G	A	H	A	S	U	E	R	U	S	■
■	L	E	I	A	■	U	B	E	■	L	E	V	I	■
■	E	R	A	S	■	R	T	S	■	S	S	A	T	■

Houses of Worship

page 47

L	A	M	B	■	E	T	N	A	■	■	J	E	H	U
A	L	A	E	■	D	I	A	N	A	■	A	D	O	S
I	L	R	E	■	G	R	I	N	S	■	N	A	P	E
T	E	M	P	L	E	O	F	A	R	T	E	M	I	S
Y	E	S	E	S	■	■	■	S	E	E	■	■	■	■
■	■	■	R	A	M	A	H	■	D	A	R	I	U	S
A	H	A	■	T	I	L	E	S	■	■	I	M	E	T
J	E	R	U	S	A	L	E	M	T	E	M	P	L	E
A	H	A	Z	■	■	S	L	U	R	S	■	S	E	T
B	E	R	I	T	H	■	S	T	A	S	I	■	■	■
■	■	■	■	B	O	X	■	■	■	A	S	K	M	E
N	A	A	M	A	N	T	H	E	S	Y	R	I	A	N
I	N	T	O	■	K	I	D	D	Y	■	A	N	N	O
T	A	R	A	■	S	E	W	O	N	■	E	D	E	L
A	H	A	B	■	■	S	E	M	S	■	L	S	T	S

Military Men

page 43

P	A	T	I	O	■	A	P	B	■	C	A	J	O	N
E	M	E	N	D	■	L	A	D	■	A	R	E	S	O
C	O	R	N	E	L	I	U	S	■	R	I	P	U	P
K	E	R	■	■	O	B	L	■	■	O	O	H	■	■
A	B	I	S	H	A	I	■	A	L	L	S	T	A	R
T	A	L	O	S	■	■	A	M	A	■	O	H	N	E
■	■	■	B	E	N	A	I	A	H	■	■	A	K	C
U	S	P	S	■	A	M	O	S	T	■	S	H	A	D
T	A	O	■	■	M	A	L	A	I	S	E	■	■	■
E	S	T	A	■	A	H	I	■	■	E	T	H	O	S
P	H	I	C	H	O	L	■	G	O	L	I	A	T	H
■	■	P	C	A	■	■	R	O	B	■	■	C	S	A
U	S	H	E	R	■	R	A	B	S	H	A	K	E	H
S	H	A	D	E	■	U	K	E	■	O	M	E	G	A
O	A	R	E	D	■	G	E	L	■	E	R	R	O	R

Horns of the Altar (Part I)

page 49

S	U	B	J	■	O	H	B	O	Y	■	I	T	C	H
A	N	O	A	■	L	O	R	N	A	■	D	A	R	A
A	C	A	C	I	A	W	O	O	D	■	A	B	E	S
B	A	T	O	R	■	L	A	R	■	S	H	E	E	P
■	■	■	B	I	P	E	D	■	I	T	O	R	■	■
T	S	U	■	A	R	D	■	V	C	R	■	N	A	S
H	A	N	A	N	I	■	J	E	H	O	I	A	D	A
E	L	K	E	■	E	N	O	L	A	■	I	C	E	R
M	A	N	A	S	S	E	H	■	B	O	I	L	E	D
E	D	O	■	O	T	T	■	R	O	M	■	E	M	I
■	■	W	N	W	S	■	J	U	D	A	H	■	■	■
B	O	N	E	S	■	V	O	L	■	H	A	L	T	S
E	G	G	S	■	R	E	V	E	L	A	T	I	O	N
A	L	O	T	■	A	T	A	R	I	■	E	Z	R	A
K	E	D	S	■	C	O	N	S	T	■	S	A	N	G

A Bevy of Priests (Part 1)

page 51

A	S	L	A	P	■	■	M	U	T	E	■	P	R	S
R	U	M	O	R	■	■	I	N	E	Z	■	R	E	A
K	I	N	G	O	F	P	E	A	C	E	■	I	A	N
■	■	■	■	P	E	A	S	■	■	K	N	E	L	T
P	A	S	S	H	U	R	■	C	H	I	A	S	M	A
U	N	T	I	E	■	■	P	R	I	E	S	T	■	■
F	I	R	S	T	■	R	E	U	E	L	■	U	C	A
F	L	A	T	■	E	A	R	E	D	■	O	R	R	S
S	E	N	■	I	S	N	O	T	■	E	L	I	A	S
■	■	G	E	T	S	I	N	■	■	L	I	A	N	A
S	T	E	P	H	E	N	■	S	H	E	C	H	E	M
T	A	F	I	A	■	■	N	C	A	A	■	■	■	■
A	M	I	■	M	E	L	C	H	I	Z	E	D	E	K
D	A	R	■	A	L	S	O	■	■	A	B	I	H	U
E	R	E	■	R	I	D	S	■	■	R	O	D	I	N

Horns of the Altar (Part 2)

page 57

B	A	A	L	S	■	C	A	G	Y	■	A	H	A	Z
A	L	L	E	Y	■	A	L	T	A	■	X	E	R	O
R	E	V	E	L	A	T	I	O	N	■	E	N	N	E
A	N	A	K	■	M	O	S	■	K	A	L	■	■	■
K	E	N	■	■	O	N	T	■	■	O	S	C	A	R
■	■	■	K	P	S	■	■	B	L	A	■	U	M	A
E	C	H	E	D	■	J	O	A	B	■	A	S	O	N
T	H	E	P	R	I	E	S	T	J	O	S	H	U	A
H	I	R	T	■	N	E	T	H	■	F	A	I	R	S
A	C	E	■	A	C	P	■	■	T	A	Y	■	■	■
M	O	S	E	S	■	■	R	J	R	■	■	A	D	J
■	■	■	M	U	Y	■	O	A	O	■	A	B	R	A
A	H	A	B	■	A	C	A	C	I	A	W	O	O	D
D	A	D	E	■	W	I	N	O	■	D	E	L	V	E
C	B	E	R	■	N	A	S	B	■	M	E	T	E	S

The Company of Apostles (Part 1)

page 53

P	A	U	L	■	■	L	E	V	I	■	S	A	F	T
A	R	P	A	■	K	A	R	O	L	■	O	L	I	O
N	A	T	H	A	N	A	E	L	O	F	C	A	N	A
E	B	O	■	P	E	D	I	S	■	L	I	N	E	D
■	■	■	L	I	L	A	■	■	D	O	A	■	■	■
S	I	M	O	N	T	H	E	Z	E	A	L	O	T	■
A	S	E	A	■	■	■	D	E	F	T	■	W	O	E
U	L	A	N	■	B	R	I	N	G	■	D	E	U	T
L	I	D	■	R	O	A	N	■	■	■	E	G	G	O
■	P	E	T	E	R	J	A	M	E	S	J	O	H	N
■	■	■	A	C	E	■	■	I	D	E	A	■	■	■
S	M	E	L	T	■	N	E	D	D	A	■	A	M	E
P	H	I	L	I	P	A	N	D	A	N	D	R	E	W
C	O	M	E	■	A	N	I	L	S	■	O	B	O	E
A	S	S	Y	■	J	U	D	E	■	■	S	A	W	N

A Bevy of Priests (Part 2)

page 59

■	T	H	O	R	■	R	A	N	G	■	C	H	A	W
■	R	U	D	E	■	A	L	B	A	■	O	E	R	A
■	E	Z	R	A	A	N	D	E	Z	E	K	I	E	L
■	■	■	A	L	L	S	O	■	■	M	E	D	E	S
E	H	R	■	I	V	O	■	A	G	O	■	E	D	H
G	O	O	D	S	A	M	A	R	I	T	A	N	■	■
A	S	S	E	T	■	■	C	O	S	E	C	■	■	■
L	E	A	L	■	A	S	C	O	T	■	R	E	L	S
■	■	■	L	E	V	A	R	■	■	P	A	L	E	A
■	■	N	A	D	A	B	A	N	D	A	B	I	H	U
R	E	O	■	I	S	O	■	O	E	L	■	A	I	L
E	A	T	I	N	■	■	M	A	G	O	O	■	■	■
U	R	I	M	A	N	D	T	H	U	M	M	I	M	■
E	L	O	N	■	B	U	N	G	■	A	A	R	E	■
L	E	N	O	■	A	H	S	O	■	R	O	I	L	■

Speaking of Churches (Part 1)

page 55

A	C	T	S	■	A	P	I	E	■	■	J	E	W	S
G	A	I	T	■	R	A	N	G	A	■	A	Y	E	S
A	T	R	A	■	B	U	R	G	H	■	V	E	E	R
T	H	E	S	S	A	L	O	N	I	C	A	■	■	■
E	S	S	I	E	■	■	■	O	R	O	■	S	T	R
■	■	■	■	T	A	B	■	G	A	L	A	T	I	A
L	A	O	D	I	C	E	A	■	■	D	U	R	E	R
E	R	N	E	■	S	E	R	V	E	■	R	O	T	E
E	D	E	M	A	■	■	P	E	R	G	A	M	O	S
C	O	R	I	N	T	H	■	L	E	I	■	■	■	■
H	R	S	■	A	R	E	■	■	■	R	A	W	L	S
■	■	■	P	H	I	L	A	D	E	L	P	H	I	A
J	O	H	N	■	A	P	E	A	R	■	P	E	N	T
T	R	E	E	■	D	E	A	N	E	■	A	R	E	A
A	T	T	U	■	■	R	O	S	S	■	L	E	A	N

The Company of Apostles (Part 2)

page 61

A	J	A	M	■	A	B	R	A	M	■	A	V	D	P
L	U	L	U	■	G	E	E	N	A	■	N	E	R	I
A	D	I	T	■	H	I	T	O	N	■	D	R	A	G
P	E	T	E	R	A	N	D	A	N	D	R	E	W	■
■	■	■	■	A	S	O	■	■	A	B	E	■	■	■
A	B	O	M	B	■	N	H	L	■	A	W	A	N	A
R	A	H	A	B	S	■	O	L	D	■	■	D	O	M
P	H	I	L	I	P	A	N	D	A	N	D	R	E	W
A	I	O	■	■	T	I	E	■	P	U	R	I	N	A
S	A	S	S	Y	■	N	Y	T	■	R	E	A	D	Y
■	■	■	I	O	U	■	■	H	O	S	■	■	■	■
■	S	I	M	O	N	T	H	E	Z	E	A	L	O	T
B	A	N	E	■	P	I	E	R	Z	■	L	E	H	I
B	U	C	O	■	E	D	R	E	I	■	S	V	E	N
F	L	A	N	■	G	E	E	S	E	■	O	I	L	S

Speaking of Churches (Part 2)

page 63

I	S	A		D	O	W	E	L	S		S	K	I	S
N	I	N		O	L	I	V	I	A		E	L	A	H
S	G	T		H	I	R	A	M	S		R	U	D	Y
P	H	I	L	A	D	E	L	P	H	I	A			
A	T	O	P						A	L	P	A	C	A
C	E	C	I	L		L	A	S		S	H	E	E	N
E	D	H		A	G	A	T	H	A		I	S	A	Y
			J	E	R	U	S	A	L	E	M			
I	C	H	O		P	R	E	L	I	M		C	C	A
K	E	A	N	U		O	A	T		T	R	O	A	S
E	N	G	A	G	E						U	R	N	S
			T	H	E	S	S	A	L	O	N	I	C	A
D	I	S	H		L	A	U	R	A	S		N	E	U
S	O	R	A		E	V	I	N	C	E		T	R	L
C	O	O	N		D	U	T	I	E	S		H	S	T

Miracles of Jesus

page 69

H	E	L	P		S	C	A	L	A		J	O	H	N
I	L	I	E		L	A	M	E	R		E	V	E	N
R	E	N	T		O	N	E	A	T		L	I	F	E
A	N	G	E	L	G	A	B	R	I	E	L			
M	A	O	R	I			A	S	S	D		J	A	I
			S	C	A	M				A	G	E	R	S
A	G	A		E	L	I	J	A	H	M	O	S	E	S
T	H	U	S		A	M	O	L	E		T	U	T	U
M	O	T	H	E	R	I	N	L	A	W		S	E	E
A	S	O	L	D				S	L	A	W			
N	T	S		G	A	R	B			A	I	S	L	E
			R	E	S	U	R	R	E	C	T	I	O	N
F	I	V	E		O	L	E	I	N		H	E	R	D
U	S	E	D		L	E	A	D	S		E	N	C	E
T	R	E	E		O	R	D	I	E		R	A	A	D

Encounters with Angels

page 65

T	W	O		M	A	S	S	I	V	E		M	O	M
O	H	O		E	T	H	A	N	O	L		A	P	A
R	E	P	E	N	T	A	N	T	S	I	N	N	E	R
T	E	S	L		A	N	T			J	E	N	N	Y
			I	I	I			B	W	A	Y			
S	A	M	S	O	N	S		A	A	H		S	C	T
U	T	A	H	N		E	N	L	S		A	W	A	Y
E	L	M	A			R	E	A			B	I	R	L
D	A	B	S		G	A	Z	A		C	A	L	N	E
E	S	O		S	O	P		M	E	D	D	L	E	R
			W	I	T	H			A	R	D			
H	O	T	E	L			H	O	T		O	R	E	S
E	T	H	I	O	P	I	A	N	E	U	N	U	C	H
L	O	I		A	C	T	R	E	S	S		S	R	I
D	E	S		M	A	O	I	S	T	S		H	U	P

Miracles of Paul and Peter

page 71

A	L	G	O	L		S	O	T	S		D	R	A	W
R	E	I	N	E		O	N	E	I		B	O	L	O
E	A	R	T	H	Q	U	A	K	E		A	L	U	M
	F	L	O	R	A		I	O	N	A		E	S	A
			P	E	T	E	R	A	N	D	J	O	H	N
S	E	S		R	A	B			A	N	U			
A	M	O	R		R	O	C	K		A	N	G	E	L
V	I	P	E	R		N	O	H		H	O	R	N	E
E	T	H	N	O		Y	E	A	N		S	E	N	T
			A	M	A			K	I	T		W	A	S
P	A	U	L	A	N	D	S	I	L	A	S			[illegible]
A	D	L		N	Y	R	O		E	I	L	A	T	[illegible]
L	I	N	A		H	O	L	Y	S	P	I	R	I	T
S	E	A	L		O	N	A	N		A	N	I	T	A
Y	U	R	T		W	E	R	E		N	G	A	I	O

Wonders of Elijah and Elisha

page 67

B	A	L	D		A	H	A	B		W	E	B	E	R
A	M	E	S		N	E	B	O		A	D	A	L	E
C	O	N	T	A	I	N	E	R	O	F	S	A	L	T
K	Y	D		L	O	R	D		P	E	E	L	E	D
			A	N	I		C	U	R	L				
B	E	A	R	S			H	O	S	S		T	L	B
A	P	H	I	K		S	O	M	E		A	R	E	O
N	A	A	M	A	N	T	H	E	S	Y	R	I	A	N
A	C	R	E		A	O	U	T		V	O	T	R	E
L	T	D		B	R	I	M			E	D	E	N	S
			C	I	R	C		O	U	T				
R	A	M	A	P	O		E	R	S	T		I	T	I
A	W	I	D	O	W	A	N	D	H	E	R	S	O	N
I	R	K	E	D		B	R	I	E		P	A	R	T
N	Y	E	T	S		A	Y	E	R		M	O	N	O

The Very Devil

page 73

T	S	A	D	E		B	L	E	S	S		H	A	S
E	T	H	E	L		U	I	N	T	A		O	C	T
R	O	A	R	I	N	G	L	I	O	N		W	H	O
	A	B	A	S	E		L	A	C			T	A	L
			T	H	E	W	I	C	K	E	D	O	N	E
R	P	M		A	D	O			S	H	E			
O	A	K	S		S	O	L	D		U	V	E	A	L
W	I	T	C	H		D	A	H		D	I	L	L	Y
A	L	G	A	E		S	E	A	L		L	A	K	E
			R	E	T			B	U	S		L	A	S
A	N	G	E	L	O	F	L	I	G	H	T			[illegible]
L	A	R			N	R	A		E	A	R	L	S	[illegible]
T	H	E		L	Y	I	N	G	S	P	I	R	I	T
O	U	T		S	A	L	E	M		E	T	O	N	S
S	M	A		U	S	E	S	T		S	E	N	S	E

A Gallery of Gods (Part 1) page 75

S	T	A	B		P	H	D				W	I	L	T
N	A	T	R		L	A	I	T	Y		I	S	A	W
A	T	T	Y		A	W	A	K	E		N	A	N	O
T	O	A	N	U	N	K	N	O	W	N	G	O	D	
H	O	R	N	S			A	S	S	E	T			
			E	D	A					B	I	B	L	E
		B	R	A	Z	E	N	S	E	R	P	E	N	T
A	S	E			A	L	E	U	T			E	C	A
T	H	E	G	O	L	D	E	N	C	A	L	F		
S	E	N	O	R					H	U	E			
			L	A	M	E	D			D	A	V	E	Y
	C	H	I	L	D	S	A	C	R	I	F	I	C	E
A	L	I	A		S	E	G	U	E		L	O	O	M
R	I	T	T		E	L	O	R	O		E	L	L	E
K	I	S	H				N	E	S		T	A	E	N

Who Said That? (Part 1) page 81

A	M	O	S		C	H	O	I	R		T	A	C	T
M	A	R	K		H	O	R	S	E		A	B	O	O
P	R	A	I	S	E	Y	E	T	H	E	L	O	R	D
S	T	L		T	E	L	L		O	B	E	Y	E	D
			H	E	R	E		N	B	A	S			
	H	A	I	R	Y		S	O	O	N		S	P	A
S	A	B	L	E		O	K	R	A		A	M	E	R
T	H	E	L	O	R	D	I	S	M	Y	R	O	C	K
E	A	T	S		E	E	E	E		A	L	T	O	S
P	S	S		A	C	T	S		S	H	O	E	S	
			L	I	E	S		C	O	W	S			
G	E	M	I	N	I		B	A	R	E		P	I	A
L	I	F	T	U	P	Y	O	U	R	H	E	A	D	S
I	N	R	E		T	E	R	S	E		S	U	D	S
B	E	S	S		S	T	E	E	L		S	L	O	T

A Gallery of Gods (Part 2) page 77

B	A	A	L			K	A	L		B	F	L	A	T
E	L	B	A		A	O	N	E		R	A	I	N	Y
N	I	B	H	A	Z	A	N	D	T	A	R	T	A	K
	M	A	R	V	E	L	S		E	S	C	A	P	E
				E	L	A		C	X	I	I			
L	A	S	E	R			T	A	I	L		D	D	T
E	T	A	T	S		O	P	E	C		K	A	R	O
T	O	T	H	E	U	N	K	N	O	W	N	G	O	D
B	L	A	S		G	I	E	S		H	O	O	P	A
E	E	N		C	A	N	S			I	X	N	A	Y
			H	O	N	E		R	E	T				
A	C	L	O	U	D		S	E	L	E	C	T	S	
T	H	E	B	R	A	S	S	S	E	R	P	E	N	T
A	I	N	O	S		C	R	A	M		A	L	A	I
P	A	S	S	E		D	S	T			S	A	G	E

What Gets Quoted Most? page 83

C	H	E	N	G		O	M	B		N	U	T	S	O
P	U	P	A	E		H	E	P		U	N	H	A	P
A	T	H	E	N	I	A	N	S		M	Y	E	R	S
				E	C	R	U		B	O	H			
R	O	D	E	S	S	A		E	Z	E	K	I	E	L
A	R	E	L	I			A	M	A	R	E	T	T	O
P	A	U	L	S			D	I	N	S		T	A	U
E	N	T	S		S	I	N	G	E		B	I	G	D
L	G	E		I	O	L	A			T	U	T	E	E
J	E	R	E	M	I	A	H			I	C	E	R	S
E	S	O	T	E	R	Y		S	A	M	O	S	E	T
		N	E	A			M	I	R	O				
A	C	O	R	N		L	E	V	I	T	I	C	U	S
S	O	M	N	I		E	A	A		H	Y	P	E	S
I	S	Y	E	T		O	D	S		Y	E	L	L	S

So Many Versions (Part 1) page 79

S	M	L		F	E	W		C	A	T		B	U	G
H	E	E		I	Z	E		A	B	A		A	R	E
A	R	S		G	R	A	V	L	A	X		A	G	T
D	I	S	C	H	A	R	G	E	B	I	B	L	E	
O	N	E	A	T			A	B	A	C	A			
W	O	R	S	E						A	L	O	E	S
		T	R	E	A	C	L	E	B	I	B	L	E	
E	C	A			E	M	A	I	L			S	I	T
C	H	I	C	A	G	O	B	I	B	L	E			
G	R	A	M	M						A	Z	T	E	C
			D	E	P	T	H			U	R	I	C	H
	M	U	R	D	E	R	E	R	S	B	I	B	L	E
S	O	N		I	N	E	R	T	I	A		I	A	S
H	O	T		U	N	A		E	N	C		A	I	T
E	N	O		M	E	D		S	A	H		E	R	S

Everyday Phrases from the Bible page 85

	C	C	C	C		S	P	O	R		B	Y	T	E
	B	O	O	N		P	A	C	E		O	O	H	S
	A	D	R	O	P	I	N	A	B	U	C	K	E	T
		L	A	S	E	R	S			P	A	U	L	A
A	P	I		S	E	I		V	A	T		M	O	B
G	I	V	E	U	P	T	H	E	G	H	O	S	T	
A	L	E	X	S			A	S	T	E	P			
S	E	R	T		P	S	S	T	S		A	S	A	N
			O	R	L	O	N			A	R	C	H	Y
	H	O	L	I	E	R	T	H	A	N	T	H	O	U
C	U	R		N	A	T		I	B	N		U	H	S
E	M	E	R	G			S	K	E	E	T	S		
S	A	L	T	O	F	T	H	E	E	A	R	T	H	
A	N	S	E		E	I	E	R		L	I	E	U	
R	E	E	S		B	O	A	S		S	O	R	B	

The Old Testament in the New

page 87

L	A	M	B		S	P	I	E	S		D	E	S	I
A	R	E	A		P	U	N	T	A		W	R	E	N
W	I	T	H	A	L	L	T	H	Y	H	E	A	R	T
S	A	E		M	I	L	O			A	L	T	A	R
			S	A	N	S		C	T	R	L			
N	E	S	T	L	E		S	O	R	T		S	B	A
U	N	T	I	E		S	A	M	E		S	A	A	B
D	R	I	N	K	A	N	D	B	E	M	E	R	R	Y
G	O	N	G		H	A	L	S		Y	E	A	R	S
E	L	K		M	A	R	Y		O	L	D	I	E	S
			S	A	B	E		P	R	O	S			
S	T	E	P	S			S	E	I	R		W	A	S
T	H	E	A	C	C	E	P	T	E	D	T	I	M	E
D	A	R	K		R	O	U	E	N		K	N	E	E
S	T	Y	E		I	N	E	R	T		T	E	N	D

Who Said That? (Part 2)

page 89

L	O	I	N	S		B	E	F		S	H	E	E	P
O	N	S	E	T		L	X	I		S	I	L	V	A
V	E	N	G	E	A	N	C	E		T	R	I	A	L
E	S	T	E	R	S		E	L	D			A	D	S
			B	E	H	O	L	D	T	O	O	B	E	Y
S	A	M		O	E	R			S	B	A			
I	G	O	T		S	D	A	K		E	T	H	A	N
T	A	L	E	S		E	R	N		D	H	A	B	I
E	G	Y	P	T		R	E	E	L		S	A	U	L
			E	A	T			L	E	S		S	T	E
I	S	B	E	T	T	E	R	T	H	A	N			
D	A	U			D	S	O		A	D	I	D	A	S
O	R	B	E	D		S	A	C	R	I	F	I	C	E
L	A	B	A	N		A	D	O		S	T	A	T	E
S	H	A	R	D		Y	S	L		M	Y	G	O	D

So Many Versions (Part 2)

page 91

T	O	R	A	H		B	O	W		W	A	T	E	R
A	Z	U	R	E		A	W	E		O	R	A	L	E
H	O	L	Y	B	I	B	L	E		R	E	L	A	P
O	N	E		R	O	E	S		P	S	A	L	M	S
E	E	R		E	L	L		W	A	H				
			T	W	A		M	A	R	I		S	E	C
P	A	T	H	S		S	C	R	I	P	T	U	R	E
E	S	A	U		S	I	G	N	S		H	E	R	D
K	I	N	G	J	A	M	E	S		V	E	R	S	E
E	S	K		E	V	O	E		H	U	E			
				Z	E	N		M	A	L		E	A	M
P	R	A	Y	E	R		B	O	R	G		M	A	O
R	A	H	A	B		T	E	S	T	A	M	E	N	T
A	T	A	L	E		H	E	E		T	A	R	D	E
M	A	B	E	L		E	N	S		E	G	Y	P	T

Beginning at the End

page 93

M	A	N	N	A		M	A	D	A	M		C	W	T
S	T	O	O	P		O	L	O	V	E		O	R	O
S	O	N	G	O	F	S	O	N	G	S		R	O	N
				S	L	E	W			S	M	I	T	E
C	A	P	I	T	A	L		R	E	I	G	N	E	D
U	N	H	O	L	Y		R	E	C	A	S	T		
S	W	I	N	E		B	O	S	C	H		H	I	S
P	A	L	S		R	E	U	E	L		W	I	D	E
S	R	I		B	U	R	N	T		T	W	A	I	N
		P	E	L	T	E	D		R	H	I	N	O	S
B	A	P	T	I	S	T		W	O	E	I	S	M	E
A	S	I	A	N			S	H	A	W				
A	K	A		D	E	U	T	E	R	O	N	O	M	Y
L	E	N		E	N	T	E	R		R	O	D	E	O
S	D	S		D	E	E	R	E		D	R	E	A	M

Between the Testaments (Part 1)

page 95

S	E	N	D		S	W	A	P	S		S	L	I	D
A	R	E	A		A	O	R	T	A		L	A	D	E
W	I	S	D	O	M	O	F	S	O	L	O	M	O	N
N	E	T		R	O	E	S			I	T	A	L	Y
			L	I	A	R		F	A	B	S			
A	S	S	I	G	N		C	O	P	E		O	B	J
S	W	A	M	I		E	R	R	O	R		P	R	E
S	E	C	O	N	D	M	A	C	C	A	B	E	E	S
O	A	K		A	R	I	S	E		L	U	R	E	S
S	T	S		L	O	T	S		T	I	R	A	D	E
			T	S	P	S		L	A	Z	Y			
A	T	A	R	I			W	I	N	E		A	D	O
B	E	L	A	N	D	T	H	E	D	R	A	G	O	N
E	R	A	S		B	O	O	N	E		S	A	M	E
L	A	S	H		S	P	A	S	M		A	G	E	S

Who Said That? (Part 3)

page 97

B	U	S	H		E	N	T	R		A	B	U	S	E
A	S	I	A		N	E	R	O		B	O	N	E	S
L	E	T	T	H	E	D	A	Y	P	E	R	I	S	H
		T	E	A			P	A	N	D	A			
C	R	I		I	V	S		L	I	N		E	P	A
R	O	N		R	I	O	S		N	E	R	V	E	S
Y	O	G	A		N	A	H	A		G	O	E	T	H
			B	O	O	K	O	F	J	O	B			
O	T	T	O	I		S	O	T	O		E	E	L	S
U	N	D	O	N	E		S	E	H	R		M	A	E
I	T	S		T	L	C		R	N	A		E	Y	E
			A	M	O	O	N			M	A	R		
W	H	E	R	E	I	N	I	W	A	S	B	O	R	N
A	M	A	I	N		E	N	O	S		E	D	I	E
D	O	R	D	T		S	E	E	K		L	S	T	S

Between the Testaments (Part 2)

page 99

S	T	A	Y		S	O	R	T	S		V	O	T	E
H	O	M	E		U	B	O	A	T		I	E	R	E
T	H	E	A	N	G	E	L	G	A	B	R	I	E	L
S	U	N		E	A	S	E			O	G	L	E	S
			B	A	R	E		P	E	R	I			
L	A	S	E	R	S		C	O	V	E	N	A	N	T
A	G	O	N	E		F	L	E	E		B	P	O	E
M	I	N	O	R		I	A	M		T	I	L	T	S
P	L	A	T		A	X	I	S		E	R	E	C	T
S	E	R	A	P	H	I	M		F	A	T	A	H	S
			F	E	A	T		E	A	C	H			
S	T	E	R	N			P	E	R	U		M	P	G
T	H	E	A	N	G	E	L	R	A	P	H	A	E	L
D	R	E	I		A	R	A	I	D		A	T	T	A
S	U	E	D		S	I	N	E	S		S	E	E	D

The Lion's Den

page 105

J	O	H	N			F	E	D			A	M	A	J
A	N	T	A		C	I	G	A	R		W	E	G	O
M	M	E	S		I	G	A	V	E		A	D	U	E
B	E	N	A	I	A	H		E	Z	E	K	I	E	L
				N	O	T	T		A	G	E			
F	A	R	A	D		S	H	A		G	N	A	T	S
A	E	O	L	I	A		E	I	O			B	E	A
S	A	U	L	A	N	D	J	O	N	A	T	H	A	N
T	E	E			D	E	E		O	N	H	O	L	D
S	A	S	E	S		F	W	D		G	O	R	S	E
			L	U	I		S	O	N	E				
D	A	N	I	E	L	S		S	O	L	O	M	O	N
U	S	O	S		S	A	T	A	N		P	O	N	E
P	O	O	H		A	D	A	G	E		E	X	E	L
E	R	N	A			D	I	E			C	O	G	S

Some Amazing Animals

page 101

A	V	I	P	E	R			N	A	B	I	S	C	O
R	O	N	A	L	D			E	L	I	C	I	T	S
A	C	A	D	I	A		T	W	O	B	E	A	R	S
M	E	N	U	S			E	T	O					
			A	H	E	R	D	O	F	S	W	I	N	E
E	T	S		A	L	E				N	A	N	A	S
L	E	U	D		W	O	O	D		L	Y	N	C	H
I	S	M	E		A	I	M	E	R		N	O	R	A
J	O	N	A	H		L	I	C	E		E	V	E	R
A	R	E	N	A				A	N	D		A	S	P
H	O	R	S	E	S	O	F	F	I	R	E			
					T	U	B			E	L	I	K	A
C	A	T	A	L	O	G	S		B	A	L	A	A	M
T	W	O	F	I	S	H			A	R	I	G	H	T
S	T	A	R	L	E	T			T	Y	S	O	N	S

Shepherds and Sheep

page 107

O	N	E		D	E	C	E	M		I	S	A	A	C
C	E	L		A	M	I	L	E		C	U	L	P	A
T	W	E	L	V	E	D	I	S	C	I	P	L	E	S
A	S	C	I	I			S	H	O		S	I	D	S
			A	D	N	A		A	I	N				
R	C	C			C	B	A		N	A	B	A	L	
A	H	U	N	D	R	E	D		S	T	E	L	A	E
B	A	B	E	R		L	O	B		E	N	I	D	S
I	S	A	I	A	H		P	A	S	S	O	V	E	R
	E	N	N	I	O		T	A	T			E	S	O
				N	E	E		S	A	H	L			
R	O	S	E		U	N	S			A	P	S	E	S
E	T	H	I	O	P	I	A	N	E	U	N	U	C	H
A	R	E	N	S		A	L	I	E	N		E	C	O
M	O	S	E	S		C	A	P	E	T		S	O	D

Snakes and Other Creepy Things

page 103

A	L	I	B	I		E	M	M	A		S	A	W	S
B	A	S	I	N		L	E	A	R		A	D	A	K
A	T	E	N	S		S	N	A	K	E	B	I	T	E
T	H	E	D	E	V	I	L			C	I	N	C	O
				C	L	E	O		J	O	N	A	H	
	P	R	A	T	T			S	I	N				
F	R	O	G	S		T	H	E	L	O	C	U	S	T
M	O	L	E		B	O	O	A	T		O	S	S	O
S	C	O	R	P	I	O	N	S		U	M	A	S	S
				A	T	L		G	N	A	T	S		
	S	T	Y	N	E		S	P	E	C				
A	T	O	O	T			T	H	E	L	E	E	C	H
N	E	H	U	S	H	T	A	N		E	S	T	E	E
I	N	I	T		I	N	T	O		A	T	A	L	L
M	O	T	H		S	T	E	M		N	O	M	A	D

Biblical Bird Walk

page 109

A	M	O	S		P	R	E	Y		B	L	E	E	D
C	A	R	A		E	I	D	E		R	A	V	E	N
A	C	L	U		E	D	E	S		U	T	I	C	A
T	H	E	L	O	V	E	R	I	N	T	H	E		
				L	E	A		A	U	S				
F	R	I	G	I	D		A	M	A	S		I	A	M
R	A	J	I	V		A	L	E	C		E	D	D	O
A	D	O	V	E	A	N	D	A	P	I	G	E	O	N
N	O	H	E		S	C	U	D		M	O	A	B	S
C	N	N		D	O	E	S		S	A	S	S	E	S
			P	A	N		O	W	L					
		S	O	N	G	O	F	S	O	L	O	M	O	N
O	B	E	L	I		O	L	O	R		D	O	T	O
E	A	G	L	E		G	O	L	D		I	O	T	A
L	Y	S	O	L		A	P	E	S		E	D	O	M

The Lowly Donkey

page 111

M	A	S	S	■	T	R	E	E	■	T	O	R	T	S
I	T	T	O	■	I	A	N	A	■	O	P	A	H	S
S	H	U	N	E	M	I	T	E	■	W	O	M	A	N
A	E	F	■	X	E	N	O	■	S	I	R	S	■	■
I	N	F	L	U	X	■	■	M	A	T	T	H	E	W
M	A	S	E	R	■	■	R	A	M	■	O	O	N	A
■	■	■	A	B	I	G	A	I	L	■	■	R	Y	N
P	A	T	H	■	L	O	R	N	E	■	G	N	A	T
I	C	H	■	■	O	L	E	S	T	R	A	■	■	■
H	A	I	L	■	N	E	R	■	■	E	A	G	L	E
A	B	R	A	H	A	M	■	■	B	A	L	A	A	M
■	■	D	I	E	S	■	H	E	A	D	■	M	V	P
L	I	D	D	Y	■	Z	E	C	H	A	R	I	A	H
A	M	A	T	E	■	P	L	O	T	■	R	E	B	A
M	A	Y	O	R	■	G	I	N	S	■	S	R	O	S

Some Earthquakes

page 117

L	I	C	E	■	S	P	A	R	S	■	A	M	O	S
O	M	E	I	■	S	I	N	A	I	■	V	I	N	E
P	E	N	G	■	G	L	A	S	S	■	I	L	E	A
■	■	T	H	E	T	E	M	P	L	E	V	E	I	L
S	O	U	T	H	■	■	E	Y	E	R	■	R	N	S
H	U	R	■	C	A	C	■	■	R	A	C	■	■	■
A	T	I	■	■	P	A	I	R	■	T	O	S	C	A
F	R	O	M	T	O	P	T	O	B	O	T	T	O	M
T	E	N	O	R	■	S	E	C	O	■	■	E	M	A
■	■	■	D	U	P	■	■	K	A	I	■	A	M	S
S	M	U	■	R	U	T	H	■	■	S	O	D	A	S
W	A	S	T	O	R	N	I	N	H	A	L	F	■	■
E	L	E	E	■	E	O	L	I	A	■	M	A	C	C
P	A	U	L	■	S	T	E	A	L	■	O	S	S	A
T	Y	P	E	■	T	E	N	S	E	■	S	T	A	R

Horses and Horsemen

page 113

I	S	A	A	C	■	A	M	O	S	■	C	A	F	E
L	I	T	H	O	■	N	A	M	E	■	A	D	A	S
■	E	L	I	S	H	A	S	S	E	R	V	A	N	T
■	■	■	■	T	A	N	■	■	■	C	A	N	O	E
Z	E	C	H	A	R	I	A	H	■	A	N	O	N	S
A	R	O	O	■	M	A	N	E	S	■	■	■	■	■
C	R	A	S	H	■	S	A	T	A	N	I	S	T	■
H	O	T	T	U	B	■	■	■	N	A	T	H	A	N
■	L	I	S	T	E	N	E	D	■	H	A	I	T	I
■	■	■	■	■	R	O	N	E	E	■	L	E	A	K
F	A	C	E	D	■	P	A	L	E	H	O	R	S	E
A	L	L	T	O	■	■	■	I	N	A	■	■	■	■
C	L	A	U	D	I	U	S	L	Y	S	I	A	S	■
T	O	R	I	■	I	S	L	A	■	T	E	A	K	S
S	R	A	S	■	M	E	C	H	■	Y	S	A	Y	E

Rivers, Brooks, Lakes, Seas

page 119

F	L	O	O	R	■	S	O	A	K	■	F	L	A	M
R	O	U	T	E	■	I	N	L	A	■	L	A	B	E
O	R	T	H	E	■	G	E	A	R	■	O	K	E	S
S	E	A	O	F	C	H	I	N	N	E	R	E	T	H
T	A	G	■	■	A	T	F	■	A	V	I	A	T	E
Y	L	E	V	E	L	■	■	■	K	E	S	L	E	R
■	■	■	E	X	I	S	T	S	■	■	■	M	R	S
■	S	E	A	O	F	T	I	B	E	R	I	A	S	■
R	E	X	■	■	■	M	A	N	T	O	N	■	■	■
E	N	C	O	D	E	■	■	■	H	I	G	B	E	E
C	A	I	N	A	N	■	C	O	N	■	■	O	N	I
I	T	T	U	R	N	E	D	T	O	B	L	O	O	D
P	O	I	S	■	E	G	E	R	■	A	U	T	R	E
E	R	N	E	■	A	G	F	A	■	S	K	I	E	R
S	S	G	S	■	D	O	G	S	■	F	E	T	E	S

The Biblical Greenhouse

page 115

C	A	S	P	E	R	■	■	■	B	R	A	C	E	D
O	P	T	I	M	U	M	■	E	Y	E	L	A	S	H
T	H	E	P	O	M	E	G	R	A	N	A	T	E	S
T	I	A	S	■	■	M	U	G	■	D	N	H	■	■
A	S	L	■	■	R	E	M	O	■	S	E	E	S	T
■	■	■	S	I	N	N	■	■	■	■	■	R	U	E
S	H	I	P	M	A	T	E	S	■	A	D	I	M	E
C	E	D	A	R	S	O	F	L	E	B	A	N	O	N
A	N	O	D	E	■	S	T	I	L	L	N	E	S	S
N	I	L	■	■	■	■	■	P	A	Y	S	■	■	■
T	E	A	C	H	■	E	L	K	S	■	■	R	E	M
■	■	T	H	A	■	Y	E	N	■	■	G	A	D	I
T	R	E	E	B	A	R	K	O	R	T	W	I	G	S
A	I	R	R	A	C	E	■	T	S	E	T	S	E	S
W	I	S	E	S	T	■	■	■	T	O	W	E	R	S

Builders of Cities

page 121

B	E	K	A	A	■	B	M	T	■	■	A	L	M	S
N	O	A	H	S	■	O	Y	E	S	■	M	A	I	N
D	A	N	A	S	■	O	L	E	O	■	A	N	N	E
■	N	E	B	U	C	H	A	D	N	E	Z	Z	A	R
■	■	■	■	R	O	O	M	■	■	L	E	A	S	T
■	■	■	J	E	R	O	B	O	A	M	■	■	■	■
W	A	S	A	■	■	■	S	O	M	E	■	D	A	S
H	E	R	M	A	N	N	■	S	E	R	V	A	N	T
O	A	S	■	G	A	T	H	■	■	■	I	N	D	O
■	■	■	■	R	E	H	O	B	O	A	M	■	■	■
L	E	A	V	E	■	■	B	A	R	N	■	■	■	■
A	N	C	I	E	N	T	B	A	B	Y	L	O	N	■
L	O	U	S	■	C	A	I	S	■	W	O	M	A	N
A	C	T	I	■	O	R	T	H	■	A	L	A	M	O
W	H	E	T	■	■	E	S	A	■	Y	A	R	E	N

Cities Great and Small (Part 1)

page 123

D	E	E	D		S	H	I	P		A	S	I	A	N
E	L	L	A		H	I	T	E		L	Y	D	D	A
R	I	A	S		I	C	E	R		A	C	B	O	R
B	E	T	H	E	L		A	G	M		H	E	S	A
E	S	H		N	O	T		A	I	D	A			
			T	A	H	O	E		S	A	R	D	I	S
S	I	D	O	N		B	K	F	S	T		I	L	A
N	E	A	R		B	E	R	E	A		N	A	I	N
U	R	N		F	O	D	O	R		M	O	S	E	S
G	I	L	G	A	L		N	A	D	E	R			
			I	T	E	R		L	O	S		A	B	A
M	O	A	B		T	A	N		T	A	R	S	U	S
A	M	B	E	R		M	I	N	H		E	K	E	S
S	O	D	O	M		A	L	E	A		M	E	N	O
C	O	I	N	S		H	E	W	N		I	D	O	S

Palatial Living

page 125

S	T	U	V		J	A	C	O	B		T	I	M	E
T	A	T	I		O	M	A	S	A		H	M	O	S
E	L	A	N		S	E	T	U	P		E	A	V	E
N	E	H	E	M	I	A	H		T	H	A	M	E	S
			Y	U	A	N		T	I	E	R			
S	P	L	A	S	H		H	E	Z	E	K	I	A	H
T	H	E	R	E		P	A	N	E	D		H	R	E
R	I	N	D		T	A	M	E	D		L	A	L	A
O	L	D		S	H	E	E	T		C	O	D	E	D
P	A	L	A	T	I	A	L		S	A	T	A	N	S
			N	O	R	N		D	U	N	S			
S	C	R	I	P	T		P	E	K	A	H	I	A	H
E	D	O	M		E	S	H	E	K		O	M	R	I
A	L	M	A		E	L	O	R	O		M	A	A	R
T	I	E	L		N	O	N	E	T		E	S	N	E

Up Against the Wall

page 127

W	H	A	T			L	C	A		S	H	E	B	A
H	A	L	O		P	A	L	P		H	A	R	A	N
A	R	D	S		E	T	U	I		A	R	O	M	A
M	E	S	H	A	K	I	N	G	O	F	M	O	A	B
			B	A	N	G		T	T	S				
J	E	R	I	C	H	O		P	A	S		S	A	L
E	P	H	O	D			F	O	R		M	A	C	E
T	H	E	N	E	W	J	E	R	U	S	A	L	E	M
T	A	T	E		H	A	D			A	K	I	T	A
A	S	T		A	I	L		S	O	L	O	M	O	N
			I	T	S		R	S	T	U				
U	R	I	A	H	T	H	E	H	I	T	T	I	T	E
P	O	S	S	E		C	L	I	N		A	N	O	N
S	A	T	I	N		J	E	F	E		M	E	R	E
A	M	O	S	S		B	E	T			P	E	E	R

Cities Great and Small (Part 2)

page 129

C	A	N	A			S	C	A	M		A	B	C	
A	R	A	I	L		M	U	S	T		F	O	R	D
R	E	A	D	Y		A	R	I	M	A	T	H	E	A
D	A	M	A	S	C	U	S			S	E	E	T	H
				T	I	G	E		I	S	R	A	E	L
A	S	S	O	R	T			F	O	O				
B	E	K	A	A		J	E	R	U	S	A	L	E	M
A	R	A	T		L	O	T	O	S		S	A	D	I
B	E	T	H	L	E	H	E	M		S	I	D	O	N
				E	E	N			C	I	N	E	M	A
T	R	O	O	P	S		S	T	O	L				
S	E	R	V	E			C	O	L	O	S	S	A	E
C	A	P	E	R	N	A	U	M		A	T	E	S	T
A	T	A	N		B	I	B	B		M	A	N	I	A
	A	H	S		A	L	A	S			S	T	A	T

Wells, Cisterns, and Other Large Containers

page 131

W	E	L	L	S		H	A	N	D		L	I	S	A
A	T	E	S	O		A	P	O	D		E	N	T	S
C	A	N	A	L		R	A	B	S	H	A	K	E	H
O	L	D		O	P	A	L			A	P	L	E	A
				M	U	S		C	I	S	T	E	R	N
C	O	T	T	O	N	S		L	E	T				
U	R	B	A	N			J	E	R	E	M	I	A	H
B	E	A	D		R	O	O	F	S		A	S	I	A
A	B	R	A	H	A	M	S			A	L	A	R	M
				A	R	E		A	D	H	E	R	E	S
S	O	L	D	I	E	R		A	E	I				
T	R	E	A	S			I	C	B	M		A	Y	N
A	B	I	M	E	L	E	C	H		A	R	T	O	O
R	I	C	E		E	L	I	E		A	B	O	U	T
E	T	A	S		B	E	E	N		Z	I	M	R	I

Gates, Doors, and Other Openings

page 133

M	A	H	A	L		S	E	A		I	S	O	U	R
I	G	O	T	A		A	N	D		T	E	R	R	A
S	H	E	E	P	G	A	T	E		S	E	T	I	N
C	A	R	U	S	O		E	L	O			H	A	O
			P	E	T	E	R	A	N	D	J	O	H	N
J	O	B		S	I	N			E	O	E			
A	S	I	A		T	O	O	K		E	S	A	U	S
C	H	E	N	G		C	P	R		S	U	M	M	A
K	A	N	G	A		H	A	U	S		S	O	P	S
			E	Z	E			P	I	Z		I	H	S
P	H	I	L	A	D	E	L	P	H	I	A			
E	O	S			S	N	O		O	L	D	E	S	T
A	S	H	E	R		D	O	O	R	P	O	S	T	S
R	E	A	D	D		O	R	U		A	P	E	A	K
L	A	M	B	S		R	A	T		H	E	R	D	S

Portable Places to Dwell

page 135

A	R	A	■	P	L	O	■	G	S	A	■	S	S	A
R	I	P	■	A	E	R	■	O	H	S	■	A	A	R
K	O	P	■	R	U	F	F	L	E	S	■	U	L	M
■	■	A	C	A	K	E	O	F	B	A	R	L	E	Y
A	L	L	A	N	■	■	R	E	A	I	A	■	■	■
R	I	A	L	■	U	S	E	R	■	■	A	M	U	■
E	F	C	■	A	S	I	F	■	■	I	M	O	N	■
■	T	H	E	S	A	M	A	R	I	T	A	N	S	■
■	E	I	R	E	■	■	T	E	N	T	■	T	A	D
■	D	A	N	■	■	A	H	S	O	■	L	I	F	O
■	■	■	S	C	A	L	E	■	■	A	L	C	E	E
T	H	E	T	A	B	E	R	N	A	C	L	E	■	■
H	A	D	■	C	A	U	S	E	T	H	■	L	A	T
E	K	E	■	A	T	T	■	G	O	A	■	L	T	S
M	E	N	■	O	E	S	■	S	I	N	■	O	A	K

Makers of Music

page 137

P	O	E	T	■	O	R	G	A	N	■	H	A	R	P
A	U	T	H	■	R	O	U	T	E	■	O	L	E	O
C	Z	A	R	■	S	O	N	I	A	■	L	A	I	N
S	O	L	O	M	O	N	■	P	L	A	Y	I	N	G
■	■	■	N	O	N	E	D	■	E	R	O	■	■	■
■	S	H	E	D	■	Y	U	M	■	K	I	N	G	S
L	O	O	S	E	R	■	B	A	T	■	L	A	L	O
O	W	N	■	L	E	V	I	T	E	S	■	O	O	O
R	E	E	S	■	D	O	O	■	N	E	T	M	A	N
D	R	Y	A	S	■	N	U	M	■	I	H	I	T	■
■	■	■	B	E	F	■	S	E	N	S	E	■	■	■
C	Y	M	B	A	L	S	■	T	I	M	B	R	E	L
L	E	I	A	■	A	T	H	I	N	■	O	I	L	Y
E	A	S	T	■	P	L	A	N	E	■	O	M	A	R
O	R	T	H	■	S	O	N	G	S	■	K	A	T	E

Artsy, Craftsy Types

page 139

B	A	R	N	A	■	S	H	I	P	■	G	O	I	T
U	R	I	A	H	■	T	A	R	A	■	E	L	L	A
L	I	T	H	O	■	A	L	E	X	A	N	D	E	R
B	E	Z	A	L	E	E	L	■	■	B	R	E	A	D
■	■	■	■	I	L	L	■	C	A	D	E	N	C	E
G	R	A	H	A	M	■	H	U	M	E	■	■	■	■
R	E	D	U	B	■	T	U	B	A	L	C	A	I	N
A	N	A	G	■	A	R	M	E	D	■	O	C	T	O
D	E	M	E	T	R	I	U	S	■	E	R	R	E	D
■	■	■	■	R	A	P	S	■	M	A	K	E	R	S
N	U	M	B	E	R	S	■	I	E	R	■	■	■	■
A	N	A	I	S	■	■	E	N	G	R	A	V	E	R
G	O	L	D	S	M	I	T	H	■	I	R	A	T	E
E	N	T	E	■	C	O	C	O	■	N	E	M	E	A
L	A	S	S	■	A	C	H	T	■	G	A	P	E	R

Glad Rags

page 141

S	A	U	L	■	■	S	O	W	S	■	C	A	R	D
E	A	S	E	■	M	I	D	I	S	■	A	S	H	E
P	R	I	N	C	E	S	O	F	T	H	E	S	E	A
I	O	N	■	A	N	T	R	E	■	E	S	T	E	R
A	N	G	■	T	S	E	■	■	S	R	A	■	■	■
■	■	■	P	H	A	R	A	O	H	S	R	I	N	G
R	O	B	E	S	■	■	G	R	O	■	■	B	A	A
A	H	A	S	■	S	N	A	K	E	■	R	A	G	S
S	I	L	■	■	E	H	I	■	■	H	A	R	S	H
P	O	M	E	G	R	A	N	A	T	E	S	■	■	■
■	■	■	L	A	B	■	■	N	E	A	■	L	I	D
A	S	I	D	E	■	A	R	O	A	R	■	I	L	E
C	A	M	E	L	S	H	A	I	R	T	U	N	I	C
T	S	A	R	■	S	I	G	N	S	■	S	E	A	R
S	E	N	S	■	R	O	U	T	■	■	A	N	D	Y

So Many Children

page 143

A	H	A	B	■	C	A	S	A	■	A	T	P	A	R
D	A	B	O	■	A	N	E	R	■	S	H	A	R	I
A	R	O	N	■	N	O	T	E	■	L	O	U	I	S
S	T	O	N	E	D	■	H	E	D	■	M	L	L	E
H	E	N	■	L	O	C	■	L	I	T	A	■	■	■
■	■	■	C	A	R	A	T	■	J	O	S	E	P	H
A	B	D	O	N	■	N	A	B	O	B	■	F	A	A
B	A	I	N	■	H	E	M	A	N	■	J	O	S	H
I	N	S	■	D	A	D	A	S	■	A	A	R	O	N
E	S	T	H	E	R	■	R	E	A	R	S	■	■	■
■	■	■	A	M	O	S	■	D	L	I	■	C	R	C
T	E	R	N	■	D	A	L	■	I	S	A	I	A	H
A	S	O	N	E	■	D	U	C	E	■	J	A	I	R
N	A	T	A	L	■	I	K	O	N	■	A	N	T	I
S	U	S	H	I	■	E	E	G	S	■	M	O	T	S

Food, Food, Food

page 145

B	L	O	T	■	■	B	A	L	S	A	■	O	F	F
L	I	M	O	S	■	C	L	E	A	R	■	C	O	O
A	F	A	T	T	E	D	C	A	L	F	■	E	R	R
H	E	R	E	O	F	■	O	R	A	■	■	A	C	T
■	■	■	M	I	L	K	A	N	D	H	O	N	E	Y
P	I	G	■	C	A	N	■	■	S	A	W	■	■	■
A	D	A	M	■	T	O	S	S	■	I	N	D	I	A
P	L	I	E	S	■	W	O	E	■	R	E	E	D	S
P	E	T	R	A	■	S	O	D	A	■	R	A	D	S
■	■	■	A	I	R	■	■	E	M	C	■	L	O	T
E	D	I	B	L	E	S	C	R	O	L	L	■	■	■
T	I	S	■	■	U	N	O	■	C	E	A	S	E	S
A	D	A	■	A	B	O	W	L	O	F	S	O	U	P
P	S	A	■	B	E	R	E	A	■	S	T	O	R	E
E	T	C	■	E	N	T	R	Y	■	■	S	N	O	W

Fasts and Breaking of Fasts (Part 1)

page 147

S	T	E	W			S	C	A	D		T	O	A	D
A	R	C	O		W	H	O	S	E		R	O	A	R
N	E	H	E	M	I	A	H	A	N	D	E	Z	R	A
D	E	O		A	F	R	O			I	N	E	P	T
			F	R	E	D		T	I	E	D			
S	P	L	I	T			B	U	N	T		T	S	R
E	L	A	T	H		A	I	N	T		L	U	N	I
P	A	U	L	A	N	D	B	A	R	N	A	B	A	S
T	I	D	Y		E	E	L	S		A	W	A	R	E
S	T	E		C	A	P	E			U	N	S	E	R
			P	A	R	T		B	E	S	S			
E	D	M	A	N			A	L	O	E		T	B	A
S	A	U	L	A	N	D	J	O	N	A	T	H	A	N
A	B	L	E		B	E	A	N	S		R	A	N	T
U	S	E	D		C	U	R	D			W	I	N	E

Spreading a Feast

page 149

S	L	I	D		S	T	U	N	T		J	A	M	B
W	A	D	I		L	O	N	E	R		O	R	A	L
A	M	Y	S	T	E	R	I	O	U	S	H	A	N	D
M	A	L	T	R	E	A	T		M	I	N	D	E	R
			O	A	T	H		O	P	T	S			
S	C	U	R	V	Y		R	H	E	E		S	H	E
T	O	R	T	E		S	E	A	T		E	N	O	S
A	N	G	E	L	I	C	V	I	S	I	T	O	R	S
R	E	E	D		D	O	E	R		D	I	O	D	E
S	S	S		B	O	W	L		G	E	O	D	E	S
			L	O	L	L		C	O	A	L			
C	E	T	E	R	A		P	A	R	L	A	N	C	E
A	G	R	E	A	T	W	I	N	D	S	T	O	R	M
N	O	O	K		R	O	M	E	O		E	S	A	U
A	N	T	S		Y	E	A	R	N		S	E	W	S

Fasts and Breaking of Fasts (Part 2)

page 151

L	O	S	S		W	I	S	H		H	A	G	U	E
I	T	C	H		I	C	K	Y		A	D	O	R	N
F	O	R	T	Y	D	A	Y	S		V	I	A	N	D
T	O	O		A	O	N	E		P	O	E	T		
E	L	L		N	W	T		L	O	C	U	S	T	S
D	E	L	O	N			M	A	I		S	K	A	T
			D	I	S	C	E	R	N			I	R	E
C	A	K	E		P	L	E	A	T		S	N	O	W
A	R	E			O	A	T	M	E	A	L			
L	E	Y	S		O	N	S			R	A	B	B	I
F	A	S	T	I	N	G		T	E	M		E	R	S
		T	O	S	S		S	O	M	E		G	O	O
A	T	O	L	L		U	P	P	E	R	R	O	O	M
D	O	N	E	E		S	U	E	R		O	N	C	E
O	M	E	N	S		E	D	D	Y		W	E	H	R

Fruit of the Vine

page 153

A	C	O	W		C	A	F	F	E		R	D	A	S
A	L	G	A		A	C	O	R	N		E	R	L	E
H	O	L	Y	S	P	I	R	I	T		P	A	L	E
S	T	E	W	A	R	D			E	S	H	B	A	N
			A	S	A		S	E	R	T	A			
M	Y	R	R	H		C	H	A		R	I	C	A	
A	M	A	D		T	H	E	S	T	O	M	A	C	H
L	C	I		A	Z	A	R	I	A	H		R	A	I
L	A	S	T	S	U	P	P	E	R		R	E	S	T
	S	A	I	S		E	A	R		T	A	T	E	S
			M	A	I	L	S		B	U	M			
C	H	L	O	R	O			S	U	R	P	A	S	S
H	A	I	T		T	A	B	E	R	N	A	C	L	E
U	H	O	H		A	P	R	E	S		G	E	O	G
M	A	N	Y		S	T	A	R	T		E	R	E	S

Fasts and Breaking of Fasts (Part 3)

page 155

S	A	U	L		L	A	M	B		J	O	N	A	H
P	E	S	O		I	D	E	O		U	N	A	G	I
E	R	E	I		L	M	N	O		M	A	T	E	S
C	O	R	N	E	L	I	U	S		B	I	R	D	S
				L	I	N			H	O	R			
A	S	F	R	E	E		T	R	E	S		D	A	Y
P	E	R	O	N		H	O	E	R		D	O	L	E
P	A	U	L	A	N	D	B	A	R	N	A	B	A	S
A	T	I	E		A	W	E	D		I	M	I	N	E
L	O	T		D	I	E	D		A	G	N	E	S	S
			S	I	N			A	T	H				
M	O	S	E	S		J	O	N	A	T	H	A	N	S
E	A	T	E	N		E	C	G	S		A	C	E	A
S	T	A	T	E		W	H	E	T		L	S	T	S
O	H	B	O	Y		S	O	L	E		F	I	S	H

Seven Suicides

page 157

W	A	R		J	A	M	A			Z	I	M	R	I
E	C	U		O	M	A	N		L	I	V	E	I	N
B	A	R	N	A	B	A	S		E	L	A	P	S	E
			A	B	I	M	E	L	E	C	H			
S	A	U	L	S				H	R	H		F	T	C
A	N	N	A		W	H	I	T	E		S	A	U	L
G	O	D		N	O	A	M			G	W	I	N	E
		A	R	M	O	R	B	E	A	R	E	R		
A	S	T	A	R			E	L	L	S		L	E	V
H	I	E	L		J	U	D	A	S		H	E	M	A
H	E	D		S	O	L				D	O	E	S	T
			A	H	I	T	O	P	H	E	L			
S	A	M	S	O	N		P	I	C	A	Y	U	N	E
S	P	R	A	T	S		E	C	H	T		S	I	B
H	E	E	D	S			R	O	S	H		G	E	N

People Getting Stoned
page 159

J	O	H	N		I	P	S	E		L	Y	S	I	N
O	P	I	A		T	O	T	E		Y	U	C	C	A
L	A	D	S		U	N	E	S		S	L	O	O	P
T	H	E	L	O	R	D	S		M	T	E	T	N	A
				V	B	S		A	A	R	E			
S	H	I	M	E	I		U	C	L	A		W	S	W
H	O	N	E	R		E	P	H	A		P	E	T	A
P	A	U	L	A	N	D	B	A	R	N	A	B	A	S
M	G	R	S		A	G	O	N		Y	R	E	K	A
T	Y	E		V	I	E	W		C	L	A	R	E	T
			K	I	S	S		A	L	O				
N	A	B	O	T	H		A	D	O	N	I	R	A	M
A	R	U	B	A		A	L	D	A		L	I	M	A
S	E	O	U	L		F	L	A	K		A	P	E	G
H	E	N	K	E		B	E	N	S		I	S	S	O

All of These Diseases
page 161

A	S	H	E	S		T	U	B	A		A	H	A	B
S	O	A	M	I		E	Z	E	R		L	E	G	S
A	L	L	E	N		N	I	N	A		T	Y	R	E
P	A	I	N	F	U	L	S	O	R	E	S			
			D	U	N	E		B	A	R		C	P	A
J	O	B		L	I	P	O		T	U	M	O	R	S
A	P	I	T		O	E	T	C		P	U	N	I	C
L	E	D	U	C		R	O	A		T	O	R	S	O
O	N	E	N	O		S	E	P	S		N	A	S	T
P	E	T	E	R	S		S	E	K	O		D	Y	S
Y	D	S		F	O	E		R	A	N	A			
			R	U	N	N	I	N	G	S	O	R	E	S
E	S	A	U		A	T	M	A		E	N	A	T	E
L	I	O	N		T	O	L	U		T	I	N	A	S
S	P	A	T		A	M	A	M		S	A	D	H	E

A Time to Weep
page 163

S	A	R	A		I	N	G	O	D		T	O	P	O
A	N	E	W		S	I	S	S	Y		R	O	H	E
H	E	H	E	A	R	D	T	H	E	W	A	L	L	S
I	T	A	S	C	A					A	N	A	M	E
B	O	N		R	E	D	F	L	A	G	S			
			B	I	L	D	A	D	Z	O	P	H	A	R
	W	A	R	D		E	D	S	O	N		E	M	A
F	A	L	A								I	M	I	N
A	L	B		E	R	M	A	S		O	R	O	S	
S	T	I	L	L	I	N	R	U	I	N	S			
			A	D	V	O	C	A	T	E		N	A	G
R	I	O	D	E					S	A	S	E	B	O
O	F	J	E	R	U	S	A	L	E	M	W	E	R	E
P	A	A	R		S	P	O	I	L		A	D	A	R
A	T	I	S		C	C	L	E	F		B	I	C	S

Rending the Garments
page 165

J	A	C	O	B		W	A	R	E		S	K	I	L
E	C	L	A	T		O	D	A	S		H	I	L	A
T	H	E	B	O	O	K	O	F	T	H	E	L	A	W
S	Y	M			U	S	G			A	L	L	Y	N
			F	C	C			O	C	R	A			
J	O	S	E	P	H	S	B	R	O	T	H	E	R	S
A	G	N	U	S		W	E	E	D	S		S	O	C
L	E	A	D		D	O	N	A	S		I	T	O	O
A	M	F		M	Y	R	O	N		A	V	A	S	T
P	A	U	L	A	N	D	B	A	R	N	A	B	A	S
			E	N	E	S			U	S	N			
P	L	A	C	E			H	E	H			A	I	S
H	I	S	T	H	R	E	E	F	R	I	E	N	D	S
A	M	I	E		E	V	A	C		U	D	D	E	R
T	E	T	R		C	A	P	A		D	E	R	N	S

Grave Matters
page 167

C	T	N	S		P	L	O	P		A	F	R	O	S
H	O	O	P		I	U	K	A		B	L	A	D	E
E	L	I	A		L	I	E	B		N	I	C	A	D
M	A	R	Y	M	A	G	D	A	L	E	N	E		
				A	T	I			A	R	T			
C	H	A	S	T	E		P	A	R	S		P	A	M
H	O	S	N	I		M	A	M	E		E	L	B	A
I	S	A	A	C	A	N	D	I	S	H	M	A	E	L
R	E	P	P		L	O	R	D		A	T	I	L	T
P	A	H		T	O	P	E		J	U	S	T	L	Y
			P	R	O			O	O	P				
		H	E	A	P	S	O	F	S	T	O	N	E	S
A	M	A	T	I		O	D	A	H		M	O	T	A
R	A	V	E	L		P	E	R	U		R	G	T	S
M	Y	E	R	S		O	R	C	A		I	S	A	K

Killed by the Beasts
page 169

E	L	I	S	H	A		T	E	K		L	I	O	N
F	E	L	L	E	R		E	L	U		E	C	U	A
S	C	L	E	R	A		S	E	R		R	A	T	S
	H	E	R	E	F	U	S	E	D	T	O	H	I	T
				S	A	P				T	I	N	N	Y
A	B	B	O	T	T		A	X	E	L				
P	R	O	V	O		O	L	E	O		A	M	F	M
S	A	N	E		S	T	I	R	S		R	U	L	A
O	T	O	N		S	H	O	O		T	U	T	O	R
				A	D	E	N		D	A	N	I	E	L
B	O	R	I	C				H	O	D				
A	N	O	T	H	E	R	P	R	O	P	H	E	T	
D	E	L	A		S	C	E		D	O	O	B	I	E
G	A	L	L		C	A	R		A	L	T	E	R	S
E	L	A	L		E	F	F		D	E	E	D	E	D

Not to Be Taken Seriously (Part I)

page 171

H	A	S	P		P	O	P	E		S	C	A	R	S
A	R	E	A		I	C	E	D		T	A	R	O	T
H	A	I	R		L	O	R	E		E	L	A	T	E
A	B	R	A	H	A	M	K	N	E	W	A	L	O	T
			D	A	T	E			P	S	I			
A	D	M	I	R	E		J	U	S		S	H	E	M
G	R	A	S	P		S	O	S	O			O	V	O
N	O	N	E	O	F	T	H	E	M	H	A	S	I	S
E	N	G			L	A	N	D		O	U	N	C	E
S	E	E	S		E	N	S		A	U	D	I	T	S
			A	T	E			S	U	S	A			
A	D	A	M	S	T	O	L	E	S	E	C	O	N	D
S	O	U	S	A		F	E	L	T		I	D	L	E
A	S	T	O	R		F	A	M	E		T	O	R	C
P	E	O	N	S		S	P	A	N		Y	R	B	K

Across the Biblical Spectrum

page 173

A	J	O	Y		B	L	A	C	K		S	L	A	P
C	O	R	A		R	A	N	T	O		P	U	R	I
D	E	B	O	R	A	H	A	N	D	B	A	R	A	K
C	L	E		A	I	R	S			L	I	E	G	E
			U	R	N	S		F	A	U	N			
S	W	I	P	E			M	A	R	E		J	C	P
T	H	A	T	S		P	O	L	A		B	E	L	A
R	I	G	H	T	E	O	U	S	P	E	R	S	O	N
O	T	O	E		T	I	N	E		N	A	U	T	S
P	E	S		P	A	N	T			C	U	S	H	Y
			L	I	L	T		L	A	O	N			
A	S	L	A	N			B	I	G	D		J	O	E
T	H	E	D	A	Y	O	F	T	H	E	L	O	R	D
E	A	R	L		U	M	B	R	A		O	H	N	O
N	Y	S	E		G	A	S	E	S		O	N	A	M

Going to Extremes (Part I)

page 175

H	O	W	L		Y	O	G	I	C		P	A	I	R
A	L	E	A		O	C	A	L	A		A	C	R	E
D	E	A	D		U	T	T	E	R		T	H	I	S
J	O	R	D	A	N		E	A	R	L	I	E	S	T
			E	C	G			C	E	E	E			
S	H	O	R	T	E	S	T		L	O	N	G	E	R
L	A	N		O	S	A	Y			S	T	O	L	E
A	V	A	L		T	W	I	G	S		S	U	M	P
T	R	I	O	S			N	O	E	L		G	O	O
S	E	R	V	E	D		G	R	E	A	T	E	S	T
			E	L	E	A			S	K	I			
S	M	A	L	L	E	S	T		T	E	N	N	I	S
C	A	M	E		P	H	I	L	A		D	I	C	E
I	D	O	S		L	O	N	E	R		E	L	A	N
S	E	S	S		Y	E	A	R	S		R	E	N	T

Hugs and Kisses

page 177

J	A	I	L		P	A	U	L		I	S	A	A	C
E	N	D	A		I	T	S	A		R	I	N	G	A
T	N	U	T		T	E	A	R		O	D	E	O	N
H	O	M	E	O	F	S	I	M	O	N		N	G	S
R	Y	E		N	A	T	R		D	O	T	E		
O	S	A		I	L	S		L	I	N	E	M	A	N
			B	O	L		G	E	N		N	Y	P	D
D	I	J	O	N		D	A	T		H	O	S	E	A
P	R	O	A		T	O	G		A	O	R			
T	E	N	T	P	E	G		A	B	M		J	C	S
		A	S	E	S		A	S	S	E		O	H	T
G	A	T		T	H	E	P	H	A	R	I	S	E	E
O	T	H	E	R		V	A	I	L		N	E	E	R
A	M	A	S	A		E	L	M	O		A	P	S	E
T	O	N	G	S		S	E	A	M		T	H	E	O

Foot Coverings

page 179

	T	H	E		A	M	O	S		H	U	T	C	H
P	E	E	N		D	I	R	T		A	B	R	A	M
E	T	T	U		A	G	N	I		I	S	L	A	M
T	H	E	F	A	T	H	E	R	O	F				
R	E	R		W	E	T			L	A	J	A	R	A
O	R	O	N	O		Y	O	N	D		O	R	A	D
			A	K	O		L	A	E		S	L	Y	E
T	H	E	H	E	B	R	E	W	S	S	H	O	E	S
B	I	D	A		E	A	I		T	H	U			
A	T	O	R		Y	U	C	K		A	A	R	G	H
S	A	M	I	T	E			A	I	N		I	L	U
				P	R	O	D	I	G	A	L	S	O	N
P	R	I	C	K		T	I	S	O		T	E	A	C
G	E	O	D	E		O	N	E	R		R	U	T	H
M	O	S	E	S		S	T	R	S		S	P	S	

Stones, Rolling and Nonrolling

page 181

G	A	S	P		A	J	U	G	A		J	O	H	N
O	A	H	U		G	O	R	E	S		O	B	E	Y
D	U	O	S		A	S	I	A	S		S	I	N	E
		T	H	E	P	H	A	R	I	S	E	E	S	
				R	E	U		N	A	P				
S	A	U	R	O		A	O	K		C	H	A	F	E
A	S	S	I	S	I		B	O	O			D	I	X
T	H	E	N	E	W	J	E	R	U	S	A	L	E	M
A	B	R			O	C	A		S	T	R	A	F	E
N	Y	S	S	A		C	H	E		A	G	I	S	T
			C	M	D			D	I	I				
	T	H	E	S	A	N	H	E	D	R	I	N		
I	R	A	N		V	E	E	R	Y		Z	U	L	U
R	A	M	E		I	N	A	L	L		O	L	A	F
A	D	M	I		D	A	R	E	S		D	L	I	T

Going to Extremes (Part 2) page 183

Z	I	M	R	I		W	A	N	G		L	U	K	E
I	S	A	I	D		I	C	A	L		U	V	E	A
L	O	R	D	S	A	V	E	M	E		E	A	R	N
C	L	A	D		P	E	D		N	E	G			
H	A	T		Y	R	S		J	E	H	O	A	S	H
			K	E	A			A	W	S		L	C	I
S	I	B	Y	L		A	B	B	E		O	L	A	V
P	S	A	L	M	O	N	E	O	N	E	N	I	N	E
O	I	S	E		B	E	I	T		L	E	E	D	S
R	A	Y		A	L	N			L	E	G			
T	H	E	G	N	A	T		W	A	M		S	H	S
			E	N	T		A	H	I		A	H	A	T
Y	M	C	A		I	M	M	A	C	U	L	A	T	E
M	O	O	R		O	R	A	L		S	A	D	I	E
A	L	B	S		N	A	T	E		G	W	Y	N	N

Not to Be Taken Seriously (Part 2) page 189

P	A	I	R		F	R	A	M	E		P	L	A	Y
R	A	L	E		R	U	N	I	N		H	O	M	E
E	A	R	P		E	N	A	C	T		A	V	O	N
P	L	E	A	S	E		T	H	E	P	R	E	S	S
			S	A	W			A	R	C	A			
F	A	S	T	D	A	Y	S		S	T	O	O	P	S
A	C	K			Y	E	T			S	H	L	E	P
T	R	I	B		S	H	R	E	W		S	I	T	U
H	E	R	A	S			A	R	I			V	E	D
A	S	T	R	I	D		P	I	T	C	H	E	R	S
			E	K	E	D			H	O	O			
A	R	U	S	H	J	O	B		T	E	M	P	L	E
T	A	L	K		E	B	O	L	I		E	R	O	S
E	S	A	I		C	I	T	E	D		R	I	B	S
S	H	I	N		T	E	H	E	E		S	M	E	E

Boats and Other Floating Things page 185

M	A	P	L	E		P	A	C	T		F	L	E	E
A	L	L	U	P		A	Z	O	R		A	T	R	Y
K	I	N	G	H	I	R	A	M	O	F	T	Y	R	E
E	I	S		E	B	E	N		P	A	A	R	S	
			A	S	E				I	L	H			
P	O	L	L	U	X	A	N	D	C	A	S	T	O	R
O	R	E	O	S		F	O	R	S			R	U	E
T	A	M	E			I	T	E			N	O	T	S
O	N	A			P	S	S	S		L	A	T	T	E
K	I	N	G	J	E	H	O	S	H	A	P	H	A	T
			R	O	D				E	N	A			
	S	T	A	I	D		G	A	R	Y		M	F	R
D	A	N	I	E	L	A	N	D	B	A	L	A	A	M
C	A	P	N		E	G	A	D		R	E	Z	I	N
I	R	K	S		S	O	W	N		D	O	O	R	S

A Sign unto You (Part 1) page 191

E	G	Y	P	T		M	A	D	D		C	A	L	C
L	O	U	I	E		I	S	I	S		A	L	I	E
C	O	L	E	S		T	H	E	M	A	N	G	E	R
I	D	E			D	R	U	G		D	A	U	N	T
D	E	S	C		J	E	R	O	B	O	A	M		
			A	B	S				A	R	N			
R	I	S	K	S		B	A	H	R			D	U	B
U	N	L	E	A	V	E	N	E	D	B	R	E	A	D
T	I	R			I	S	T	S		B	O	W	L	S
			T	P	N				P	C	P			
		J	E	R	E	M	I	A	H		E	S	E	K
S	T	E	N	O		O	B	S	T			E	D	Y
G	R	E	A	T	F	I	S	H		L	I	V	I	A
T	O	R	N		F	R	E	E		W	R	E	C	K
S	Y	S	T		F	A	N	S		M	I	N	T	S

As a Reminder page 187

P	S	S	T		P	A	S	T	A		S	L	U	R
A	T	O	W		A	R	E	A	R		H	I	S	T
R	A	L	E		R	O	U	S	T		E	R	S	E
T	H	E	L	O	R	D	S	S	U	P	P	E	R	
S	L	A	V	S		I	S	E	R	E				
			E	O	N					D	R	I	P	S
W	P	A			T	H	E	R	A	I	N	B	O	W
I	O	L	E		S	O	D	A	S		S	E	L	A
T	H	E	S	A	B	B	A	T	H			T	O	P
S	L	E	P	T					E	S	E			
				T	A	R	A	S		O	S	H	E	A
	J	E	S	U	S	E	M	P	T	Y	T	O	M	B
C	O	C	A		C	U	E	R	O		H	O	M	O
L	U	F	T		O	S	S	I	E		E	K	E	D
I	R	A	S		T	E	S	T	S		R	Y	N	E

The Bible on Screen (Part 1) page 193

O	M	E	N		S	A	U	N	A		M	I	G	S
N	O	D	E		E	P	S	O	M		S	O	R	T
E	R	N	E	S	T	H	E	M	I	N	G	W	A	Y
S	E	A		I	T	I	S			E	R	A	S	E
			B	L	E	D		A	P	E				
S	L	E	E	V	E		H	A	R	D		B	C	H
M	E	R	G	E		A	E	R	O		S	I	L	O
E	D	W	A	R	D	G	R	O	B	I	N	S	O	N
A	G	I	N		I	R	O	N		N	O	O	N	E
R	E	N		F	E	E	D		S	K	U	N	K	S
				U	S	E		S	P	I	T			
A	T	O	N	E			S	O	O	N		S	C	I
C	H	A	R	L	E	S	L	A	U	G	H	T	O	N
T	O	R	T		N	O	O	K	S		M	A	L	T
S	U	S	A		D	O	W	S	E		S	T	A	R

A Few Bits of Potpourri
page 195

H	E	R	A		S	E	R	R	A		K	N	I	T
A	L	I	T		I	M	E	A	N		N	A	Z	I
D	I	C	H		G	I	S	T	S		O	B	A	N
J	O	H	A	N	N	G	U	T	E	N	B	E	R	G
			N	O	S		M	A	L	O				
A	C	C	A	D		P	E	N		T	R	A	L	A
B	O	D	S		Q	T	S		O	M	E	G	A	S
A	N	X	I	O	U	S		T	H	E	E	A	S	T
C	O	L	U	S	A		A	R	M		D	R	E	I
I	R	I	S	H		I	R	A		A	S	S	A	R
				E	L	I	M		O	P	T			
T	H	O	M	A	S	J	E	F	F	E	R	S	O	N
W	U	S	A		A	O	N	I	A		I	A	T	E
A	S	T	R		T	H	I	N	G		P	R	I	E
S	H	E	K		S	N	A	K	E		S	I	S	S

The Bible on Screen (Part 2)
page 199

S	T	A	R		L	I	M	E	S		A	R	M	S
T	A	P	E		I	C	A	N	T		C	A	S	A
A	L	A	S		O	U	I	D	A		A	V	E	R
S	C	R	E	E	N		M	O	B	Y	D	I	C	K
			R	A	S			W	A	V	E			
Q	U	O	V	A	D	I	S		T	E	M	P	L	E
A	T	I	E		E	D	T			S	Y	R	I	A
T	E	L			N	O	I	S	E			O	B	S
A	R	E	T	E			N	O	N		O	S	E	E
R	O	D	H	A	M		G	O	D	S	P	E	L	L
			E	S	T	A			T	O	E			
E	V	E	R	T	O	L	D		I	N	N	I	N	G
N	E	B	O		S	P	A	S	M		I	D	O	L
G	R	A	B		S	E	D	G	E		N	E	R	O
R	O	L	E		A	S	S	T	S		G	A	M	P

A Sign unto You (Part 2)
page 197

A	D	A	M	S		N	A	I	L		R	G	T	S
S	A	M	O	A		I	B	R	I		I	R	A	E
P	R	I	A	M		G	R	I	M		T	A	M	A
	N	E	B	U	C	H	A	D	N	E	Z	Z	A	R
				E	S	T	H			A	Y	E	R	S
M	O	B	I	L	E		A	V	I	S				
A	T	E	S				M	I	S	E		A	P	S
P	H	A	R	A	O	H		S	O	L	O	M	O	N
S	E	R		C	L	A	M				T	I	K	E
				R	E	N	I		F	E	A	R	E	D
P	H	I	L	A			L	C	D	R				
R	A	H	A	B	T	H	E	H	A	R	L	O	T	
O	N	A	N		Y	E	T	I		A	U	B	E	R
E	N	T	E		P	A	U	L		N	C	A	A	S
M	A	E	S		E	T	S	I		D	E	L	T	A

. . . And Things Left Over
page 201

L	E	S	S		S	T	R	I	P		T	S	C	A
O	P	I	E		C	H	I	N	A		R	E	O	S
F	O	R	T	Y	Y	E	A	R	S		E	V	A	S
A	X	E		E	L	S		I	S	R	A	E	L	I
T	Y	N	D	A	L	E			A	T	T	N		
			E	T	A		E	D	G	E		D	E	A
W	I	F	E	S		S	P	I	E	S		A	T	M
A	R	O	D		P	O	E	M	S		G	Y	R	O
H	O	R		T	H	R	E	E		M	O	S	E	S
A	N	T		E	A	T	S		K	O	A			
		Y	E	A	R			T	E	N	D	A	Y	S
F	I	D	E	L	I	S		H	R	E		T	A	U
A	L	A	N		S	E	V	E	N	Y	E	A	R	S
K	E	Y	S		E	N	A	R	E		O	N	E	A
E	A	S	Y		E	D	S	E	L		L	Y	N	N